HOSTILE CITY

By the same author

The Barra Boy
All We Cannot Leave Behind

The Cal Jackson Novels
Full Sun

The State Trilogy
A Justified State
State of Denial
State of War

HOSTILE CITY

IAIN KELLY

The Book Guild

First published in Great Britain in 2026 by
The Book Guild Ltd
Unit E2 Airfield Business Park,
Harrison Road, Market Harborough,
Leicestershire. LE16 7UL
Tel: 0116 2792299
www.bookguild.co.uk
Email: info@bookguild.co.uk

Typeset in 11pt Minion Pro

Printed and bound in Great Britain by 4edge Limited

ISBN 978 1835743 478

British Library Cataloguing in Publication Data.
A catalogue record for this book is available from the British Library.

For

Chloe Dawn and Caden Daniel

And

all the readers who continue to give their support

hostile (hos·*tile*) *adjective*

a: of or relating to an enemy

b: marked by malevolence: having or showing unfriendly feelings

c: openly opposed or resisting

d: not hospitable

e: having an intimidating, antagonistic, or offensive nature

The aim is to create, here in Britain, a really hostile environment for illegal immigrants.

Home Secretary Theresa May MP, introducing the UK Home Office Hostile Environment Policy

For too long, people coming to this country have taken advantage of our famous welcoming spirit. From now on we must look on these illegal immigrants with hostility, rather than hospitality.

Fergus Bennett, Leader of the Scottish First Freedom Party, conference speech

PART 1

OUT OF THE PAST

1

Twelve Years Ago

Tony insisted on buying another round.

'Don't you have to get home?'

'I don't have to do anything I don't want to do,' Tony answered.

Which was true, thought Cal. Tony would inherit his family's business empire one day – he could do what he wanted and there were few consequences – but the one person Tony still had to answer to was his father, Francis McArthur.

'Don't you have to be at the opening tomorrow?'

Tomorrow was a big day for Francis McArthur. His latest venture was complete – a new skyscraper in the city centre housing a restaurant, office space and luxury apartments. The grand opening was a big deal in the city and Francis insisted his family be there.

Tony waved Cal off. 'I'll be fine.'

'I need to study this weekend.'

'What are you talking about? You're going to work for me. I'm going to run my dad's business and bring you in as my right-hand man. You won't need a college course certificate.'

Cal admired Tony's certainty. At no point did he think that perhaps Cal did not want to be his friend's assistant, or that Cal might want to make his own way in the world.

Cal heard his father's voice: *Don't hang around with Tony McArthur. That boy is trouble. His family is trouble. Always has been.* Joseph Jackson, Cal's father, was a mid-level official in the city council planning department. He was jealous of Francis McArthur's money and success. Tony had been Cal's friend since primary school. They had grown up together. Cal ignored his father's warning.

'One more,' Cal caved in, 'then we split.'

'I'll get them in.'

Juliet was already drunk. It was after ten and they had not left the flat yet. Rose checked her phone again. Sarah had messaged to say they were on their way, but that had been half an hour ago.

'At this rate we'll make it just in time for last orders.' Rose checked herself in the mirror and reapplied lip gloss. She swept her dyed-blonde streak back from her face and tucked it behind her ear. She was tired of her fringe cut; it made her look too young. She would grow the streak out and get a new cut. Her make-up was good though. It made her face look thinner. She was never happy with her round face. She thought about more eyeliner but resisted and threw it into her bag.

'Are you ready to go?'

'Relax,' Juliet called from the bathroom, 'if we're late we can just head straight to the club.'

'We were supposed to be there ten minutes ago.'

'I doubt Bex and Fraser will notice that we're not there. They're so into each other.'

'Jealous?'

'Of Fraser? He's lucky Bex sees anything in him. He's punching well above his weight.'

Rose's phone pinged. 'Sarah is downstairs. Come on.'

'Get her to come up for one.'

'If she comes up here, we'll be here for another hour.' Rose was already feeling the effects of the couple of vodkas she had downed. She had lost count of how many Juliet had already had.

'Alright, alright. Anyone would think you were anxious to meet a certain guy in the pub tonight.' Juliet finally emerged from the bathroom.

'Don't even go there.'

'What? You ashamed?'

'I don't have a crush on Logan.'

'Of course you don't. We just always have to go to the same pub where he works every weekend and you spend the whole time standing at the bar instead of sitting at the table with us.'

'Get your coat on. We're leaving.'

The air was filled with smoke, the ceiling was low and the lights flashed in time to the pulsing music. As Tony crossed the floor, he greeted everyone he passed. He was well known in the clubs around Glasgow. Cal stood at the side of the dance floor and watched a group of girls dancing in front of him. One of them, a blonde, had been making eye contact with him for the last ten minutes. Or at least, he thought she might have been. He was never very good at picking up on the signals. He lacked the confidence that Tony had. She looked his way again and Cal managed to smile at her.

Tony appeared at his side and handed Cal a beer and a shot glass. 'You could do a lot worse.' He nodded at the blonde, who smiled and turned back to her friends.

'We need to go.'

'Your loss. Got us a couple of chasers.'

Cal shook his head. 'I said one more. You're meant to be driving.'

'I'm fine. One more isn't going to make a difference.'

'Cheers, you daft eejit.' Cal downed the shot in one gulp and felt the aniseed taste burn his mouth and throat as it went down. 'That stuff is mingin.' He raised the bottle of beer and slugged a quarter of it down to wash away the taste of the shot.

'Sure you don't want to stay longer? You could be in there, and her friends are not bad-looking either.'

'Calm down. You're like a dog on heat. There'll be plenty more opportunities for you to chase the local girls in your dad's new nightclubs.'

'Aye, I can't wait.' Francis McArthur had recently acquired a portfolio of clubs from a reluctant seller, adding the venues to his growing collection of land, restaurants, offices and accommodation around the city. 'I'm going to manage them, or one of them at least.'

'You? In charge of a nightclub?'

'What? You don't think I could do it?'

'I think you might be too easily distracted by the clientele and the drink. Come on, let's get out of here.'

'Alright, but you owe me a proper night next weekend.'

'Sure, whatever you say.'

Cal hooked his hand under Tony's armpit and dragged him around the side of the dance floor towards the exit. They paused at the cloakroom.

'Leaving so soon?' the girl behind the counter asked.

'Big day tomorrow,' Cal answered.

Tony was fumbling about with his hands in his pockets, trying to find his ticket. His car keys spilled out and fell to the ground. He bent to pick them up and swayed. Cal managed to catch him before he toppled over.

'Forget it, I know which jacket is yours,' the girl said and went to collect it from the rack behind her. She brought it back and handed it over. 'Don't think he should be driving.'

'Don't worry.' Cal took the car keys from Tony. 'I'll get us home.'

'Be careful. See you next weekend.'

They had made it halfway around Victoria Circus. A taxi passed them. Rose tried to wave it down, but it was a private hire and someone was in the back. She cursed.

'Relax, lover. We'll pick one up on Great Western Road and be there in plenty of time for you to chat up the barman.'

Rose ignored Juliet, who stopped and fumbled in her purse, eventually finding her vape. She put it in her mouth, adjusted her skirt and hitched up her low-cut top. Sarah took her arm and they walked together, Sarah propping up and guiding Juliet along the pavement.

Sarah's phone rang and they stopped again. Rose turned back and waited.

'That was Cass,' Sarah said, when she'd finished the call. 'They're waiting for us at the junction.'

'Did you tell them to try to wave a taxi down?'

'Should I have?'

'Never mind.' Rose gave up. She would just have to relax and go at their pace. Logan would be behind the bar next weekend. It was wishful thinking on her part anyway. He wouldn't be interested in a second-year student; he was almost thirty. He probably had a girlfriend. But whenever she did manage to get his attention, they always hit it off. 'Come on, you two,' she called back to her friends. 'I'm starting to sober up here.'

Cal pushed Tony up the stairs and out of the door on to the pavement. The pounding music faded into the background. The fresh air hit them and revived Tony.

'I'm fine to drive.'

Cal watched him stagger across the pavement. 'One too many tonight, pal. I'll drive.'

They crossed Great Western Road at the traffic lights. Tony's Volkswagen Golf was parked on the road. His dad had bought Tony the car for his twenty-first birthday. Tony had added a spoiler and alloy wheels, tinted windows and a large exhaust that made the engine growl. Cal opened the passenger door and bundled Tony in. It wasn't the first time he had driven them home after a night out. On other occasions Tony had taken charge when Cal had had one too many.

Cal got behind the steering wheel, leant across and strapped Tony's seat belt on. When he sat back he felt a moment of wooziness. When he went to put the key in the ignition, it took him three attempts to find it. It did not occur to him that the alcohol was affecting him more than he realised.

'Can't believe you turned down your chance with that blonde,' slurred Tony. 'You need to take those chances when you can, looking as ugly as you do.'

'Thanks, pal.'

'She was way out of your league anyway. Once she heard your boring patter she would've lost interest.'

'You're probably right. Would probably prefer your stimulating conversation.'

'Just my natural charm.'

'Now I know you're pissed.'

Cal started the engine. The stereo came on at the same time, blaring a loud dance track through the speakers Tony had installed in the back of the car. Cal pulled out without checking the mirrors and a passing car blared its horn and swerved to avoid them.

'Fuck off,' Tony shouted out of the window.

Cal started moving again. They pulled up at the traffic lights behind the same car. 'You should get out and have a word with him,' Tony said.

'Not worth it.'

'At least race him.'

'Probably best if I don't. Don't want the police to be pulling us over, the state you're in.'

The lights changed and they pulled away. The car in front turned onto Great Western Road. Cal followed. The road was a dual carriageway. 'Get past him,' Tony urged him.

'Why's he going so slow?' Cal put his foot down and pulled out from behind the slow-moving car, but as he pulled alongside, the other driver increased his speed. Tony looked across and gave him the middle finger. The driver was about their age. He put his foot down harder. Cal matched him. They hit seventy miles an hour. The road was long and straight and there was no traffic in front of them.

'You better beat him. My reputation is on the line.'

'No problem.' Cal gunned the engine again, the exhaust roaring as he shifted down to fourth gear and surged ahead.

'You got him,' Tony shouted. The speedometer hit ninety. The other driver backed off.

'Showed him,' said Cal, looking in his mirror as the road sloped up to a gentle summit and then started to dip down again. Beyond the dip was the next intersection. Cal didn't see the traffic lights turn to red. He was too busy looking at the car behind him. By the time he turned back, it was too late.

They met Cass and Fiona at the traffic lights on the main road.

'I'm bursting for a pee,' announced Juliet as they hugged and greeted each other.

'We could have been at the pub half an hour ago,' said Rose.

'Excuse our Rose,' Juliet told the other girls, 'she's on her period and is missing her favourite barman.'

'We'll get a taxi here,' said Cass. 'Look, there's one heading into the town now.' She pointed at the black cab that was on the other side of the road, pulling up as the traffic lights turned from green to amber and then red.

'Thank God, come on.' Rose stepped off the pavement as the green man appeared, determined to get the taxi driver's attention before he missed them.

Cal slammed on the brakes. He was going too fast to stop in time. He shot through the red light. A couple of the girls in the group stepped back. One did not. The car was still doing forty miles an hour when it hit her. The left-side headlight shattered as it smashed into her legs. She flew up over the bonnet and her head hit the windscreen.

The impact made a sickening thud of flesh and bone against metal. The windscreen shattered. The car skidded on for another sixty feet along the road before stopping. When it did stop, her body rolled off the bonnet and landed on the road with another hollow thud.

'Jesus fucking Christ,' shouted Tony, 'what the fuck have you done?'

Cal's hands gripped the steering wheel, his knuckles white. Smoke from the brakes swirled around them. The engine was still running. There was a moment of nothing, of time suspended, of no sound. Then he heard the screams.

'Fuck, fuck, fuck.' Tony pulled his phone out. 'I'm calling my dad.'

Her friends sprinted along the road. One of them was calling an ambulance. They gathered around her. One couldn't look and turned away.

Cal undid his seat belt, opened his door, got out and walked around the front of the car. He saw the dents to the bumper and bonnet and the shattered hole in the windscreen, and he noticed the hair and blood stuck there.

'What the fuck were you doing?' a girl screamed at him. 'Look what you've done.'

Cal looked at the girl on the ground. She was covered in blood. Her eyes were closed. Her clothes were ripped and torn. Her legs lay at an unnatural angle, twisted the wrong way.

'Is she dead?' he mumbled. His hands were shaking. No one answered him.

He heard Tony speaking into his phone as he got out of the car. 'Dad, it's Tony. Something really bad has happened.'

'Have I killed her?' No one answered him. Two girls sat over their friend. The others huddled on the pavement.

Cal staggered to the kerb. He felt faint. It had all happened so fast. He looked again at what was left of the girl lying on the road, a mound of flesh that had once been a human being. He felt his stomach heave and he vomited.

He slumped down on to the pavement and sat with his head in his hands. What had he done?

Rose felt the cold tarmac underneath her. Her head pounded. The world had spun out of control. She tried to breathe and her chest felt like it had been crushed. Her ears were ringing; she couldn't hear properly. She thought she heard screaming and Juliet shouting her name. Why was she screaming at her? She tasted the blood and bile in her mouth. She was shaking, but it wasn't cold. She was looking up at the night sky. All the stars seemed to be streaking across the sky, spinning and swirling above her. A blurry face came into view. She tried to move her head over and focus her eyes, but she could do neither. She convulsed and coughed and blood came out of her mouth. She worried that it would stain her dress. She had to get up and get off the road, but she felt strange. It wasn't just that she couldn't control her legs and arms, it was that she had no sense that they were there at all. Everything was numb and cold and lifeless. The only pain came from her head. Her brain felt like it had been beaten and her skull had been cracked open by a hammer. The pounding was relentless. The only way she could make it stop was if she closed her eyes. She had to let the calm blackness take her. That was better. If she could just sleep forever then the pain in her head would stop. She felt hands on her shoulders. She still heard screaming and crying. She wanted it to stop. She slipped away into the night, and the sounds and pain faded away to nothing.

Six Months Ago

Rose had felt like this before.

She remembered lying on the cold tarmac and she remembered the taste of blood in her mouth. She remembered that strange feeling of leaving her own body.

The stars streaked across the sky, spinning and blurring.

A face came into view. 'Juliet?' Rose mumbled, but it was not her friend this time. It was a man – the same man who had stabbed her.

'I'm sorry,' he said. Then he was gone.

There were differences this time, she realised. It was quiet; there was no screaming. She was not in pain.

That strange feeling returned. Everything was cold and numb and lifeless. Maybe it was the layer of snow on the ground that was making her cold.

She convulsed and coughed and blood came out of her mouth. She had survived this once before. She could do it again.

She closed her eyes and let the calm blackness take her.

She slipped into the night and faded away.

This time Rose would not be able to pull herself back from the death that awaited her.

2

Present Day

Cal woke up from the same nightmare he relived every time he slept. He shivered and the last remnants of the horror evaporated. He left Rose lying on the cold pavement. She did not die the night he hit her with the car. She survived the coma and shattered bones and her brain healed. The scars eventually faded. Until the night she had been murdered six months ago.

The morning sunlight peeked through a gap in the curtain and brushed across Cal. Jenny shuffled and turned over and her arm fell across Cal's chest and held him under the duvet. Cal gently lifted her arm away and sat up and looked at her. The shaft of light caught her bare shoulder and neck and her skin glowed. Her long black hair fell across her face. She had saved Cal. If not for Jenny he would have slipped back down into the pit of despair he had struggled so hard to free himself from.

Detective Simone Millar had come to the nightclub six months ago. It was two days before Christmas. Millar told Cal that Rose Black was dead. Millar knew their history. Millar knew Cal had become obsessed with Rose after she had recovered from the car accident.

Millar knew Cal had followed Rose. She knew Cal had taken an unhealthy interest in the young woman he had almost killed.

'The detectives running the investigation will want to speak to you,' Millar warned him as Cal tried to absorb the news. He was slumped against the wall in the nightclub. Millar knelt next to him. 'I had to tell them about your past with her.'

'I haven't seen her in over two years,' Cal stuttered. He couldn't take it in, he couldn't make sense of it, he couldn't breathe. 'How did she die?'

Millar shook her head. 'I can't say anything just now, but I thought you should know.'

He couldn't remember how he got home that night. Jenny must have given him a lift back to his flat because it was her who woke him the next morning, Christmas Eve.

'There's a police detective here,' Jenny had said. 'He wants to ask you some questions.'

Cal sat in his living room facing Detective Michael Dykes, Millar's partner. Dykes started by explaining why he had come to see Cal.

'Because of your previous relationship with Detective Inspector Millar, she has recused herself from this line of inquiry. However, she has informed the detectives leading the investigation of your past interactions with Rose Black.'

Dykes was being diplomatic. He knew Cal Jackson had been an informer for Millar in the investigation into corrupt Glasgow businessman, Francis McArthur. Cal had worked for McArthur. He had just been released from prison and wanted to be left alone, but Millar persuaded him to rethink his decision. Millar knew Cal had been following Rose Black, the girl he had almost killed twelve years ago. She knew Cal had been stalking her. Cal told himself it was to protect Rose, to see that she had recovered and moved on with her life. Millar showed him it was an unhealthy obsession that could send him back to prison if Rose found out about it. Instead,

Millar offered Cal an alternative. Work for her as an informer and leave Rose alone for good.

Now Cal was a person of interest in the murder of Rose Black.

'These are preliminary questions. You haven't been charged with anything and you don't have to answer if you don't want to. You aren't obliged to have a legal representative with you, but I will be recording what you say and it may be used in the future as part of the investigation.'

Cal nodded. He had nothing to hide. It had been over two years since he had last seen Rose, before he had been put in prison for assaulting a police officer. He did not know where Rose lived now. He had not tried to find her. After the McArthur case ended, Cal had been freed from helping the police; he had moved on. He had met Jenny. He had never forgotten Rose, but he had got over his obsession with her.

'Twelve years ago, you were driving a car that hit a pedestrian and caused severe injuries.'

'Yes.'

'That person was Rose Black.'

'Yes.'

'You avoided going to jail and received only community service after pleading guilty to driving under the influence and causing injury by dangerous driving.'

'Yes.'

'Those crimes would normally carry a custodial sentence. How did you avoid going to prison?'

'My lawyer made a deal.' The truth was his friend, Tony McArthur, who had been in the car with him that night, had a father with powerful contacts. Francis McArthur had pulled strings and cut deals and Tony and Cal got light sentences.

'Rose Black spent two months in a coma, suffering a severe brain injury, several broken bones and significant scarring. Life-changing injuries. Did you feel any guilt about what you had done?'

'Of course I did,' Cal said. He left it at that. He didn't say he had been riddled with so much guilt that it set him on a destructive path that ruined his own life.

'You became obsessed with Rose after the accident, is that right?' So Millar had told him. Cal couldn't blame her. If they had found out she had known and had not informed the investigation, Millar would have lost her job. 'You followed her? Stalked her?'

'I kept an eye on her recovery. I wanted her to get better,' Cal tried to rationalise his behaviour. Dykes didn't believe him.

'Did you ever approach her? Threaten her?'

'No. I wanted her to have a normal life. I wanted her to recover from what I had done to her and get back the life I had taken from her after the accident.'

'When was the last time you saw Rose Black?'

'Before I went in to prison.'

Dykes flicked a page in his pad and checked a previous note. 'That was two years ago. You assaulted an off-duty police officer?'

'I was drunk and on drugs and not in a good place. I didn't know he was a police officer.'

'You pleaded guilty and served twelve months of a two-year sentence, then got released on parole for good behaviour.' Dykes looked at him. 'Did you try to make contact with Rose Black after you got out of prison?'

Dykes worked with Millar. He had seen Cal sitting outside of the flat Rose Black used to live in. There was no point in lying. 'I tried to find out if she was doing okay, but she had moved on and I never found out where she had moved to.'

'You didn't search for her or try to find her?'

'If I had tried to, Detective Millar would have put me back in prison. You know that.'

'Did you know of anyone else who might want to harm Rose Black?'

'No.'

Dykes had reached the end of his questions. He flipped his notepad closed and put it in his pocket. 'We'll be in touch if there is anything else. I would advise you not to leave the city for the next few days in case we want to contact you again.'

Cal had to ask the question that had been eating away at him since Millar had told him Rose was dead. 'How did she die?'

'I can't tell you that.'

'Did she suffer?'

'I'm not going to give you any details about an ongoing investigation, Cal. You know I can't.'

Dykes left him in the living room. Jenny saw the detective to the door.

The police never spoke to Cal again. They were satisfied he had nothing to do with Rose's murder.

Cal learnt the details of her death from news reports. Rose had worked as a human rights lawyer. She took on cases of refugees and immigrants seeking asylum in Scotland. She worked against the criminal gangs that trafficked vulnerable people into the country. She had been stabbed as she left her office late in the evening. An anonymous witness came forward and described a man of Middle-Eastern or Eastern European appearance fleeing the scene of the murder. The man was never found. The police suspected people-trafficking gangs may have had something to do with her murder, but they couldn't get close to them. The gangs operated abroad and out of reach of the police.

Far-right leaders made the most of the description of the suspect. People like Fergus Bennett, a self-described activist and failed politician, who had retired and had been largely forgotten by the Scottish public, resurfaced. His newly founded Scottish First Freedom Party suddenly had a purpose and a following. Stirred up by rumour and false information, protests against immigrants followed – protests that soon became an excuse for riots and violence. Communities of ethnic minorities around the country became targets. Immigrants were terrorised and harassed. People of colour were targeted. Political leaders appealed for calm. Police and prosecutors stepped in. Order was restored on the streets of the city, but the anger continued to simmer.

Millar and Dykes worked on the investigation. After four months there were no suspects and the investigation stalled. The team was rotated to bring in a fresh perspective and regain momentum. Millar and Dykes were reassigned.

Cal had a new nightmare that haunted him now, alternating with his memory of the accident. It had been snowing on the night Rose had been killed; a fine dusting of white had covered the city streets. Cal pictured her lying on the pavement, the white covering turning a dark red as blood seeped from her body. Cal saw the life drain from her. He saw her twelve years earlier, lying on another street, battered and broken and bathed in blood. The two images conflated in his mind. He had killed her, after all. It was all his fault.

She had been stabbed three times. Twice in the chest and once in her neck. Cal saw her try to fight the darkness that was creeping over her. He saw her cough and splutter. He saw her stop moving.

Cal left Jenny lying in the bed and made his way to the kitchen. He made a coffee, took it to the living room and sat on the sofa. It was after ten. They had been working at the club and had got in after three in the morning. Jenny always slept longer than Cal. Three or four hours a night was all he needed – a hangover from the unsettled nights in prison.

The street outside was quiet. The morning rush hour had passed. The air was mild and the sky grey, another underwhelming day as the city waited for any sign of summer weather arriving.

Cal flicked through the news headlines on his smartphone. The top story was about a small boat sinking in the English Channel. Twenty immigrants were missing, presumed drowned. Politicians were outraged. All agreed the illegal crossings had to stop. No one ever came up with a solution that worked. Statistics painted a grim picture, but missed the one vital element that was always forgotten – each number represented a human being. A person stripped of their dignity, of their home, of their family – forgotten as leaders argued over targets and worried about optics and votes. Rose had seen these immigrants as people. She had wanted to help them. She had cared about them and fought for them.

He heard Jenny get out of bed and go to the bathroom. She appeared in the living room five minutes later, her hair tied up in a loose ponytail. She wore his t-shirt that she had slept in.

'Morning,' she said, folding her arms and leaning on the door frame.

'Morning,' Cal replied. 'Sleep okay?'

'Great. I needed it.'

'Anything planned for today?'

'I need to go back to my place and get a change of clothes before work tonight.'

'We can swing past on the way in later.'

'You want another coffee?'

'I'm good, thanks.'

Jenny smiled and went into the kitchen. Cal watched her go. He still struggled to understand what she saw in him. They had met when Jenny was hired as the bar manager at the nightclub. They were both in their early thirties. Most of the staff in the club were students, ten years younger than them. Even Carmen, the club owner and manager, was only twenty-five. Gradually they developed a friendship that had naturally progressed into something more over the last six months. Now they spent most nights together. It was comfortable for both of them. They enjoyed each other's company. It had recently moved from a casual arrangement to something more meaningful – at least, that was how Cal felt. At some point he would have to find out if Jenny felt the same way about him. For now, he was happy that she still wanted to wake up next to him.

Later, after stopping at Jenny's flat so she could grab a change of clothes, they arrived at the Carnival for work. When Cal had started working there last summer, it had been called *Plein Soleil.* When Carmen became the owner, she rebranded. *Alô, Alô, Carnaval* was a Brazilian film starring Carmen Miranda with a bowl of fruit on her head. Carmen Carmichael had been named after the Bizet opera by her father, but the association with the Brazilian carnival worked better for a nightclub.

Carmen was in tonight. She spent less time at the club now that she had Jenny to take care of the day-to-day running. Cal had no doubt Carmen knew about their relationship, but she had never said anything. If it didn't affect their work, then there wasn't a problem with Jenny and Cal sleeping together. They were all adults.

Being a bartender suited Cal: a steady, if unspectacular, income; night hours that helped with his insomnia; and little stress. After everything that had happened to him over the last few years, all he was looking for was a quiet life.

The Carnival was quiet. The university term was almost finished for the summer break; many students had either gone home or gone travelling. Most of those who had ventured out for a drink sat in the garden area outside, huddled around heaters under an awning. Few wanted to spend the long summer evenings downstairs on the basement dance floor. The music reflected the mood – chilled vibes providing a relaxed background for the couples and groups enjoying a few drinks and easy laughter.

Carmen came down from her office and circled the room, checking everything was in order. She had let her hair grow out in the last few months, though she still kept it bleached blonde. She was slim and petite and still managed to dominate the room. Georgia was working the floor, delivering drinks to tables and clearing away empty glasses. She would be graduating in the next couple of weeks and moving away. Only Lauryn would remain from the young staff that had originally been at the club a year ago when Cal started. A fresh set of students would take bar jobs ahead of the new term, and Cal would feel that little bit older again. Carmen shared a brief word with Georgia and the doormen who provided security.

Then she came over to the bar. 'So how does it feel to be a free man at last?' she asked Cal.

'I didn't think you would have heard already.'

'I got an email this afternoon confirming your period of parole had ended and you were no longer under supervision or subject to any restrictions. Congratulations, you can now work here without needing special dispensation.'

'That mean you're going to keep me on?'

'I'll think about it.' As usual, Cal struggled to tell if she was being serious or not. 'Meanwhile you can treat yourself to a glass of champagne to celebrate, on the house.'

'Thanks.'

'Just one, mind. You're still on shift.' She walked away and went through the double swing doors that led back up to her office.

Jenny came over. 'A freebie? You must be in the good books.' She placed her hand on his shoulder. 'I tell you what, you take the free glass, I'll pay for the rest of the bottle and we can celebrate properly back at mine later.'

She moved away to serve a customer. Cal watched her and again wondered how he had managed to land on his feet. He was finally ready to leave the past behind him and move on.

3

Riz rolled the cigarette on the plastic table top, lifted it to his mouth, licked the inner edge of the paper and folded it closed. He flicked the cheap plastic lighter. The flame lit up the dark room, covering his face in a flickering orange glow. He felt the heat for a brief second and the tobacco leaves sticking out of the end of the roll-up caught light and glowed. He put the lighter on the table and leant back in the well-used armchair. He took a long drag, inhaling deeply. He closed his eyes and tried to calm himself. The constant shake in his hands became still, his breathing slowed. It had been like this for six months now. When he'd got to this country, he thought the hard part was over. He thought his life would be better. That was what they had promised him. Instead, it had turned into a living hell.

Riz wished he had never left his home. He pictured Durrës in his mind: the blue Adriatic Sea along the coast; the industrial port where he managed to find scraps of work; the rectangular white hotels along the seafront; the narrow beach and the warm air. He walked through the town in his mind, away from the water and the modern malls. Here was the Durrës of his childhood – scruffy and full of character. He passed along the grids of narrow streets, no more than rocky tracks, with low white walls and metal gates on either side, surrounding small gardens and square houses with flat roofs. Half-built blocks were scattered between finished buildings and empty plots of land where wild flowers and weeds thrived. There were no streetlights, but telegraph poles stood every twenty-five yards along the road, and from them electricity cables ran overhead, spiralling off to various houses. Ramshackle pipes, wires and walls appeared in all directions. The land around the buildings was uneven with piles of dirt and rubble. It was so different to the paved, structured city he was trapped in now. It was also warmer and drier, and the sky was blue instead of grey.

His memory took him to the block of apartments on Rruga Koder Stan. The lime-green paint on the walls was flecked and crumbling, but gave the three-storey building a distinctive appearance. He walked up the stairs to the second floor and into their small apartment. Leandra stood on the balcony, taking in the afternoon sun. She glowed as she turned to him, her blonde-brown curls backlit by the orange sun, like a halo around her angelic smile. Zerina was at her feet playing with sand in a red plastic bucket, scooping it out with a spade. Her hair was dark like his, but with curls like Leandra's. She still had the roundness of baby fat in her face.

He longed to pick up his little Zerina and cuddle her. Leandra would join them and they would be one and together – a family once more.

Noise from across the hallway brought Riz back to the present that he was desperate to escape. There were twelve of them in the small apartment; six slept on the floor of the living room, six in the only bedroom. They all shared a single toilet and small kitchen. The only furniture was an old television in the corner, a plastic table and two collapsed armchairs with ripped leather coverings dotted with cigarette burns. The white walls were scratched and dented and in one corner a damp green-brown patch of mould spread across the ceiling.

Most of them were around their mid-twenties, although a couple were still only teenagers. All had young families back home. All had worked as low-paid casual labourers or delivery drivers, or had been unemployed. All were sold the same lie about coming to the United Kingdom to earn money to support their young families. Riz was the only one from Durrës. He had no one to share his memories of home with. The rest were from the capital city, Tirana.

The men talked about home and their lives before coming to Glasgow. They talked about their journeys to get here. They had come along various routes; some were driven across Europe and crossed the English Channel before being trucked north through England; others had spent time in London before being moved. Some left Albania by boat and sailed across the Mediterranean Sea before being dropped at various ports – Marseille, Lisbon, Genoa, Barcelona – and then moving north. Fatmir had been flown in on a plane, stowed away in the baggage hold. He had no idea where the flight had stopped en route. Someone had met him at Edinburgh Airport and brought him to the apartment. Riz had come on the back of a truck that took him across land – going north from Albania through Croatia, Slovenia, Austria and into Germany. He had stayed there for three months, until they had told him it was time to move on. He had not intended to come to Britain, but he was told there were better opportunities here. They drove him to Calais, where he lived in the camps until he was put on a dinghy that crossed the Channel. He met Erjon and Lorik there. They came north together and now shared the same room in Glasgow.

Each had their own story to tell. Each had done things they'd never imagined they would be asked to do.

His hands were shaking again, but he could not stop them. It was happening more and more often. It used to happen only when he thought about what he had done. What he had been made to do. The tremors and the anxiety were getting worse. He could not talk about it with any of the others. They had not been involved. It had been him alone and he had been sworn to secrecy.

Riz tried to shut out the memories of the things he had done. He tried to think of Leandra and Zerina. His solace was the money that was sent back to them. That made his sacrifice worthwhile. Just a few more months, he thought, maybe a year, and then he could return. They would be richer than he had ever dreamt they would be – richer than casual shifts at the dockyards or part-time work in the cigarette factory could ever make him. They would have a future to look forward to. Zerina could go to a good school and grow up with opportunity, not in poverty with no chance of a better life. He tried to cling to the belief that this could still end well.

One day they would be together again. Then he could start to forget the things he had done here. At the start they had worked on building sites. Riz had expected that. Then they had been selected for a different line of work. They had no choice but to do as they were ordered to do. They were beholden to the men in charge. They knew about Leandra and Zerina. They knew about all the loved ones left back home. They threatened to do terrible things to wives and girlfriends, parents and children, unless they did as they were told. The men were threatened and blackmailed, but at the same time, they were told they would be rewarded. Riz clung to the dream of the bright future that awaited him back in Durrës, no matter how far away that seemed right now.

He smoked the last of the roll-up and stubbed it out on the table. Around him, others started to stir. They had been told to rest. They had a job to do tonight.

That was bad news.

When they were told they had a job to do, it meant someone was going to get hurt. Someone or something. They were never given any explanation. It meant violence.

Erjon's head emerged from the sleeping bag next to him. '*Përshëndetje*.'

'Hi.'

'*A fjete mirë?*'

'I haven't slept well since my last night in Durrës,' Riz answered him. 'Speak in English, remember.' Their masters warned them to always speak English. They told them it would help them acclimatise to their new country. Riz had been here long enough to know speaking the language would make no difference. They were not wanted here, no matter what.

The front door to the apartment banged open.

'Up, all of you. Let's go,' Konstandin shouted from the hallway. He was not a big man. Riz had thought often how easy it would be to overpower him; he was a foot taller and twice his weight. But Konstandin was the lieutenant for their masters. Whatever Konstandin ordered, they obeyed. If they dared to disobey, he would threaten to report them and there would be consequences, either here or back in Albania.

'Come on, you lazy bastards,' he yelled in his accented English.

The men stretched and extricated themselves from their sleeping bags, then threw on jumpers and trousers and shoes.

Konstandin checked outside the front door, then he waved them out. They trooped down the stairwell. Outside, a white Ford Transit van, rusting around the edges, was waiting for them. They all got into the back and sat on the floor. In the middle of the floor was a selection of baseball bats and sledgehammers.

4

The car had crashed through the metal shutter and the glass panel behind it, and ploughed on through what had once been a reception counter. Detective Simone Millar picked her way over the broken glass that covered the floor. Curtains and wall hangings had been pulled down and set on fire. Mirrors and decorative lights had been shattered. Chairs and desks had been upended and smashed into pieces. The flooring had been ripped up. Green and red paint had been daubed across the walls. Beyond the reception area, the rest of the property was in a similar state. Whoever had trashed the place had done a thorough job. They had also been professional. They had hit early morning when the place was empty; no one had been hurt or killed.

Millar edged past the abandoned car and emerged back out onto the street through the gaping hole where the front of the property had once been. The incident team had set up a cordon with police tape sealing off the scene and keeping the public at a distance. There was a steady flow of commuters on their way to work. Some kept moving without breaking stride; others stopped to have a good look and take photos on their smartphones.

Millar turned and looked up at the damaged sign over the smashed window. “Peaceful Dove Thai Massage”, although the “-age” had fallen off and lay in the rubble on the pavement. A streetlight had taken a hit too and leant at a slant, although the election placards that adorned it still clung on.

This was the third incident in the last two months. DeVito’s, an Italian-American restaurant on the south side, and the Bellagio nightclub in the city centre had both suffered a similar fate. So far, Millar had been unable to get a lead on who was responsible, but she was sure they had to be connected.

Michael Dykes picked his way around the abandoned car and rubble to join her. ‘The owner is on her way. A Mrs Chen. Her English seemed pretty good on the phone, but I’ve asked for an interpreter at the station just in case.’

‘Get on to the Specialist Crime Division. Better check if this place is on their radar. See if it’s a genuine massage parlour or a front for something more.’ Millar walked back into the building and made her way to what was left of the reception desk. Dykes followed. Millar bent down, pulled on a pair of forensic gloves and moved twisted plastic and metal and pieces of wood. Underneath she found the chassis of a computer. It was dented and bashed. ‘Take this. If we’re lucky, the hard drive can be salvaged and we can get a list of clients and workers. If not, I suspect Mrs Chen won’t give them up without a fight. Check her visa status with the Home Office. This could turn into a mess and a lot of paperwork.’

Dykes went to find a forensic officer who could bag up the computer. Millar continued into the massage parlour. Behind the reception area, a door led through to a cloakroom where clients could leave their belongings and change out of their clothes and into a towel. The towels lay in a charred heap on the floor. Another door opened onto a narrow corridor, painted in a calming teal colour with a tiled floor. Off the corridor was a series of rooms. The doors to the rooms had been ripped off their hinges. Each room had been identical inside, tastefully decorated in cool yellow and orange, with Eastern symbols and artwork on the walls. There was a massage table in each one, and a sink with a collection of bottles of various scents and oils, and candles. The tables had been upturned and the sinks had been smashed, and the various bottles lay empty and broken. The mix of strong aromas made Millar sneeze. She went into one room and started picking through the rubble. It didn't take her long to find what she suspected she would – a pack of condoms had spilled out across the floor. There was a pot of lubricating oil next to them.

She stood up and looked around. At head height she saw a cupboard door that was cut into the wall. It was locked. Millar took out her tension wrench and lock picks and selected the one that looked the right size. It took her ten seconds to spring the lock open. Inside she found small bottles of amyl nitrate, branded as "Love Aroma", and a collection of rubber sex toys and various straps, harnesses and whips. That answered her question about the legality of the Peaceful Dove massage parlour.

Dykes came into the room and found her holding a large bright-pink vibrator. After a momentary pause, he decided not to mention it. 'Mrs Chen is here.'

'What do you think? Rival gang?' Millar placed the vibrator back in the cupboard and closed the door.

'Could be, fighting over territory.'

'Or locals unhappy at the cheap immigrant labour moving into their patch.'

'"Coming over here, taking our jobs."'

'Something like that. Let's take Mrs Chen to the station and question her there. I want to find out the names of all the women who work here and where they are. We'll need to get Immigration Services and Special Crimes involved. I'm pretty sure we'll find some of them are illegal immigrants, if not all of them. If we're looking at human trafficking and slavery, the National Crime

Agency will need to get involved.' She waved her arms at the destruction around her. 'Whoever demolished this place wanted to put them out of business, and they've succeeded.'

They walked back to the front of the store. The crowds had thinned out as the morning rush hour ended.

'Any CCTV coverage?'

'Two cameras out on the street. We'll get the footage from them; they should show us the front of the place.'

'Any security cameras inside?'

'Mrs Chen isn't saying, but forensics found these amongst the rubble in reception and in the rooms in the back.' Dykes pointed to a selection of battered cameras that had been bagged and tagged.

'I guess the footage will be on that PC. If we can access it, let's identify anyone we can.'

'Think they used it to blackmail clients?'

'It's not like they have moral scruples that would stop them stooping that low. What about the car?'

'Reported stolen last night by a Mr Anderson. Taken from outside his work in Uddingston.'

The forensic team, dressed in their SOCO oversuits, were already dusting and fingerprinting the inside of the vehicle and pulling it apart. 'We won't find any prints in there,' Millar said. 'Who else should we be looking at?' she thought out loud.

'Church-going puritans unhappy about prostitutes selling sex in plain sight?'

'Not impossible, but I can't see them taking this sort of action.'

'An unhappy customer? Maybe they blackmailed the wrong person.'

'Could be, but this was a team, not one person. They were organised and knew what they were doing. In and out in five minutes and destroyed the place. It fits with the Bellagio and DeVito's.'

'So it's a gang then. The same one who did the other places.'

'That would be my bet. Question is, which gang, and why? Dig into these places a bit more, see if there is any connection between them.'

'Someone trying to set up an empire, expanding into new territory?'

'There's no pattern so far. Different types of businesses spread across the city.'

'All owned by immigrants.'

'Only if you count second- or third-generation.' The upcoming election had stoked the fires on immigration numbers once again. Although Glasgow was a reasonably tolerant city, some of the anger and bitterness that dominated political discussion south of the border had made its way up to Scotland. But there was nothing to suggest these attacks were racially motivated. Millar dismissed the connection for the moment.

A scene of crime officer came towards them, brandishing a heavy weapon of some kind. He held it up for Millar to see. It was a sledgehammer, a block of heavy metal on top of a long wooden handle. 'They left this behind,' the officer said.

It was something at least. Maybe they would get a print from it. It was the first mistake they had made, assuming the same gang was responsible for all three attacks. The SOCO took the sledgehammer away and put it in the back of the van along with the other evidence they had seized so far.

Millar was sure it was business rather than a personal vendetta. No one had been harmed physically and the properties were all owned by different people. It was about establishing territory and muscle. Millar had seen how criminal networks like this expanded before. She had helped to take down the last person who had tried to rule the city, but Francis McArthur would never have operated like this. He was subtle and kept his illegal activities at arm's length, behind respectable companies. This was something else. This was open warfare, a declaration from someone that they were going to move into the power vacuum McArthur's absence had left in the city. They made no pretence of being civilised.

'We need to get the word out with our contacts. Any information on new players on the scene,' she said to Dykes as they headed back to the car. 'Drugs, prostitution, trafficking. Someone must know something. We'll question Mrs Chen and then leave her to the Home Office. We need to start getting information from the streets.'

5

Millar ordered her usual drink – a spiced dark rum straight up on the rocks – and sat in her usual stool at the end of the bar.

The Carnival was busy. It was Friday and groups of students were celebrating the end of exams. Millar could have done without them. She preferred it when the bar was emptier.

Cal wondered sometimes why Millar came at all. When she had first started appearing regularly, Carmen had disapproved. Having a police detective prop up the bar every night wasn't great for business. On the other hand, it would not be a wise move to make an enemy of the local police force.

At ten, the dance floor and small bar downstairs opened and the crowd thinned out as the exuberant students made their way below. Cal had time to collect empty bottles and plastic cups from the bar and wipe it clean. Georgia cleared the tables.

'Another?' Cal offered Millar as she slugged down the last of her rum. 'I could make it more interesting for you? I do a mean Daiquiri now.' It had taken Cal most of the last year, but he had finally mastered some of the cocktails on the club menu.

'Do I look like a cocktail kind of girl?'

'I wouldn't like to judge.'

'Same again.' She shook the empty glass at him.

Cal poured a measure of rum into a fresh glass and scooped in the ice. 'Everything okay?' He could tell something was bothering her.

'Another place got hit today.'

'The massage place in the city centre?'

'Brunswick Street,' Millar nodded. 'Someone is trying to take over the hospitality business in the city.'

'I wouldn't have thought a massage parlour would be of much interest to a criminal gang.'

'There was evidence to suggest it offered something more than simple rest and relaxation.' Millar raised a suggestive eyebrow. 'A restaurant, a nightclub that used to belong to McArthur, and a massage parlour that was a front for prostitution. Can't be coincidence that all three have been targeted and put out of business in the last month.'

'No idea who it could be?'

'Nothing so far. We've put out feelers on the streets.'

'Someone new?'

'Has to be. Someone wanting to make their mark in the city.'

'I mean, you don't think Tony would—'

She cut him off. 'Tony McArthur has gone legitimate. He's only interested in keeping the McArthur construction and demolition business going. He's got no intention of getting back into nightclubs.'

After Francis McArthur had been killed and his corrupt practices exposed, his empire had been split apart. Tony had managed to cling on to the construction business.

'How's Marie?'

'She doesn't get in touch.' Cal's sister was still married to Tony, although the last he had heard, there were tensions in the relationship.

'And your niece?'

'Marie sent me some pictures. She seems cute, like most babies.'

'You haven't met her yet?'

Cal shrugged. 'Not had an invite.'

'You're her uncle, you don't need an invite. How old is she now?'

'Two months.'

A customer came to the bar. While Cal poured a pint of Guinness and a Bacardi and coke, Millar downed the rest of her drink.

Carmen appeared through the double doors that led to the top floor. She came over to the bar. 'How are you this evening, Detective?'

'I can't complain. I was just updating your barman here on today's events.'

'What events?' asked Carmen. She tolerated Millar in her nightclub, but it wasn't ever going to be a warm friendship between them. Like Cal, Millar had used Carmen in her investigation into Francis McArthur. Carmen had never committed to whose side she had actually been on – McArthur gave her a start at the nightclub, had put her in charge and trusted her to run the place. Millar had got in the way.

'Another business trashed. A massage parlour in the city centre.'

'Same as the Bellagio and that restaurant?'

Millar nodded. 'You should keep an eye out. There's no pattern at the moment other than they are targeting hospitality venues. The Carnival could be on the list. It's a former McArthur nightclub with a new owner, just like the Bellagio.'

'Thanks for the warning. We've got security in place.'

'Don't be complacent.'

'I'll bear that in mind. Don't keep my barman from his work, will you?' Carmen walked away and continued her tour of the nightclub floor.

'Wouldn't dream of it,' Millar said to her departing back. She turned back to Cal. 'Guess that's my cue.' She put her glass on the bar and picked up her jacket.

'You don't have to go,' Cal said.

'I need to be in early to work this case.'

'You don't really think they will target this place, do you?'

'Who knows?' She shrugged. 'It's as likely to be this place as any other in the city.' She pulled her jacket on and fastened it. 'Don't worry. They seem to always appear when the business is closed and no staff are about, so you should be safe.' She gave him a salute and headed out of the front door.

Cal watched her go. He didn't know why Millar kept coming back to the nightclub to see him. Was she lonely? As far as Cal knew, she didn't have any family or a partner waiting for her at home. It was ridiculous that he didn't know more about her after all this time. Whenever he asked how she was, Millar always related the question to work and her latest case. He never managed to break through her exterior. He made a note to make more of an effort the next time she was here.

Part of him suspected she was here because of Rose Black. She had been on the team that investigated her murder and they had not got close to catching anyone. They had never been able to establish a main suspect – the closest they had come was the description of the man seen fleeing the scene of the crime. They had never picked up a promising trail of him.

Millar had never known Rose, but she knew about her history with Cal. She had blackmailed Cal into helping her investigation of McArthur by threatening to expose Cal's behaviour. Despite that, at the end of the investigation, when Francis McArthur was dead, Cal and Millar had become friends of a kind.

Did Millar feel guilty about Rose's death? About never catching whoever had killed her? Was that why she continued to come into the nightclub and talk to Cal? Was she looking for him to forgive her in some way? Did she need Cal to absolve her of any blame?

Jenny came up the stairs from the basement. 'You okay there? You're a million miles away.'

'I'm fine,' Cal said, picking up Millar's empty glass and washing it.

'It's crazy down there tonight. You've got the easy shift up here. Your friend gone for the night?'

'Yeah, she's working early in the morning.'

'I need these brought to the bar downstairs. Can I leave it with you?'

'Sure.' He took the piece of paper from her and started collecting the various bottles.

6

They rode over another pot hole and the back of Riz's head hit the metal side of the van. He looked round at the other men – heads down, eyes staring at the floor, no one willing to speak. It was three in the morning when they were woken in the flat. Konstandin had crashed through the door and shouted at them to get up. They had another job to do. It had only been three days since they had demolished the massage parlour; now they were hustled into the back of the van again.

There were ten of them in the back. Lorik and Afrim sat on the floor, the others on the makeshift benches along the sides. Konstandin sat in the front, next to the driver and Fatmir. Riz could see the backs of their heads through the cage that separated them. All he could see through the windscreen was black night and the glow of streetlights as they streaked past. There were no windows in the back of the Transit.

The baseball bats and sledgehammers lay on the floor in front of them. Riz felt panic rising inside of him. He had made a mistake at the massage parlour. He had dropped the sledgehammer in the confusion and left it there, somewhere amongst the rubble of destruction. When they had returned to the flat, Konstandin supervised the return of the equipment. When he saw Riz was empty-handed, he screamed at him and hit him. He would lose a month's wage because of his stupidity. If he made a mistake again, he would be beaten and killed.

Riz thought about what he had done since he had arrived in this cursed country. He was not a violent man before he arrived here, but he could no longer believe that about himself. He had committed violence here. He had been forced to do it, but he could have resisted. He could have said no.

If he had done so, he would be dead.

He thought of Leandra and Zerina. All he wanted was to make them proud. To go back to them a rich man who could provide them with the future they deserved. Could he return to them at all after what he had done? They could never know the truth about the violence he had committed. If they did, they would no longer love him.

He felt the rage inside him. The sickness, the bile. He could not fight it any longer. He had given in to it. He had become a monster, someone he could no longer recognise from his past life in Durrës.

Erjon pressed against his side as they rocked over another bump. 'The roads here are worse than in Tirana,' he mumbled.

Riz gave him a weak smile but did not reply. Each of them was lost in their own thoughts of home, of what they had been through to get here and of what lay ahead tonight. Riz wondered if any of the others had committed the same evil that he had. He doubted Erjon could have. He was still an innocent boy. Erjon still believed he would return home a rich man one day, to the life and family that waited for him in Albania.

'Where do you think we are going this time?' Erjon said to him above the thrum of the diesel engine.

'I do not know.'

'Why do they keep getting us to destroy these places?'

Riz shrugged. 'They must have a reason. I doubt it will ever be explained to us.'

'We just do as we are instructed.'

'Exactly. Do not ask too many questions, Erjon. It will only get you into trouble.'

Erjon fell silent. The van swayed around a corner. Konstandin turned and looked over his shoulder. 'Two minutes. Get yourselves ready.'

They each took the black cloth balaclava they had been given and pulled it over their heads. Riz adjusted it so the holes for his eyes and mouth were in the right place. He double-checked his shoelaces were tied tight. One by one, each man leant forwards and picked a weapon from the pile on the floor.

The van slowed and rolled forward. The noise from the engine fell to a murmur as they crept along.

Konstandin gave them their instructions. 'You know what to do, boys. This is a nightclub. A den of iniquity where the morally corrupt heathens of this country commit many sins. We must put a stop to it. We must teach them the pure ways, the proper way to live their lives. We must destroy it. We will not leave until this place has been punished.'

Riz did not believe this religious nonsense. They were not on a mission to cleanse the decadent West of their loose morals. Maybe Erjon and some of the others still believed that was why they were doing these things; Riz was not so naïve. These missions were about something else. They were being used as pawns by the men who had brought them here, to fight some sort of war against other criminals.

The driver pressed down on the brake pedal and the van came to a stop with a soft jolt. Konstandin and Fatmir got out of the front. The driver stayed where he was and kept the engine running.

The back door opened. 'Go now,' Konstandin ordered them. 'Follow Fatmir.'

They filed out one by one, crossed the dark pavement and disappeared up a narrow alleyway between two buildings.

Riz was the last to leave the van. Konstandin caught him by his jumper as he stepped out into the night air. 'I am watching you, Tariq Rizwan. No mistakes tonight. You do as you have been told. You hold back, you will not see the morning. Understood?'

Riz did not answer him. Konstandin let go of his jacket. They remained standing, their eyes locked, for a moment more. It was the only defiance Riz could offer. He followed the others into the alleyway.

Konstandin brought up the rear and waved his arm. 'Go,' he commanded in a hushed order.

Fatmir heard the command. He swung a sledgehammer. It crashed into a metal door. The sound echoed around the alley, bouncing between the walls of the buildings. Fatmir swung the sledgehammer again and the door started to buckle. After a third attempt, the lock gave way and Fatmir put his body weight against the door and forced it open. The men followed him inside.

By the time Riz entered, the nightclub had been flooded with bare yellow light. Tables and chairs were upended and smashed. There was a bar at one end of the room. Two men were behind it, smashing the optics and glasses with baseball bats. Riz was shoved in the back as he stood watching.

'What are you waiting for?' Konstandin growled in his ear. 'Get on with it. You smash those lights.' He pointed at a series of wall fittings, decorative curved glass lampshades that ran around the room.

Riz ran to the corner of the room, making his way through the splinters and shards of wood that flew in the air as tables were broken and crushed. He swung the baseball bat at the first light and shattered it into pieces. He moved on to the next one.

'Two minutes,' shouted Konstandin. 'Faster, you lazy bastards.' They were in a frenzy now, a destructive mob savaging anything in their path. 'Fatmir, take two men upstairs.' Fatmir obeyed and a trio of them ran up the stairs. Soon tables and chairs were raining down from the balcony above into a large heap in the middle of the dance floor. The panels of the floor itself were being ripped up.

Riz had made his way around half of the room when a gut-wrenching cry made everyone stop. Riz turned in time to see a body flying through the air, thrown from the balcony above. The scream stopped with a sickening thud as the body hit the ground. There was silence. All of them looked at the crumpled body on the floor, and then to Konstandin.

The body was that of a white man. He was on his back. His leg lay at an unnatural angle. A shard of bone was visible poking through the skin where it had shattered. He coughed and blood spilled from his mouth.

Fatmir and the two men who were with him ran back down the stairs. 'He surprised us,' Fatmir explained. 'He was waiting for us. It was a trap; he had a knife. Afrim saved us.'

Konstandin turned to Afrim. 'You threw him over the balcony?'

'I had to. He attacked us.'

Riz could see in Afrim's eyes that he was terrified. They had been told no one would be there. This man lying on the floor was either a security guard or a worker at the nightclub who had not left.

'You have done well.' Konstandin smiled and put his arm around Afrim, who was visibly shaking. 'But now you must finish what you have started. You understand?'

Afrim nodded. Konstandin led him over to the stricken man and then stepped away. Afrim looked at each of the men who stood around him. He raised the sledgehammer above his head. The white man on the floor raised a weak, pathetic cry of resistance, choked by the blood that had gathered in his mouth. Afrim shrieked in despair as he brought the sledgehammer swinging down from above his head.

There was a deadening thud.

'Come now,' Konstandin yelled. 'Finish what we have come here to do. You have one minute.' He took Afrim away and started leading him out of the club. The men did not move. 'Now,' screamed Konstandin, 'or you will all be lying there like that bastard.'

They returned to their tasks. Riz turned back to the lights. He felt the anger and bile inside him. He took it out on the lamps. How had he ended up here? What had he done to deserve this punishment? He screamed as he smashed another light fitting. He swung and missed the next one. He could feel only rage. He reached out and punched the lampshade with his fist. The glass shattered and he felt it slice into his hand. Red blood appeared over his brown skin. He felt faint and put his hand on the wall to stop himself from falling. A smudge of red blood stained the white wall.

'Enough!' shouted Konstandin. 'Out now, all of you.'

The men ran for the door and out into the alleyway. Riz looked back and saw Konstandin with a petrol can. He splashed some through the door, then bent down and used a lighter to spark the fire. It spread across the floor in a sweeping blanket.

'Shit,' cried Konstandin. His sleeve had caught fire. He beat his arm against the wall and patted it with his other arm until the flame had gone out.

'Get in the van,' he grabbed Riz and pulled him along the alley. He threw Riz in the back and slammed the door closed.

As soon as Konstandin jumped into the front seat, the driver floored the accelerator and the van leapt forward. They drove away into the night. Behind them, Riz heard faint sirens as the emergency services arrived at the nightclub. They had got away just in time.

Riz picked himself up and put his back against the door. He held his sliced hand against his chest, trying to stem the bleeding.

He looked at the other men. They sat in silence and stared at the floor again. Each was trying to process what had just happened.

In the far corner, Riz saw Afrim. He was sobbing. He had pissed himself. The adrenalin had worn off and Afrim had realised what he had become. He was a killer, a murderer, a monster.

Riz recognised the look on Afrim's face. He could relate to the turmoil he was going through. Riz had been there himself.

7

'Nathan MacDonald. Twenty-two, Caucasian, in his final year at Strathclyde University studying Philosophy. Lived in a flat not far from here. Originally from Kirkcudbright in Dumfries. His family are being notified just now. Worked at The Shed on weekends to earn extra money. The manager says he volunteered to stay late last night to get the place ready for a private function that was due to happen this afternoon.'

'What was the private function?' asked Millar.

Dykes checked his notes. 'A retirement bash for a Mr Franks.'

'Anything on Mr Franks? Any criminal record?'

'Nothing on record. A teacher who spent forty years at the local school. He's clean.'

'So not linked to this in any way.'

'Doesn't look like it. Looks like Nathan was just in the wrong place at the wrong time.'

Millar replaced the sheet over the bruised and bloodied face of Nathan MacDonald. They had got his identification from the wallet in his pocket. His face was battered beyond recognition. Millar stood up. 'Send someone round to have a chat with Mr Franks, just in case.'

'You think it's the same gang?'

'Hard to think otherwise, although they're getting more frequent and the dead body is new.' Millar gestured at the broken furniture and shattered glass that surrounded them. 'Everything else fits.'

'Could it be someone else? Maybe another gang retaliating for the previous attacks?'

'Could be, but which attack? All the previous locations were owned by different people.'

'The Fuscos would have the muscle,' Dykes suggested. The Fusco family owned DeVito's restaurant.

'Not their style, though. If they were going to burn a place down, they would do it properly, and they wouldn't kill an innocent kid.'

The call had come in just after three in the morning. A passer-by on his way home from a night out saw a group of men, wearing black clothes and balaclavas and carrying hammers and bats, spill out of a white Transit van and break into The Shed nightclub. The witness didn't hang around to see what happened after that, but he did have the presence of mind to call the police and alert them.

By the time the first responders arrived, the men and the van had gone, but the fire had not taken hold of the building. The fire engines arrived in time to contain it and there was only damage to a small section around the side door where the men had broken into the club. They were too late to do anything for Nathan MacDonald though. His body was found in the middle of the floor. His head had been crushed, caved in by a solid object. All that was left was a bloody pulp. His legs were broken. The forensic team were pretty sure he had been thrown or had fallen from the upper balcony and landed on the floor. Then someone had finished the job with a blunt instrument to his head.

Millar started pacing around the floor, careful to avoid the broken chairs and smashed glass. Dykes followed her. 'They thought the place would be empty. They weren't expecting to find someone here. They started out with the same plan as before. Break in, wreck the place, put it out of business and leave.'

'But they found Nathan inside.'

'Probably he ran upstairs when he heard them breaking in. He tried to hide, but they came upstairs and found him.'

'Whoever found him panicked, or got carried away and threw him over the balcony.' Dykes pointed up at the raised level and they both followed the drop from above to the body lying under the white sheet on the floor.

'The fall didn't kill him, but they couldn't leave a live witness behind.'

'Whoever is in charge finished him off.'

'Or he made someone else do it as an example. It breeds loyalty. They had committed murder now and all the rest were complicit in the act. They're tied to him now.' Millar continued. 'Either way, it leaves behind more evidence than he would like. They're not stupid, we know that. From three previous crime scenes, we've managed to lift one partial fingerprint.'

'So the attempted arson is a reaction to the killing.'

'Exactly. They didn't plan to burn the place down until the situation changed and they quickly tried to adapt. Lucky for us, they botched it.' They stopped at the far end of the room and took in the scene. The floor was crawling with scene of crime officers, all wearing white suits and blue plastic overshoes. They were picking their way carefully through the scene, looking for anything that might have been left behind.

'They're getting careless,' Dykes mused. 'They didn't plan this one as well as the others. They exposed themselves. We have a witness that saw them arriving. Reckons there were about twelve or thirteen of them. We know they came and left in a white Transit van.'

'Number plate?'

Dykes shook his head. 'Afraid not.'

'They will ditch the van. Put a call in for any reports of stolen or abandoned white Transits across the country.'

Dykes headed off to put in the request. Millar bent down and poked through a pile of shards and dust with her gloved hand. She could feel that they were getting close to a breakthrough. They had managed to pull a partial fingerprint from the sledgehammer that had been left behind at the massage parlour. The prints had not been matched to anyone on record so far, but it was something to build on. Across four crime scenes, they had to get lucky at some point. No one was that good at hiding all the evidence. She knew patience was key, but at the same time, Nathan MacDonald was lying dead in front of her. That raised the stakes. There would be pressure from above to crack the case quickly. The media would start digging and getting involved. More importantly, Millar knew that once their crimes had escalated in violence, criminals were more likely to do it again. Now that the gang had got a taste for killing, they may decide to do it deliberately next time. She had to put a stop to it before any more innocent people got caught up in the violence.

'Over here,' shouted one of the forensic team. They were standing by the wall, pointing at something. The scene of crime officer in charge made his way over. Millar followed. 'On the wall.' The officer pointed to a dark smudge.

Millar looked at it. It was a deep red mark, a blood stain. A handprint.

'Can we get prints from that?' the scene of crime officer asked.

'We should be able to get at least partial prints.'

Millar allowed herself a small moment of victory. Finally, they were getting somewhere.

Back outside, Millar found Dykes by their car.

'We got a good print on the wall. One of them must have cut themselves and left a nice bloody handprint for us. They will prioritise it at the lab for us.'

'That's something at least,' Dykes replied. 'Not such good news about the white Transit.'

'What?'

'They found a white Ford Transit in Barrhead this morning. No plates, completely burnt out. They didn't make a mistake setting the fire this time.'

It was a shame, but it was not the end of the world. 'Send someone along to oversee the recovery. You never know, maybe our luck is changing and we can get something from the remains.'

They are rattled, Millar thought. If they had got rid of the van, they would need to find another one. She made a note to have her team informed of any reports of stolen vans in the next few days.

They are having to adapt and react and when that happens, they will start to make more mistakes. She could feel the thrill of the chase and the adrenalin rising. She had not had that feeling for a while. It was the feeling that made her love her job.

They left the scene of crime team to finish up at the nightclub. Millar had a passing thought about Cal and the Carnival. The Shed was the second nightclub to be targeted. She made another mental note to warn other nightclubs and business owners about the pattern they were seeing, and she would stop by and see Cal later on to tell him to be on his guard.

Just as they opened the doors of their car, the police radio crackled into life. It was an all-points bulletin. All available officers and cars were commanded to respond.

'Reports of violence breaking out at George Square,' the dispatcher said. 'Clashes between a far-right protest and other groups. Repeat. All available units to respond and assist. Over.'

'That's Fergus Bennett and his mob.'

'Do we go?' asked Dykes.

'No choice.' They could have done without it, but if command had decided it was worth all units responding, then they had little option.

8

Dykes pulled up in front of three police vans that barricaded Queen Street. Flashing blue lights warned people to stay away. A group of uniformed officers stood in a line across the top of the street, where it led onto George Square. Millar and Dykes stepped out of the car and were hit by the noise of several hundred people jeering and shouting. A police loudhailer tried to make itself heard over the din, urging the crowd to move back and stay calm, but only succeeded in adding to the racket. A cloud of smoke hung in the air, produced by flares that continued to be lit and thrown at the police line.

Dykes handed Millar a stab vest. Millar grabbed one of the uniformed officers as he passed. 'Where's command?' She had to shout to make herself heard.

'Other end of the square,' the officer pointed towards the south-east corner. 'South Frederick Street.'

'Thanks.'

They slipped through the police line and into the square. The main crowd of protesters were gathered in the centre. The statue of Sir Walter Scott looked down from the top of the pillar at a stage erected at its base. Homemade flags and banners were attached to the scaffolding that held up the temporary structure. "Keep Britain for the British", "British People's Party", "Scotland First", "Stop the Boats". Among them were placards urging the public to "Vote for Scottish Freedom".

A group of men stood on the stage. At the front of this group, Millar recognised Fergus Bennett in his trademark long beige coat. This was his election rally. He was the leader of the right-wing Scottish First Freedom Party. Bennett stood to attention, his head held high, his hands crossed in front of him, surveying the unfolding drama in front of him with no hint of emotion.

Fergus Bennett had been on the fringes of the political scene in Scotland for many years, although he had never managed to get elected to any seat of power, despite standing for the European, Scottish and United Kingdom parliaments. He had even stood for the local council elections in Glasgow. He had failed every time. He presented himself as a man of the people, a hero fighting for the working class – despite a past life as the wealthy son of an international banker. Bennett had been privately educated and had made a fortune on the stock exchange. He made a lot of noise, caused a lot of disruption and used his connections to gain a disproportionate amount of media coverage, but he could usually be dismissed as a rabble-rousing irritant.

That had changed after Rose Black's murder. When news broke about a suspect of Eastern European or Middle Eastern heritage, Bennett had seized his moment. He used social media to spread his message. He skirted around the laws of hate speech and incitement to violence. He encouraged his followers to take to the streets and protest. While his followers ended up in jail in the police crackdown that followed, Bennett's popularity and public profile soared. The Scottish First Freedom Party surged in the polls. They expected to capitalise on their new-found notoriety in the upcoming Scottish Parliament elections – and Fergus Bennett finally had a chance of claiming an election victory and a seat in an elected body.

Bennett remained impassive on the stage. He had achieved what he wanted from this rally. He was flanked on either side by a selection of white men, all cut from a similar cloth – well-built, mid-thirties to mid-forties, close-cropped hair, dark sunglasses – ex-military, Millar thought, some sort of private security.

Another flare flew across the sky, launched from within the crowd in front of the stage. Millar followed the arc of the red smoke. It landed on the ground, twenty yards short of the police line. Riot police in black combat gear and black helmets, armed with riot shields and batons, formed a U-shape along the south, east and west sides of George Square. Behind them, mounted police were forming up. The large horses bucked and stamped and strained as they were brought into position. Riot vans were in place on the roads around the square, metal shields covering their reinforced windscreens.

The loudhailer again tried in vain. 'Please disperse immediately. If you do not disperse, we will be forced to take immediate action. I repeat…'

No one was listening. It was a legal formality – the warning had to be issued. Once it had been ignored, the police were within their rights to take further action.

Sticking close to the buildings, Millar and Dykes made their way along the south side of the square until they reached the corner at South Frederick Street. They slipped beyond another line of uniformed police. In the middle of the road, the mobile command unit had been set up, a large white portacabin with "POLICE" emblazoned across the side. Millar saw the tall figure of Deputy Chief Constable Aileen O'Hara. She had operational command. Millar and Dykes arrived just as O'Hara was addressing her officers.

'Okay, they've had fair warning. Let's start moving them. Everyone clear?'

There was agreement from those around her and the group broke up to carry out their orders.

O'Hara turned to go back inside the command unit. Millar caught her attention. They had been at the academy together, two women drawn together in what had still been a man's world at the time. O'Hara had worked her way rapidly up the chain of command, while Millar had followed her ambition to make detective rank. They had kept in touch through work functions and occasional operations where their paths had crossed.

'What happened at the nightclub? I heard a body was found,' O'Hara asked Millar as she approached.

'Looks like another attack on a business, only this one turned violent. Are we needed here?'

'We're short on detectives. Stick around for a bit. If we arrest some of the ring leaders, I want experienced detectives to handle them. You don't have to get involved with the rest of it.'

'Understood,' Millar replied, trying to hide her frustration. They were to stand about and do nothing, wasting time while she had a murder to investigate. Political elections were the least of her concern, and every time they occurred, valuable resources were used up to police them. The overtime would be welcomed by the rank and file, although they could have lived without the rioting.

'Goddamn elections.' O'Hara tipped her head and disappeared inside the portacabin.

'I guess we wait,' said Dykes.

'Might as well watch the show. Come on.'

They made their way back up the street to the square. Millar stepped up on a concrete bench to gain height. Dykes joined her. From their elevated position they had a good view over the square. A whistle sounded and the lines of riot police started to walk forward. They were met by a re-energised roar and a fresh volley of verbal abuse from the crowd. More flares were lit and thrown. Glass bottles flew. Those that reached their intended target battered against polycarbonate shields.

'They're going to try to move them up North Hanover Street,' shouted Millar. She had seen this tactic before. George Square had a long tradition of attracting protests from all sides, on all arguments – football supporters, strikers, political rallies, Unionists and independence supporters. When things turned ugly, North Hanover Street, a steep hill flanked by solid brick walls on either side, provided a convenient route through which to funnel a crowd.

The political rally that had been granted a licence to stage their event by the city council had broken the limits imposed on them. Banners and placards with insulting slogans had been seized upon arrival. The chanting of anti-immigration and anti-Muslim slogans was incessant. The organised speakers on the stage had been little better. No doubt Fergus Bennett would later claim the police had over-reached and abused their power. He would become the victim, silenced and cancelled and unable to practise his democratic right to freedom of speech.

Millar looked across to the stage. Bennett and his group had disappeared. They had seen what was coming and left before becoming caught up in any violence. Having whipped up his followers into a blind frenzy, he had abandoned them to face the consequences. *Typical of a coward,* thought Millar. She pointed out the disappearance of the ring leaders to Dykes.

'Looks like there won't be anyone for us to deal with at the end of this.'

'Rats deserting a sinking ship,' replied Dykes.

The trouble was, the ship wasn't sinking. The rise of the intolerant, extremist views of the far-right seemed to continue unabated. The rise of the far-left matched the far-right. In the middle were the majority and the police, trying to maintain some sort of order. The root causes were not being dealt with. Divisive politicians seized on public anger and added fuel to the fire. Facts and figures on immigration and refugees were twisted to suit agendas. Religion and skin colour, and wars and genocides taking place thousands of miles away, were used to stoke discontent. Polarised views were cemented. It was hard to see how they would ever be changed.

The police lines kept marching forward. The cordon around the protestors grew tighter. Some of the crowd saw what was coming and started to back away, taking the escape route left open to them up North Hanover Street. The majority held firm. Some had come to the gathering in the hope and expectation of a confrontation. They welcomed the opportunity to face the police. It proved they were being oppressed and society had become overrun and ruled by a woke minority. It proved the immigrants flooding into the country were a threat to their traditional way of life and culture. Millar knew those who believed these things had been grossly misled, but nothing would change their mind. She knew some of the officers in the police force held private views similar to some of the protestors they were now facing. Others were here because they just wanted a fight and would admit their political beliefs and knowledge were sketchy at best.

The front line of riot police met the front line of protestors. There was scuffling and pushing and the volume rose again. Shouts of "scum" and "pigs" echoed around the square.

Millar saw the first fire bottle as it arched through the sky and fell behind the front line of police, bursting into flames amongst the officers backing up the riot police.

Then hell descended on George Square. Tear gas was deployed. The police pushed forward. The mounted police galloped into action. More Molotov cocktails arched through the air and exploded in sheets of flame.

'Come on,' shouted Millar. She jumped down from the bench.

'Where are you going?' Dykes shouted as he followed.

Millar sprinted across the square to the rear of the police lines. They continued to push forward. More flaming bottles and flares fell around them. There wasn't much Millar could do on the front lines – she wasn't wearing the right equipment and wasn't part of the tactical team – but she wasn't going to stand by and watch while her colleagues were under attack. She fought her way through to an injured officer who had been hit by a glass bottle. He was dazed and blood ran down the side of his face from a cut above his eyebrow. Millar got him to his feet and guided him back through the square to a waiting paramedic.

'We shouldn't be in here,' shouted Dykes at her shoulder.

'Get in there and help anyone who is hurt,' she yelled at him. Dykes knew not to argue with the look of anger on Millar's face.

A smoke bomb went off close by. Millar felt the sting of the gas in her eyes. She turned and headed back towards the retreating crowd, searching for anyone else who had been hurt. Dykes did the same.

The television cameras caught the unfolding events and later tried to present a balanced report of what had occurred. Hundreds of clips filmed on mobile phones flooded the internet and police brutality started trending across social media.

The only winners were those who wished to further stoke the fires of division for their own personal gain. Somewhere, Fergus Bennett would be toasting a successful day.

There were a number of superficial injuries to protestors and police officers and thirty arrests, but there were no serious casualties. Deputy Chief Constable Aileen O'Hara judged it to have been a successful operation given the circumstances they had faced, and made her case on the broadcast news.

Millar and Dykes stayed until the embers began to die down. As Millar had guessed, there was little for them to do once the dust had settled. The ring leaders were long gone. Other officers could deal with the minor arrests.

Millar had her own investigation to get on with. She had already lost an afternoon.

9

'Not brutal enough,' was Lauryn's assessment as they watched the clip on her phone. It showed a police officer in riot gear striking a white male, leaving him with a cut to his forehead and blood streaming down his face as he was carted off by other officers. The caption on the social media post read: "Police brutality against peaceful protestors! Britons are being oppressed in their own country! Imagine the media outcry if the victim was a Muslim!"

The Carnival was quiet. After the riot in George Square that afternoon, the police and civic leaders had appealed for calm and restraint. Politicians spoke of dialling down the divisive rhetoric that had marred the election campaign so far, and warned against false information on immigration being spread on social media.

They had also asked the public to think twice about entering the city and to stay away from the city centre for the rest of the day. Carmen had decided to open the club despite these warnings, but the only customers were a group of four women celebrating a fortieth birthday. The DJ booked to play the dance floor downstairs had been cancelled half an hour ago. Georgia had been sent home early.

Cal stood behind the bar with Jenny. Lauryn sat on a stool on the opposite side, holding her phone out to them to let them see the clip she was viewing.

'You wouldn't be saying that if it was a climate change protestor or a union striker they were attacking,' said Jenny.

'They wouldn't be starting a fight with the police or shouting racist abuse though,' Lauryn replied. 'There's just as many clips of police officers getting battered as there are of protestors.'

'I'm amazed no one was killed.'

'I think that was by luck rather than design,' said Cal.

'They were busy cleaning up the square when I walked over,' said Lauryn. 'Glass and rubbish everywhere. All the benches had been trashed.'

'You shouldn't be walking about the city on your own,' warned Jenny.

'I'm a big girl.'

'I'm serious. You heard what happened at The Shed last night?'

'That's not the same.'

Jenny shook her head at Lauryn's bravado and turned to Cal. 'Has your detective friend not said anything about it? I notice she's not here tonight.'

Cal shrugged. 'I guess she's working the case, but I haven't heard from her since she was in the other night.' Cal wondered if Millar had been caught up in the riot that afternoon. She would normally make an appearance on a weekend evening, but he guessed she would be busy.

One of the women came to the bar. The club was so quiet, they could hear her high heels clicking across the wooden floor. Jenny served her.

'Jenny's right,' Cal said to Lauryn. 'You should be careful for the next few days until things calm down. The city feels like it's ready to explode.'

'It's only going to get worse building up to the election. There's going to be more and more of these protests, from all sides. I might even go to some of them.'

Cal knew Lauryn was passionate about countering the rise of the far-right and populism. 'Just promise me you'll be careful and don't do anything daft.'

'Yes, Dad,' joked Lauryn, a painful reminder to Cal of the ten-year age gap between them.

Jenny finished serving the woman and she clipped back across the floor to her table. 'They're having this last round and then moving on to try to find somewhere livelier.'

'Good luck to them finding that tonight,' said Lauryn. She held her phone out towards them again. 'Look at this. That was before the police had moved in. You can hear their racist chants.' She turned the volume up on her phone and played them another clip she had found scrolling through her timeline.

Carmen came through the doors from her office and saw them. 'No phones at the bar. You know that.'

'Sorry.' Lauryn pulled her phone back and stopped the clip playing.

'I'll let you away with it, given the circumstances. You may as well head home. The three of us can manage for the rest of the night. I don't think it's going to suddenly pick up.'

'If you're sure?'

'I'll call you a taxi to get you home,' said Jenny. 'You're not walking through the city on your own at this time of night.'

Lauryn headed down the stairs to the staff area to collect her belongings. As she exited, the curtain over the main door opened and Roddy, the doorman on duty tonight, came in. He saw Carmen at the bar and gestured to her. Carmen went over and disappeared through the curtain.

'Could be an early finish tonight. You fancy coming over to my place?' Jenny asked Cal.

'I don't have anything else planned. I'll think about it,' Cal joked.

The four women in the corner finished up the last of their drinks, put on their jackets and gathered together their purses and bags, and a large helium-filled balloon with "40" imprinted on it. Cal made his way over to clear their table as they headed for the door.

'Have a good night,' he called after them, and started collecting their glasses and the ice bucket with the empty Prosecco bottle in it. He took them to the bar and placed them on the counter. He turned as Carmen re-entered through the main door.

Cal froze on the spot. One look at the face of the man following Carmen brought back a series of painful memories.

He was tall and broad, a mixture of muscle and fat that combined to make a heavy, immovable object. His hair was the same black buzz cut that Cal remembered from a year ago.

Carmen brought him over to the bar. 'I think you already know Cal. This is Jenny, our bar manager. Jenny, this is Patrick.'

Jenny hadn't noticed Cal's reaction yet. 'Hi,' she said breezily and held her hand out to greet him. Patrick took it, his bear-like paw enveloping her small hand.

'I've brought Patrick in to help out with security for the next few weeks, just until things calm down. After what happened at The Shed, the police have been in touch again warning us to take extra precautions.'

Cal recovered from his initial shock. 'Millar has been in touch?'

'Not Millar, but someone from her team.'

'You know Detective Millar arrested this guy last summer? You were there, right? You haven't forgotten?'

Before Patrick could defend himself, Carmen beat him to it. 'Of course I remember, Cal. Let's be grown-ups about this.'

'Grown-ups? So I should just forget about him kidnapping me out of my house and driving me to be tortured by McArthur and his crew?'

'To be fair,' Patrick said, a smile spreading across his face, 'all I did was drive the car.'

Patrick had been one of McArthur's drivers, working for Francis and his son, Tony. When they had learnt about Cal's duplicity with the police, they had come for him, not once but twice, at the club and later at his home. Millar had come to Cal's rescue on both occasions.

'Also,' continued Patrick, 'I was never charged with any criminal offence. I was just an employee caught up in it all.' The smile on his face told a different story from the words leaving his mouth.

'Look, we all know what happened last year,' said Carmen, acting as a peacemaker. 'Right now, we need some extra help, so I reached out to Patrick as someone who can do a job for us. It's only until this investigation comes to an end.'

'Is he going to be here every night?' Cal asked.

'Just until this blows over.'

'And you trust him?'

'He was loyal to McArthur.'

'McArthur was a criminal.'

'We both worked for McArthur too.'

'I didn't have a choice; I was made to work for him.'

'McArthur is dead. We all made mistakes, maybe did things we didn't want to do.' Carmen tried to draw a line under the argument. 'You don't have to be best friends.'

'If it makes you feel any better,' Patrick said to Cal, 'I don't have any hard feelings about it.'

'It wasn't you that was tied up in a warehouse having his face beaten in.'

'Fair point.' Patrick shrugged.

'Enough,' said Carmen. 'Come on, I'll show you the rest of the place. It hasn't changed that much since you were last here.'

Carmen took Patrick away and they headed down the stairs just as Lauryn reappeared at the top of them. She pointed over her shoulder. 'Isn't that—'

'Yes, it is.'

'Why's he here?'

'Extra security,' answered Jenny.

'Bit awkward,' understated Lauryn.

'Let's not talk about it.' Cal went back over to the table to finish clearing it. There wasn't much he could do. Patrick was an unwelcome reminder of the recent past, but Carmen was right. They needed the extra muscle and Cal could attest to Patrick's suitability for the role. It was better to have someone like Patrick on your side instead of fighting against him.

PART 2

DETECTIVE STORY

10

Dr Pat Golightly's assistant called and asked Millar to come over right away. The forensic evidence from the Peaceful Dove Massage Parlour and The Shed nightclub had moved up the priority list after Nathan MacDonald's death, but Millar had not expected to hear anything this soon. The technology team were still trying to salvage anything from the hard drive of the computer that had been recovered from the massage parlour, but it did not look promising, and so far Mrs Chen had failed to cooperate.

'Can't you tell me over the phone? Or just email the results?'

'Dr Golightly insisted you should come over right away.' If Pat Golightly wanted to see her, it must be something important, although Millar could not think what it could be.

She hung up and left Dykes in the incident room. He could spend the morning ensuring the paperwork on Nathan MacDonald was correct. When they did catch these bastards, Millar wanted the case against them to be watertight. The family of Nathan MacDonald deserved that at least. His parents were travelling up from Kirkcudbright by train to formally identify his body today.

She took an unmarked squad car from the car park. Dalmarnock Police Station was busy as the aftermath of the riot was dealt with. Working on the property attacks and Nathan MacDonald's murder kept Millar and Dykes out of it. The automatic barrier rose and Millar turned left and crossed over the Rutherglen Bridge to the south side of the river. She stretched her shoulders and arms as she drove. They still ached from her exertions at George Square the day before, reminding her she was no longer as fit as she had been when she was a beat cop.

She joined the motorway at the Polmadie interchange and followed the M74 across the south of Glasgow until it merged onto the M8. From the elevated road she looked north and saw the city skyline, dominated by tall glass buildings that had sprung up over the last couple of decades – sheets of glass that reflected the bright sun against the clear blue sky. Millar put her sunglasses on to shut out the glare. Yellow and red cranes stretched skywards as work continued on more office blocks. Her city was changing in other ways. Shopping centres and high-street stores were being demolished and refurbished to bring living space back into the centre of the city. A modern and sleek financial sector had taken over the famous Broomielaw, once renowned as the heart of the shipbuilding industry, with all the pollution that came with it. The street now marked the boundary of the low-emission zone that covered the centre of Glasgow. The collapse of high-street shopping in the technological age had been another blow to a city that was once famed for its "style mile" of fashion stores that ran along Argyle Street, up Buchanan Street and onto Sauchiehall Street. Empty units and shuttered shop fronts now dominated. The city would have to reinvent itself once more. The demolition and construction industries would be in rude health for the foreseeable future.

The motorway dipped down and the city across the river disappeared. Millar took the exit for Govan and turned onto Helen Street. She passed the supermarket and the fast-food restaurant and pulled up at the entrance to the Police Scotland compound. The gatehouse window slid open and Harry's familiar face appeared. Harry had been sitting in the gatehouse for as long as Millar could remember. Music from a radio drifted out of the opening.

'Busy morning?' She gave him a cursory wave of her identification.

'Lot of coming and going,' Harry answered, taking a sip of coffee from his mug. 'Not had a good riot for a wee while.' He put down his drink, picked up a pen and a clipboard and made a note of Millar's arrival.

'I'm not sure how you manage to cope,' said Millar.

'It's taken a lot out of me.' Harry leant forwards and hit the button that raised the barrier in front of Millar.

'You take it easy now.'

Harry didn't have to tell her where to park. Millar moved forwards and left him to his morning paper and the radio.

She pulled up outside the building that housed the Moorepark Laboratory, a brand new purpose-built forensic facility run by the Scottish Police Authority and named after the small enclave of Moorepark in Govan where it was situated.

At the reception, she announced she was here to see Dr Golightly and was waved through.

She walked along the pristine corridors with bright white walls until she reached the room on the first floor, with windows overlooking the industrial estate that covered the rest of Moorepark. Dr Patricia Golightly had the blinds drawn to keep out the bright daylight, while white LED lights in the ceiling lit her laboratory. Air conditioning whirred in the background.

'I still can't believe they gave you new digs as good as this,' said Millar as she knocked and came through the door.

'I'm worth every penny and you know it.' Golightly didn't smile. Her demeanour was always serious. Millar liked to have some fun with the stern technician. Golightly turned off the electronic microscope she had been peering through and stood up from the stool she had been resting on. 'Thanks for coming over.'

'I dropped everything as soon as I was summoned.'

'You're going to want to see this.' She walked to the workbench at the back of the room and picked up a beige folder. Millar wondered if her demeanour was a reaction to her surname. There was nothing light about Patricia Golightly. Her presence was heavy and stern. She was only in her late thirties, not much older than Millar, but she looked and acted like she had been trudging around the laboratory for an entire lifetime. Her white lab coat and the spectacles that hung from a chain around her neck added to her aged appearance.

Millar opened the file and started to flick through the report inside. Golightly summarised it for her. 'Some good news for you. The partial print we got off the sledgehammer from the massage parlour matches the print we took from the wall at the nightclub.'

'They're from the same person?'

'Highly likely. There's enough there to make it a highly probable match.'

'So it's the same gang?'

'That's for you to investigate, not me. I'm saying the same person was probably in both places and was probably involved in both incidents, given that one print was from a weapon recovered from one scene and the other was a blood-stained mark on a wall.'

'The bad news?'

'We're still checking, but so far there's no match with any prints we have on record.'

It would be too much to hope for, to have a name pop up and blow the whole investigation wide open. Still, Millar was encouraged. Find the person who did match these prints, and they had evidence to pin two of the attacks on them.

'Keep checking. You never know, they might be on file somewhere.' Millar saw Golightly looking at her. There was something else. 'What?' she asked.

'We don't have a match with anyone identifiable, but the prints do match with another open case. One that you were involved with last year.' Golightly handed Millar a second file.

Millar took it from her, a puzzled look on her face. She flipped open the front cover and read the name of the case file. It was named after the victim in the case. It read "Black, Rose".

Millar's head started to spin.

Golightly was still talking. 'The prints from the massage parlour and from the nightclub match the prints taken from the murder weapon used to stab Rose Black last year, the knife that was recovered from the scene. Whoever was at the nightclub and the massage parlour was also at the scene of Rose Black's murder.'

11

Superintendent Douglas Forsyth was at the head of the table in full dress uniform. He had spent his day dealing with the fallout from the riot in the city. Millar thought she saw a few more tired lines on his face, a few more grey hairs in his short crew cut. It had been a stressful couple of days for the head of the force. And now this.

Millar sat next to Dykes. Across from them sat Detective Inspectors Boyle and Scott. They looked downbeat rather than energised. They were in the room that adjoined Superintendent Forsyth's office in Helen Street Police Station, five hundred yards from Patricia Golightly's new laboratory. The room was plain – white walls, white ceiling tiles, white window blinds, and four white tables grouped together to make one large table. There was no clutter, no files or boxes and nothing on the walls. Investigations were not run out of this room. This room was for the superintendent to meet with senior officers and detectives when extraordinary events required it.

Marcus Boyle was the lead investigator in the murder of Rose Black. Finlay Scott was his partner on the case. Millar had called Superintendent Forsyth from Dr Golightly's office as soon as she had heard the news. Dykes had driven over from Dalmarnock. Boyle and Scott were working out of the city centre station on Stewart Street. On Superintendent Forsyth's command they had dropped everything and made their way to the south of the city. An hour later, the superintendent and the four detectives were sitting together.

'This is the break we've been waiting for,' Forsyth told them. It was no secret he had been frustrated with the lack of progress in the Rose Black investigation. A lone woman stabbed to death on a city street had generated a lot of publicity. It had focused a lot of attention on the police and what they were doing to stem the unrelenting tide of violence against women. People questioned how safe the streets of the city were. It had brought politicians to the superintendent's office, and he did not like to have politicians interfering with his work. Six months had passed and the initial public outcry had died down. The public disorder had abated, but the political clamour had not, especially with an election looming. The failure to catch the perpetrator was a black mark against Forsyth and his force. The press returned to the lack of progress in the hunt for the killer on their front pages every few days. The family of Rose Black were outspoken in their disappointment at the lack of progress. 'Marcus, this lead is now the priority for your investigation.'

'It's one of a number of lines of inquiry open to us. A new one that opens up a new avenue,' Boyle answered diplomatically.

'Bollocks.' Forsyth shut him down. 'You've had nothing for weeks. This is the first solid lead we've had in the whole bloody case.'

'We've been reviewing CCTV and going back over statements. Detective Scott has been re-interviewing everyone involved—'

'And getting nowhere. This is your priority. Drop everything else and work this angle. Millar and Dykes are reassigned back on to your team. They'll come at it from their side – the attacks on property and Nathan MacDonald's murder.'

Millar felt Boyle bristle with indignation. No detective liked to be undermined on their investigation – it was nothing personal against Millar. Boyle was old school. He was six feet tall and balding. His youthful muscle was running to fat but he was still a formidable presence. There was no personality clash or animosity between them, but she was ten years his junior and she was a woman, and Millar knew both those things counted against her in Boyle's eyes.

'Sir, it's definitely an important lead, but I would really like to continue with the lines of inquiry we are going through at the moment. I don't want to drop everything and just concentrate on this alone—'

Millar cut him off this time. 'Dykes and I will work the Rose Black connection to our case and come at it from our side. We'll share everything with Detective Boyle.'

'Fine,' said Forsyth, 'and no fuck-ups. I need this case put down, and quickly. Unsolved murders and riots in the city are not what I need.'

'We'll do our best, sir,' said Boyle.

The superintendent dismissed them and returned to his office. The four detectives left the meeting room and made their way along the corridor.

'What do you think then?' Boyle asked Millar. 'How does your case connect to Rose Black?'

'We have a gang going around the city destroying property, perhaps trying to muscle in on the scene in the vacuum left after the McArthur empire was broken up.' Millar didn't need to remind Boyle that it was her investigation that had taken down the McArthur empire. She did not know if Boyle had been one of the officers on the take from McArthur, but she knew McArthur had had a lot of police officers on his payroll. 'And we know that at least one of the members of this gang was at the scene of Rose Black's murder, potentially the murderer himself.'

'The man seen running from the scene of the crime?'

'Our Eastern European mystery man. Could be. Have you ever got closer to finding him?'

Boyle shook his head. 'Nothing. For all we know, he never existed. He was just a convenient excuse for the far-right wingnuts to go on the rampage. We looked into her cases and got nowhere.'

Rose Black had been working as a human rights lawyer, representing immigrants and refugees who had arrived in Scotland illegally. She was helping them claim asylum and protecting them from deportation. It had brought her indirectly into contact with some unsavoury people – the gangs of people traffickers who made money smuggling these desperate people across the borders from Africa, the Middle East and elsewhere.

The police had looked into those connections, pointed in that direction by the anonymous witness statement. They had interviewed all of the clients Rose had been representing. They found nothing that directly linked these gangs to her. Her clients were desperate people, but every one of them considered Rose a hero. She was one of the few people they trusted, who treated them with dignity, listened to their stories and worked tirelessly to defend them. There was no motive for them to hurt her.

But now her murder was linked to a gang that was trying to muscle into the city. A new player on the scene, perhaps a new player who had not been in the country before, who had come from overseas. A new player who shipped men into the country and then put them to use in building their business. A new player who would not want an ambitious and dedicated human rights lawyer getting too involved in their people-trafficking business. It made sense as a working hypothesis if Rose had stumbled into something she should not have.

Millar kept her thoughts to herself. 'I'll look into her cases again, see if anything new jumps out. Are all the files on the database?'

'Sure.'

'We'll need access to them.'

They exited the building and split up – Boyle and Scott to return to Stewart Street, Dykes to return to Dalmarnock.

Millar gave Dykes his instructions before he left. 'Start going through her case files again. Get names together of people she was representing at the time of her death and in the months beforehand. Go through their statements and look for crossovers, any names that crop up, people who might be involved in trafficking these people over here.'

'You think the gang we're looking for is a people-trafficking gang? Expanding their business?'

'It would make sense. They have a ready-made workforce in debt to them in the city. Men with no income, no home, here illegally with no one to turn to. Desperate men.'

'So they keep them on as employees?'

'That's a polite way of putting it. They use them to carry out muscle work for them. They have a hold over these people.'

'Okay, they use them to commit these crimes and move into the city, I can see that, but why kill a lawyer?'

'I'm speculating, but what if Rose found out about them? One of her clients says too much about the people that smuggled them into the country, she starts snooping around where she shouldn't, gets too close.'

'That's a reach. They want her out of the way because she's meddling with their illegal immigrants? If anything, she's helping them by keeping their men in the country. Killing a lawyer only brings more heat on to the gang. It's counterproductive for them.'

'Has it been, though? It fits with the witness statement. The gang gets one of their men to kill Rose.'

'Alright, it's worth looking into,' Dykes conceded.

'If it is linked to people trafficking, the NCA will want to get involved. Start making some calls and see if there is anyone there who can tell us anything about gangs operating in Glasgow.' The

National Crime Agency led the response to people trafficking and modern slavery in the United Kingdom.

Dykes opened the door to his car. 'I'll see you back at the station.'

'I'll meet you there in a bit. I have to make a detour on the way.'

'Anything I should know about?'

'It's personal,' Millar answered, which was her way of telling Dykes it was better he did not know.

12

In recent years the south side of the city had been flooded with upmarket restaurants and trendy bistros. The Cathcart Road Café was very much an old-style café, a place to go for a standard hot-filled roll and a plain cup of tea. Nothing fancy, nothing extravagant. The café had its regulars and the owner, Big Mags, knew all of them by name. If a stranger entered, they could expect to be judged by Big Mags, and the warmth of her welcome was adjusted accordingly.

Cal entered during the lunchtime rush. He ordered his usual – a roll, square sausage and potato scone with a black coffee – and took a table at the back against the wall. Workers from a construction site further up the road had all come in for their lunch break. It was noisy with chatter and laughter.

'No Jenny today?' asked Mags as she delivered Cal's roll on a chipped plate.

'Meeting someone else.'

'Oh, aye? You better not be messing that lassie about,' warned Mags. 'She's way too good for you.'

'I know it.'

Mags returned to the counter and Cal squirted ketchup on to his roll and waited for Millar to arrive. She had insisted on seeing him alone.

He was halfway through his roll and the lunchtime rush was beginning to die down when Millar arrived. She stopped at the door and looked around, saw him and made her way to his table. Big Mags watched her cross the room with interest, a new face to be evaluated.

Millar slid into the seat opposite him.

'You want anything to eat?'

Mags came over with a notepad. 'Normally you order at the counter.'

'Coffee, please.' Millar usually preferred a latte, but she could read the type of establishment she was in.

'Milk?'

'Please. No sugar.'

'Nothing to eat?'

'No thanks.'

Mags retreated back to the counter to fetch the coffee.

'What is it?' He could tell something was troubling Millar. She was not great at hiding her feelings if something serious had happened.

Millar waited until Mags had returned with her drink and then watched her return to the counter.

'She thinks I might be cheating on Jenny with you.' Cal's attempt to lighten the mood did not raise a smile from Millar. 'So what did you need to see me about?'

Millar took a sip of the hot coffee. She clasped her hands around the mug and looked down at the table. 'I shouldn't really be telling you this.'

'You're not telling me anything at the moment.'

'I mean, it's a breach of protocol. I could be fired for telling you.'

'So don't tell me. From the sound of it, I might not want to hear it.'

Millar looked up at him. She knew she was about to crush the small amount of happiness Cal had managed to rebuild in his life over the last few months.

She had debated whether to tell him or not. Even after she had called Cal and arranged to meet him, she wasn't sure if it was the right thing to do. She knew it was legally wrong. Cal was connected to Rose Black only because of what he had done to her over a decade ago. He had left her in a coma and had got away with it. Cal had not been able to let Rose go. Millar had used that against him when their paths had first crossed. Maybe that's why she felt like she owed him something now. He was just a member of the public like anyone else. He had no right to be informed about a development in the investigation.

If Boyle or Forsyth found out, Millar would be taken off the case, suspended and probably fired.

She took another sip of the coffee. It was horrible, but she liked the burn as it went down her throat.

'It's about Rose Black,' she said.

Cal sat back in his chair, as if he wanted to distance himself from her and what she had to say.

'They found out who did it?'

'No, but we've had the first break for months.' Millar kept going. She had crossed a line and there was no going back. 'It's linked to the case I'm working on right now.'

'The massage parlour thing?'

'You heard about The Shed nightclub?'

'That was linked too?'

'We found the same fingerprint at both places.'

'I heard someone was killed at the nightclub.'

Millar nodded. 'We don't have a match for the fingerprints yet, but we did have them on record from an earlier investigation.'

Cal saw it coming. 'From Rose's murder?'

'From the murder weapon.'

Cal reeled. The person who had killed Rose was still out there in the city, still free, still going around killing people and trashing nightclubs. 'Are you back on the case?'

'Yes, working it from the angle of the property attacks. Boyle is still running it overall.'

'How is Rose linked to the property attacks?'

'Working hypothesis: it could be to do with her work, through people-trafficking gangs. They could use the people they bring into the country to trash these places.'

'And Rose found out about them? She knew who the people traffickers were?'

'The problem with the investigation was always the lack of motive. Why would someone kill Rose? Sure, men attack women on the street, we know that, but usually, if they don't know each other, there's a sexual angle. Or they kidnap them first and abuse them before killing them. Rose was stabbed in the middle of the street and left there.'

'Find the gang trashing these properties and you find Rose's killer.'

'It could be that simple. We thought they were a professional outfit up until the last nightclub attack. But they panicked when they found the kid in the nightclub and killed him. They might be run by professionals, but these men are no experts. They didn't react well to an unexpected occurrence. They tried to burn the place down to hide the body and failed.'

'So you think they're amateurs?'

'I think they could be normal people like you and me, forced into doing something they don't want to do and aren't equipped to do. Not many people are cut out for violence and murder. The gang leaders could be blackmailing them and they have no one else to turn to.'

'Except maybe a human rights lawyer who wants to help them out, and when the gang leaders find out about her, they do something about it.' Cal paused. It made sense. It was a possible motive at least. 'What do you want me to do?'

'Nothing. I just wanted you to know. I'm going to catch the bastard that killed her.'

Cal believed her. He had seen Millar like this before, when she was hunting Francis McArthur. When she set her mind to do something, she was impossible to stop.

'Have you told her family?'

'Boyle talks to the family, no one else.'

'They have a right to know more than I do.'

'I don't disagree.'

The conversation paused. Cal ate the last piece of his roll. Millar looked around the café. Mags was still keeping a wary eye on them.

Cal had thought he had left his past behind him. Now he seemed to be surrounded by it once more. 'You remember Patrick Healy?'

'McArthur's driver?'

Cal nodded. 'With a sideline in kidnapping. He was in the club the other night, meeting Carmen. She was consulting him on extra security.'

'Makes sense. I guess you weren't too enamoured to see him again.'

'Not really, no. I don't seem to be able to escape that part of my life.'

'It's a smart move, at least for the moment. There are only so many nightclubs in the city. If this gang is looking to move in on the territory, the Carnival has as much chance as any other club of being their next target.'

'That's reassuring.'

Cal stayed in the café after Millar had gone. His past swirled around him. He thought he was done with all of it. Last summer he had confronted that part of his life and had drawn a line under it. Then Rose had been killed and it had sent him spiralling back to a dark place. Jenny had saved him. But the killer had never been found and the investigation remained open. He should have known at some point Rose would come back to haunt him once more. The feelings of guilt and shame about the young life he had wrecked returned. He felt the weight of his past. The accident with Rose had led to everything that had gone wrong in his life. A year later, Cal's dad had killed himself, driven to it by the debt owed to Francis McArthur. Then followed the fall into drug addiction, alcohol and the self-destructive cycle that had finally ended when Cal had been put in prison for assaulting a police officer.

There was so much Cal could not put right, but he could not sit and do nothing while Rose Black's killer was still walking around the city.

13

Millar grabbed a pre-packed sandwich from the staff canteen when she got back to the station and took it to her desk in the incident room. Dykes was on a call with someone at the National Crime Agency. Every so often he mumbled "uh-huh" and scribbled something on his notepad.

Millar started eating while she logged on to the computer. Detective Scott had emailed her access details to get back into the Rose Black case files. Millar followed the link, entered the details and the folder structure appeared on her screen.

There were a lot of folders; it was a high-profile and lengthy case. She skipped through witness statements and forensic reports. She had already memorised those when she had been involved in the case.

She found what she was looking for. A folder titled "Rose Black – Libertio Files". Libertio was the name of the law firm Rose had worked for. Millar clicked on it. It was password-protected. There would be sensitive legal information in the files that could not be shared outside of the few detectives involved in the case. She emailed Scott to request access and waited for his response. While she waited, she ate the rest of the tasteless sandwich. She felt like eating something more substantial. Her diet had gone to pieces in the last fortnight, as had her regular trips to the police gym. She was drinking too much and snacking on the wrong sort of food. It always happened when she got too involved in a case.

Dykes shifted in his chair, leant forwards and made another note. Michael Dykes was two years younger than Millar, just the wrong side of thirty and recently promoted to full detective inspector rank. He was typical of the new batch of detectives that were coming through behind Millar – well trained, smart, diligent and clean-cut. He was also innocent. He hadn't spent enough time on the street, out in the real world, getting to know the city and the people and the real way that criminals worked. He was a bright, shiny new penny that needed to be dented and rusted. Millar had tried to show him some of that. There was a decent detective in there somewhere, behind those clear-blue innocent eyes and the boyish clean-shaven face.

Finally, Dykes wrapped up the phone call and put the receiver back in the cradle on his desk.

'Well?' asked Millar.

'Spoke to one Higher Executive Officer Rohan Chopra.' A higher executive officer was the equivalent of a police sergeant, a middle-ranker. Not an administrator, but not an inspector either.

'Anything useful to tell us?'

'I'll type it out for the files,' said Dykes.

Always sticking to the correct protocol, thought Millar. 'Bullet points?'

'He's circumspect about a gang of people traffickers branching out into other areas of crime, especially within a city. They're more likely to use their connections to spread into drug smuggling or counterfeit goods. He's also pretty certain they would not attack or kill a human rights lawyer. These gangs like to keep a low profile. They wouldn't do anything that might bring unwanted attention. They very much like to keep in the shadows.'

'Great.' Maybe they were reaching after all.

'He did give us a bit of a rundown on the people-trafficking scene in Scotland. Unlike the perception given by the media and certain politicians, it's actually a small-scale industry, especially if you compare it to London and the south-east of England. Scotland isn't swamped with illegal immigrants desperate to make a home here.'

'Must be the weather that puts them off.'

'The main countries of origin are what you would expect – Syria, Afghanistan, Iraq, Iran and a few others around the Middle East, and Albania. Other nationalities make up less than ten percent, although that still amounts to around ten thousand immigrants. Ninety percent of the immigrants are males and most arrive via small boats across the sea, claim asylum and get swept up in the system.'

'But there must be some who don't claim asylum? Who slip through the net and disappear into the country without appearing on any records?'

'The figures they have only cover the illegal immigrants they know about, but he did stress it was very difficult to get into the country completely undetected.'

'Right, but we're talking about twelve men, according to our eye witness from the nightclub. Even allowing that they might be part of a larger group, there could easily be fifty, a hundred, undocumented immigrants in the city.'

Dykes shrugged. 'Anything's possible.'

'Anything about Glasgow in particular? Any gangs they know about operating in the city?'

Dykes shook his head. 'They don't operate on a city-by-city basis. They look at the overall country and they concentrate on ports and borders. Once the immigrants enter the asylum system, the Home Office takes over. They don't have any open cases in the Glasgow area for slavery or people trafficking.'

'A dead end.'

'Pretty much.' Dykes tossed his notebook onto his desk. 'If we're looking for a criminal gang made up of illegal immigrants, where do we start?'

Millar looked out of the window. There wasn't much of a view. The flat ground around the station was brownfield ex-industrial land that was awaiting its next reincarnation, probably as a housing estate. Warehouses and storage facilities crept up to the boundary of the police station. Beyond them the outer edges of the east end of Glasgow rose up in the form of new-build council flats, the neighbourhoods of Bridgeton, Dalmarnock, Parkhead and then the Gallowgate heading west into the city. That was where they needed to be looking, she realised. The answer was not going to present itself to them as they sat in their office block on the edge of the city. They had to be out there, on the streets, asking the people who really knew what was going on in their city.

'Come on, let's go,' she said to Dykes, getting up from her chair and picking up her jacket.

'Go where?'

'Out there,' said Millar. 'I know some people we can ask about criminal gangs in the city.'

14

Jenny insisted on coming with him. Cal could not refuse her. He owed it to her to include her in what he was going through; she had earned that much.

Libertio's office was on Bath Street, at the peak of the sloping hill that ran down to Charing Cross on one side and Buchanan Street on the other. They were a civil and human rights law firm, specialising in immigration cases and the rights of refugees and immigrants. The bulk of their workload was Legal Aid cases, fighting for those who did not have the means to hire an expensive lawyer. It was not glamorous work and it was not well-paid work. The firm relied on the bankroll of wealthy philanthropists and concerned donors.

Rose had worked her way up through the company having joined as an intern after graduating from university. She had worked diligently and earned the qualifications to become a solicitor. She was admitted to the roll at the age of twenty-seven.

Cal found this out after she had died. She had been at university when he had almost killed her. He had followed her career, and her life, for a time after that, watching her recover from the harm he had done. She had never needed his help. He had never found a way to make amends.

Jenny found a parking space a block away from the sandstone terraced building.

'What now?' she asked him.

'I'm not sure. I go in and ask to speak to someone, I guess.'

'You haven't thought this through. They are a law firm. They will only talk to the police about something like this.'

'You're probably right, but I have to try.'

Jenny walked with him back along the street. Across the road from the office was a sandwich bistro, situated in the basement of an office block, with steps leading down to a brightly lit window. She would wait for him there. 'Good luck,' she said and kissed him on the cheek. She had to let him try, even if she knew it was pointless.

Cal crossed the road and walked up the steps and through the glass entry door. There was a directory on the wall. A number of different firms occupied the offices of the four-storey building. Libertio shared the third floor with another law firm. Cal climbed the carpeted stairs.

He exited the staircase and went through a door that had "Libertio" stencilled into the glass panel.

A young man sat behind a desk. Legal files were stacked in piles in front of him. There was barely room on the surface for the computer monitor and the two telephones. He was on a call when Cal entered. He smiled and raised a finger to let Cal know he would be with him just as soon as he could be. Cal listened to him as he spoke into the phone. He had a European accent, German or Polish.

The furnishings were sparse and jaded. This was not the image of the successful, big-money law firm familiar from television dramas. This was a place where hard, difficult work was done for little reward. Beyond the reception area was a carpeted corridor. A series of doors lined each side of the corridor. A couple of smartly dressed women bustled out of one door and along the corridor, then disappeared into another room.

There was a small waiting area with low cushioned chairs and a coffee table. On the coffee table was a vase of fresh flowers and next to it was a photograph. The face of Rose Black stared out at him from inside the black frame.

It was a professional headshot photograph, like one that would be used on the company website. Rose wore her auburn hair tied back and had light make-up on. She wore a black blouse and jacket. She smiled at the camera. The photograph favoured the left side of her face, her head turned over her right shoulder and her body angled to the side. Cal knew the right side of her face bore the scars he had left on her.

The receptionist finished the call. Cal guessed he was some sort of office clerk who doubled up his duties by manning the front desk. 'Sorry for the wait, sir. How can I help you?'

Cal had not given enough thought to what he should say. He decided on the direct truth. 'I wanted to talk to somebody about Rose Black.'

'Do you have an appointment with someone?'

'No, sorry.'

'I'm afraid we're very busy. It would be better if you made an appointment and came back. Can I ask what it's regarding?'

'Did you know Rose?' Cal asked.

'I'm afraid I started here after she…' He trailed off. 'Were you a friend of hers?'

'No, I was a…' It was Cal's turn to stumble. What exactly was he to Rose? Not a friend. A stalker? A protector? 'I took an interest in her career. Is there anyone here who would be able to talk to me about some of the cases she was involved in before she was killed?'

'I'm sorry, who did you say you were? I'm afraid no one will be able to talk about legal cases with you unless you have the authority to—'

A woman appeared from a room at the top of the corridor. She paused and stared at them. Cal did not notice her.

'My name is Cal Jackson. I'm helping the police with their inquiries. If there was someone I could have a quick word with?'

The receptionist was having none of it. 'I'm afraid that is out of the question. It's a bit irregular for a member of the public to come in and expect us to talk about our cases. I'm afraid I'm going to have to ask you to leave.'

The woman had started to walk along the corridor when Cal had said his name. Now she stood on the other side of the desk from Cal, staring at him. Cal thought she had come to offer moral support to her colleague, but when he looked into her eyes he saw something else. She was looking at him with a mixture of disgust and hatred.

'What the hell are you doing here?' she asked, with more than a hint of venom.

'I wanted to talk to someone about Rose Black.'

'You've got some bloody nerve after what you did to her.'

'I'm sorry, do I know you?'

The receptionist tried again to get Cal to leave. 'If you want to make an appointment for another day, sir.'

The woman cut him off. 'It's alright, Alexander, I'll talk to this piece of shit. I can't wait to hear what he has to say for himself.'

Alexander was taken aback. Even if Cal was an unorthodox visitor, there were certain levels of politeness that professional law firms had to maintain. 'Juliet, that is no way to talk to someone.'

'You don't understand, Alexander. This man almost killed Rose years ago and somehow didn't even go to prison for it. I was there the night he ran her over in his car. He has got no right to be here at all.'

'Perhaps I should leave.' Cal had not been prepared for this. He wanted to confront his past, but he had not expected to confront it so literally.

'No, you don't get to run away again. You want to talk about Rose? Let's talk about Rose. Follow me.' Juliet turned and swept the nearest door open. She held it for Cal to walk through. Her eyes followed him as he passed her and entered a small meeting room.

'Should I call anyone else, perhaps one of the senior partners?' Alexander said behind him in his polite, clipped Germanic accent.

'No need to trouble them. I'll deal with him,' answered Juliet, and swung the door closed behind her with a definite slam.

15

Mid-afternoon, Duke Street. The pubs were open. They tried The Dennistoun Arms and The King's Head without success. They walked further on, passing a convenience store, Nim's Thai Massage, the Essence of Beauty salon, Laser Teeth Whitening, a vaping store and a Cash Converters pawn shop. Millar found the sort of person she was looking for in The Red Lion.

Tacky McGee sat in the corner, nursing a pint of Tennent's Lager. He had earned his nickname – bad luck stuck to Tacky like glue. He had a terrible habit of being in the wrong place at the wrong time. His criminal record was a hit list of minor misdemeanours. It was well known that if you needed a fall guy to take the blame, Tacky was your man. One more bullet point on his file would not make much difference at this point. Millar was responsible for two of those bullet points. She had arrested him when she was a constable and the east end had been her patch.

Tacky looked up when Millar and Dykes entered. There were no windows in the Red Lion. The only natural light came through the open door. Orange wall lamps provided gloomy illumination. It took a moment for Millar's eyes to adjust to the dark interior. A haze of smoke hung around the room. Charlie stood behind the bar. He had run the Red Lion for the last forty years. Not much had changed in that time. The red carpet and red-upholstered chairs were worn and stained; the dark, varnished oak walls and bar were scratched and chipped. Ashtrays still sat in the middle of each table. Behind Charlie, a portrait of the late Queen Elizabeth II in full royal regalia kept an eye on events. The east end was traditionally the Celtic-supporting, Catholic-minded side of the city. The Red Lion was a Protestant outlier.

'Constable Millar, it's been a long time,' Charlie greeted her. He placed his palms on the bar, his arms spread out, supporting his portly frame.

'It's detective now,' Millar replied with a smile. She looked into the corner and saw Tacky McGee trying to hide behind his pint glass.

'Times have changed,' said Charlie.

'Not in here, they haven't. Aren't you going to update that?' Millar pointed at the Queen's portrait.

Charlie ignored the remark. 'A social call? Can I get you anything to drink?'

'Afraid it's business, Charlie. I'd like a wee word with our friend Tacky here.'

'By all means, make yourself at home.'

Dykes followed Millar over to the corner table. They pulled across two chairs from the next table and sat on either side of Tacky. Dykes looked uncomfortable in the downbeat surroundings. *This is the trouble with the fast-tracked generation of detectives,* Millar thought. *They've never had to get their hands dirty. They've been taught in classrooms, not on the street, in the real world.* Dykes looked as out of place in The Red Lion as a Catholic at an Orange Lodge meeting.

'You know, it's illegal to smoke in a public indoor space these days,' Millar said. It had been for almost twenty years in Scotland. The Red Lion must have been the last holdout.

Tacky meekly stubbed out the roll-up he held between his index and middle fingers. 'There's no one else here,' he reasoned.

'You wouldn't want poor Charlie to suffer from your second-hand smoke?' On cue, Charlie let out a loud, hacking cough from behind the bar.

Tacky leant back and became even smaller in his chair. His jacket and trousers were old, worn and stained. His fingers and teeth were yellow, matched by the slack skin around his face. His hair was a greying mop, unstyled and unwashed.

'How have you been, Tacky?' Millar asked.

'You know how it is. Surviving and thriving.'

'How long has it been? Ten years?'

'Must be close to it. So you're high up now. I hear you took down Francis McArthur.'

'It's good to know you've still got your ear to the ground, Tacky. That's why I wanted to see you.'

Every constable who pounded a beat in Glasgow had one or two contacts like Tacky. Informant was too strong a word for people like him. They would never be on the police payroll; they would never betray the people in charge. It was too dangerous. But at the same time, Tacky knew everyone and always knew what was happening in his particular part of the world. He was a fountain of knowledge when it came to the less salubrious parts of the underworld that petty criminals could access, and the police could not.

'Oh, I don't mix with those sorts of people anymore, Millar.' He picked up his pint and took a slug of the cloudy golden liquid.

Millar would have to play his game. 'You need your glass refreshed, Tacky?' She didn't wait for him to answer. 'Detective Dykes, fetch Tacky another pint from the bar, would you?'

Dykes looked at her uncertainly. She motioned for him to get up and leave them.

'Tennent's, if you're buying,' said Tacky, 'and a bag of salted peanuts.'

Dykes got up and made his way to the bar, his feet sticking to the carpet with each step. Charlie had already started pouring a fresh pint.

'I'm looking for some people.'

'I know lots of people, Millar.'

'Specifically, I'm looking for a group of people. Newcomers to the city, moving in on the turf. Picking up some of McArthur's old business.'

'The nightclub attacks? DeVito's restaurant?'

Millar nodded. It amazed her that Tacky could appear so pathetic and so astute at the same time. 'And the massage parlour.'

'You think it's one gang doing all of them?'

'It's a theory. Heard anything about them?'

Tacky shook his head. Flakes of dandruff fell onto the shoulders of his dark jacket.

Millar sighed. Some things never changed at all. She took out her wallet, pulled out a twenty-pound note and placed it on the table between them, keeping her hand on it.

'Take a look around outside, Millar. There's new places and new faces all the time now. Massage parlours, nail bars. Hell, even the sweet shops are fronts now. Say what you like about the old gangs, but at least they kept the streets clean and the place civilised.'

Millar tried not to laugh at Tacky's skewed view of history and the violent gangs that had once ruled the streets around the city. Reminiscing about the romanticised and sentimental memories of the good old days was a national pastime for some, and belied the reality of Glasgow's past. To get what she needed, it was easier to play along. 'You mean immigrants?'

'Foreigners, yeah. I'm not racist, you understand,' said Tacky, immediately preparing to contradict himself. 'But the likes of Mr McArthur treated people with a bit of respect. These immigrants just take advantage of people, and they've got no respect for the traditions.'

Don't argue, thought Millar, *just keep him talking.* Dykes returned, placed a full pint in front of Tacky and dropped a bag of peanuts next to it. He raised an eyebrow at the money under Millar's hand and looked at his partner.

'I fancy some peanuts too, and a soft drink. Do you mind?' Millar said to him. Dykes took the hint and left them alone again.

Tacky raised the fresh pint to his mouth. 'Cheers.'

'Any chat about foreign gangs that might be looking to expand?'

Tacky swallowed and put the glass back on the table. 'I told you. I don't get involved with that sort of thing anymore.'

Millar slid the twenty-pound note closer to him, but he only shrugged, picked up the packet of peanuts and ripped them open. Maybe he didn't know anything. Maybe Millar had been away from the streets for too long and had lost that connection.

Tacky crunched his way through a handful of nuts, dropping crumbs down his front. 'If you want to help, you should talk to Charlie. His old dear has a bunch of them living in her estate. Up and about at all hours, so they are.'

'A bunch of who?'

'Foreigners. Group of them, all men staying in the one place.' Tacky raised his voice across the pub. 'Isn't that right, Charlie? Up at the high-rises in Possilpark.'

'What's that?' called Charlie from behind the bar.

'Your maw was telling you about a bunch of asylum seekers all staying in a flat in her block.'

'Aye. Middle Eastern, she says, or something like that. They all look the same to her. Boarded up their windows, made the place look like a ghetto. Reckons they get bussed out and work on the building sites. She's seen them all getting put in a Transit van together.'

'A Transit van? What colour?'

'How the hell am I supposed to know that?' Charlie answered. He disappeared behind the bar.

It was too much of a coincidence, thought Millar. There were a thousand Transit vans around the city, and thousands of construction workers getting picked up and dropped off in them every day, working at developments all across the urban sprawl.

'Sorry I couldn't be of more help, Millar,' said Tacky, between crunching peanuts. 'Like I said, times change. I've left those days behind me – or rather, those days have left me behind.'

Dykes returned with another bag of peanuts and a glass of Coke. Millar stood up. 'Come on,' she said, 'we've got someone else we should go and see.' She headed to the door. 'See you around Tacky. Look after yourself.' Dykes left the Coke on the table, pocketed the bag of nuts and followed Millar.

Tacky slid the twenty-pound note from the table and stuffed it into his pocket. The rest of the week looked brighter now. Another pint and he could pick up a fish supper on the way home.

16

If Cal ever needed a solicitor in the future, he could do a lot worse than Juliet White.

He sat on an uncomfortable chair behind a table in the interview room. Juliet stood on the other side of the table and stared down at him. Her brown hair was cut just below her ears in a bob, her skin was tawny-brown and soft-looking. If she was the same age as Rose, she looked younger than her years. Her youthful appearance hid her fearsome attitude. Cal could picture her defending a client with the same determined energy she was directing towards him at that moment. He was not enjoying being on the receiving end of it.

'You don't remember me from that night?' she asked.

'I don't remember a lot from that night. I have nightmares about that night, but I find it hard to recall specifics.'

'I still have nightmares too. I was right next to Rose when you hit her.'

'I understand that,' stuttered Cal.

'You never even told her you were sorry.'

'Of course I was. My lawyer told me not to get in contact with her or her family. I wanted to.'

'Did you feel any sort of guilt? You walked away from it with a slap on the wrists and community service.'

'Believe me, I felt so much guilt. I hated myself for years. I still do.'

'Cry me a river,' she dismissed him. 'And you appear here now, six months too late.'

'I'm trying to help,' Cal pleaded. 'I'm trying to find out who killed her.'

'Are you some sort of private investigator?'

'Not really. I just…' Cal faltered as he tried to make a convincing explanation that would encompass everything he had been through in the last twelve years and how it had led him to this point. 'I just want to help. I owe Rose that.'

'You don't owe her anything. She was doing just fine without you.'

'Was she, though?' Cal tried to steer the conversation away from Juliet's anger about him and towards Rose. 'That's what I wanted to ask someone. How was Rose in the weeks before she was killed? Was there anything that was upsetting her? Anything at work that might have put her at risk?'

'The police looked into that six months ago. We told them all we knew. We handed over all her case files. We work with people in desperate situations. We work with people under extreme stress. There's always an element of risk involved, but none of our clients wants to harm us. We're often the only people trying to help them.'

She paused and took a breath. 'Why now? Why are you here now, after all this time? Has something happened?'

'I can't really say.'

'You're going to have to, or you can leave right now.'

He had no choice but to tell her. If she was Rose's friend then it would do no harm. 'There's a new angle to the case. You heard about the attacks on the nightclubs and other properties?'

'Yes.'

'There's a link between those attacks and Rose's murder.'

'What sort of link?'

'Fingerprints at the scene.'

That made Juliet stop for a moment, then she paced across the room as she digested the news. 'The same person behind these attacks killed Rose?'

'Potentially. Someone was in both places, that's for sure.'

'So what are you suggesting? Illegal immigrants who Rose was trying to help killed her and are now rampaging across the city?'

'It's just a possibility.'

Juliet cut him off with a sarcastic laugh. 'That is just typical of the police and people in this country. "There's a gang of violent offenders running around the city killing women and destroying property. It must be those awful illegal immigrants that are swarming over here, ruining our good old British way of life."'

'It's just an avenue the police are looking into.'

'Of course it is, and at no point is their thinking clouded by prejudice against immigrants. Give me a break. These people have nothing. They are more likely to be the victims of crime than the perpetrators, and they have no one to help them when they *are* the victims of crime. Instead, they get persecuted even more.' She thumped her fist against the table and then relented. She walked over to the window and stood facing out into the street.

Cal waited a moment before speaking. 'You were Rose's friend at university?'

Her face softened. 'We met on the first day of high school. Black and white. Ironically, she was the one with the pale complexion. After that we were inseparable, your classic best friend cliché right through school. We went to the same clubs, had the same interests, hung out together all the time, and took the same classes. It was inevitable that we applied for the same course at university and moved into a student flat together. Then you almost killed her.'

There was nothing Cal could say in response.

Juliet continued, 'Rose was already the strongest person I knew. She was away from university for six months recuperating. When she came back, she had scars and walked with a limp and a crutch, but she hadn't changed. She was the same amazing person I knew before the accident, only more determined than ever to graduate and use her degree to help people.

'You expect me to say she suffered mental agonies as well as physical ones? She didn't. She powered through any obstacle in her way and moved on to the next thing. No regrets, just kept moving forward. She was a force of nature. Right up until the night someone killed her.'

'What happened that night?' Cal had heard Millar's clinical police version of the events of that night, and the sensationalised media version. He wanted to hear it from someone who knew Rose and had been around her at the time.

'She worked late as usual. It's a thankless task, what we do here. Too many people needing help, not enough money, not enough staff and not enough time. I usually stayed late with her, but I had a family party to go to. I left about six. She stayed on until nine. It was two days before Christmas. She wanted to get paperwork filed before the courts shut down for the festive break. It was pitch black by the time she left. Everyone else had left the office. She took some files with her to work on over the break, locked the door and came down the steps, and someone stabbed her. She bled out on the pavement right there.' Juliet pointed out of the window to the street below.

'There must have been witnesses. The city would have been busy with festive parties. Someone must have walked past and seen something.'

'They appealed for witnesses. They only got that one anonymous tip-off. They found the knife at the scene. Whoever killed her dropped it and fled. A passer-by found Rose lying in the snow ten minutes after she had been stabbed, but it was too late.'

'I'm sorry,' Cal said.

Juliet turned to him, 'She didn't need anyone to be sorry for her.'

'I meant for your loss.'

A resigned smile, 'She was like my sister, you know? Life just isn't the same without her. I know it's a cliché, but I still expect her to be in the office when I come in sometimes. And I can still hear her laughing when someone says something ridiculous, or I imagine her anger when another client has another injustice forced upon them.

'I keep thinking I should move on from here, that I need to move on to get over her loss, but part of me doesn't want to let go of the memories that are here, or give up on the work we started. If I leave then I lose her all over again.'

Juliet shook her head. She was on the verge of tears and Cal knew she did not want to break down in front of him.

'What was she working on when she died?'

This time Juliet was more forthcoming. 'We were both working with a group of Albanians. You would have seen it on the news. There was a spike in illegal immigrants coming from Albania, arriving in small boats. The government has clamped down on it now, here and over there, but that still left thousands here.'

'Why were they coming here?'

'The promise of making money and sending it back home to family, and returning after a couple of years with enough to make them rich in Albania. Economic migrants. The reality was that when they got here, they couldn't work without the correct legal documents. Some claimed asylum, but they didn't have a case. Others slipped through the system and ended up working illegally – cheap labour in construction, car washes, nail bars, manufacturing, food packaging and delivery drivers. The really unlucky ones end up in the sex trade or criminal gangs.'

Cal thought about what Millar had said in the café – a criminal gang, new to the city, moving in on territory and business. It could mean something; it could mean nothing.

Juliet sensed Cal was leaping to conclusions. 'I was working with these clients too; so were a whole bunch of us. They had no reason to hurt any of us and no reason to single out Rose.'

'What do you think happened?'

She gave a deflated sigh, 'Maybe it was just a random attack. Maybe Rose was just in the wrong place at the wrong time again.'

She emphasised "again". Cal knew what she was referring to.

'I'll go,' he offered. 'Thanks for talking to me.' He stood up to leave and walked over to the door.

'If you want to do something to make yourself feel better about what you did to Rose, find the bastard that killed her. And when you do, let me know. I want to look the son of a bitch in the eye.'

Cal nodded and closed the door behind him as he left.

17

'Hit him again.'

Riz looked up at Erjon. He could see the fear in his eyes. He knew Erjon did not want to beat him. It was not Erjon's fault.

Riz looked at him and reassured him. It was alright.

Erjon drew back his fist and threw it forwards. Riz fell to the ground again.

'Get back to your place,' Konstandin ordered the younger man. Erjon stumbled across the room and collapsed on to his threadbare sleeping bag.

Konstandin hauled Riz to his feet. 'One more mistake and it will not just be you that is punished,' he spat on Riz's bruised face. 'Your wife and child are not safe. Do I make myself clear? One call from me and you will have nothing to return home to.'

He let go and Riz dropped to the floor. Konstandin slammed the door behind him as he left. They heard the key turn in the lock.

The men had not left the flat since the night of the attack on the nightclub, when the boy had been killed. They judged the fallout from the comings and goings of Konstandin, and the mood he was in.

On that night, they had heard angry confrontations through the locked door. Konstandin was berated by another man and tried to defend himself. The door had been flung open and Afrim had been hauled out. No one had seen Afrim in the days since. No one expected to see Afrim again.

Konstandin had appeared the next day with a black eye and bruises across his face. He had been beaten. Whoever was in charge held him responsible for the job going wrong and the unwanted attention it would bring. Konstandin in turn lashed out at the men who had not followed his orders as they should have. They were lazy, sloppy, useless nobodies whom he would crush like bugs if it was up to him. They had ruined their own chance of a magnificent future. Now they were wanted men, the police would not leave them alone. They were useless to their masters. They could not work, they could not carry out any more assignments. They would have to hope that the boss was merciful and spared their families and loved ones back home.

They were to be kept locked in the room together until a decision about their fate was made. In the early months, they had been allowed to come and go from the flat. They were picked up each morning and taken to a building site, where they worked for long days. One day a week and in the evenings they were free to do what they wanted. They were only warned not to draw attention to themselves. That changed when their new duties began. They were no longer taken to the building site and in between the night-time raids they were kept indoors and out of sight. The outer door to the flat was kept locked. Now the doors inside the flat were locked. Their freedom was being eroded one door at a time.

Riz wished the doors had been locked from the first day he had arrived here. Then he would not have become a monster. Then he would not have committed the greatest sin.

After Konstandin had berated them, they had been left alone for days. No light came through the boarded-up windows. It was difficult to tell how much time had passed.

There were five of them in the room now that Afrim had gone. The other six men were in the bedroom across the hallway. For the first few hours they had communicated with each other through the walls, trying to keep spirits up. Gradually both rooms had fallen silent.

In the dark there was nothing to stimulate them. They had dozed away the hours. They grew hungry. The bottles of water were finished. The room stank of their waste as the buckets filled up and remained unemptied.

Then Konstandin had returned, crashing through the front door and into the room. He found Riz and dragged him out of the room into the hallway. He pinned Riz to the wall, their faces an inch apart.

'*I haftë djalli shpirtin*!' Konstandin yelled in their native tongue, breaking his own rule to only speak in English. *The devil ate my soul.* 'I warned you not to make any more mistakes.' He slapped Riz hard across his face, and slammed his back against the wall. 'No money, you hear me? No more money for you or your family.' He slapped Riz again. 'If it was up to me, I would kill you now. Idiot!'

Riz slid to the floor. He had done something wrong, but what?

'Please, *zotëri*. What is it that I have done?' Riz asked with deference, trying to avoid reigniting Konstandin's anger.

Konstandin wheeled round and bent down over him, his finger in Riz's face. 'I almost think you have done it deliberately. First you leave the hammer, now you leave your fingerprint. I advised throwing you to the police, but no one listens to Konstandin.'

'I don't understand.'

'The police have your fingerprints from the nightclub and the massage parlour. They are looking for us, for foreigners, for men. You have led them to us with your stupidity.'

'I am sorry, *zotëri*.'

'Do not call me "sir". Do not talk to me at all. You have landed all of us in the shit. You understand? And all I am allowed to do is warn you and punish you when I should kill you with my own hands.'

Konstandin had picked Riz up and threw him back into the room. Then he had ordered Erjon to administer more punishment. He forced Erjon to beat his friend. Erjon did as he was told through tears.

Riz felt the blood pulsing across his bloated and battered face as he lay in the dark. Erjon had finally stopped sobbing and slipped into a fitful sleep.

Riz tried to close his eyes and picture Leandra and Zerina. He tried to see them in Durrës, on the shore, with the clear turquoise sea meeting the clear blue sky behind them. He tried to connect with them and remember why he had come here in the first place. He tried to return to the world before all his wrongdoing.

He felt tears run across his bruised skin. The saltwater stung where the skin was broken.

Their faces remained blurred. It was them, his wife and his daughter, but they were hazy, out of focus. They were slipping away from him, receding from him, like the humanity that was seeping out of his soul and vanishing in wisps of smoke.

He was losing them, not just separated by thousands of miles across land and sea, but spiritually too. He could never return to them now, not after what he had done. Every moment he was trapped in this hell, he fell further from them. The life he dreamt of, the life they had all dreamt of together, was a spectre now, a ghost that had died when he had killed.

He told himself again that he had had no choice, but that was not true. He could have said no. He could have refused. They would have beaten him or abused him or killed him. Only now did he realise that would have been better than trying to live with the thing that he had done.

A new face flashed across the darkness. This one was clear and distinct. It was her. The pale white face of the woman. He relived that moment again. He saw the look of shock in her wide eyes.

Silently, in the dark, Riz wept.

18

Millar picked Cal up outside his flat. Dykes was in the car with her.

'Twice in one day,' said Cal as he slid into the back seat and closed the door. It was early evening. Jenny had dropped Cal back at his flat after his meeting with Juliet White. Cal had the evening off from the Carnival; Jenny had left for her shift. He had planned a quiet few hours in front of the television to unwind. Then Millar had called him. Cal repeated now what he had told her on the phone. 'I think this is a terrible idea.'

'You're probably right,' Millar agreed as she pulled away from the kerb. 'That's why I'm bringing you along.'

On the journey from the south side of the city to the west end, Millar updated Cal on what they had learnt from the National Crime Agency and Tacky McGee.

'They come from all over, but the biggest numbers are from the Middle East – Syria, Afghanistan and Iraq. We're getting some of our liaison officers to get in touch with leaders in those communities and see if anyone is willing to talk to us. And the other group is Albanians, but we don't really have any links to them.'

'Albanians?' Cal repeated. Juliet White had said Rose had been helping Albanian clients.

'I spoke to a colleague of Rose's this afternoon.' Cal didn't tell them that he had visited Rose's work.

'Christ, Cal,' exclaimed Millar. 'I spoke to you this morning to keep you in the loop. Now you've started your own investigation?'

'She mentioned they had been working with a group of Albanians.'

'Could just be a coincidence. She worked with a lot of different groups,' said Dykes.

'One of the main industries that uses this illegal immigrant labour is construction,' Millar continued.

'Hence your bad idea,' said Cal.

'We have to use all the connections we can.'

They turned on to the motorway and crossed the River Clyde, and at Charing Cross turned towards the Mitchell Library building as the evening sun was setting behind it. They turned onto Claremont Street at the impressive modern Central Gurdwara Singh Sabha, its golden domes and minarets glowing in the dusk. Every parking space was taken. Millar looped around Royal Terrace and Royal Crescent twice before giving up.

'We'll jump out here. You stay with the car,' she instructed Dykes. 'Get an ice cream in the park.'

She pulled up outside the sandstone building on Royal Terrace. The buildings were similar to those of the Libertio offices in the city centre – square, three storeys high, with the addition of entrance porches held up by imposing Doric columns. Millar and Cal got out of the car. Dykes moved over to the driver's seat and took off to find somewhere to wait for them. Across the road, Kelvingrove Park was busy with local residents, workers finishing their day and students still in the city for the summer, all out enjoying the good weather. Children ran around the play park.

'Ready?' asked Millar.

'Not really,' replied Cal.

She led the way up the steps and into the vestibule. On the door entry panel she pressed the button next to "McArthur Construction".

It was Tony McArthur who met them at the door to the office on the ground floor. It consisted of only three rooms – a small reception area with a desk, a larger room that served as Tony's office, and a side room filled with filing cabinets with folders and files piled on top of them.

Tony's reaction when he saw them was better than Cal had expected it to be. He looked from Millar to Cal and managed to contain the flicker of irritation that passed across his face. The last time Cal had seen him, Tony had been bleeding on the floor from a gunshot wound to his leg and his father, Francis McArthur, was lying dead next to him, stabbed through the heart. Millar had seen Tony since then as part of her investigation into the McArthur business. Tony had faced trial only a few months ago. He had avoided a jail sentence, probably due to the remnants of his father's connections within the justice system, and with the mitigation of Francis McArthur's death taken into account. As part of the deal, the McArthur property portfolio was torn apart. The nightclubs, bars and restaurants were sold off. Tony was allowed to keep a portion of the construction and demolition business, the business with which Francis had started out.

Millar broke the silence. 'How's the leg, Tony?'

'Aches every day.' He turned to Cal. 'Your sister was wondering if you were ever going to visit your new niece.'

Cal hadn't spoken to Marie since December, when she had told him they were expecting their first child.

'Just letting you all get settled. I'll come over soon.'

'I'm assuming you haven't turned up here to congratulate me on becoming a father?'

'Can we talk?' Millar cut in.

'I thought you were off my case now?' The lawyers and the Crown Prosecution Service were still picking through some of the minor details from the fallout of the collapse of the McArthur empire. The threat of fresh charges still hung over Tony's head.

'This is something different. We need your help.'

'You want my help?' Tony laughed. 'I'm barely managing to hold what's left of the business together. We're losing the house. I'm getting harassed by ex-clients threatening to sue me and I have to get up at six every day to do physio on my leg. All thanks to you two. And now you want my help?'

Millar waited to see if he had finished. 'It could be worse, Tony. You should be in prison.'

Tony ignored her comment. 'Do I have a choice?'

'Of course you do, but a little cooperation might look good for you right now.'

Tony gave in. The sooner he got this over with, the sooner Millar and Cal would be out of his office. He sat down behind his desk. Millar sat in the one seat opposite him. Cal stood behind her, leaning against the wall and letting Millar ask the questions.

Tony leant forward. 'So what is it you want to talk about?'

'We need information on the construction industry, specifically the use of illegal immigrant labour.'

Tony raised his hands to stop her. 'I don't get involved in any of that. I'm totally clean now.'

'Relax, we're not accusing you of anything. You heard about the attack on your old nightclub?'

'I've got nothing to do with that place.'

'I know. And the attacks on the massage parlour, DeVito's restaurant and The Shed.'

'Sure, I've heard about them.'

'We're trying to find out who is behind them.'

'You think they're all linked?'

'You don't?'

Tony shrugged. 'Sure, makes sense. You think it's a gang of illegal immigrants?'

'Or someone using illegal immigrants to do their dirty work for them.'

'I guess that could happen, but like I said, I don't have anything to do with it. There are no illegal immigrants on our sites and you know I'm not allowed to work in the entertainment industry anymore.' A judge had barred Tony from working in the hospitality industry indefinitely. 'I don't see how I can help you.'

'Rose Black,' said Cal.

That caught Tony by surprise. 'Rose Black?' Tony knew Cal had struggled with that night ever since it had happened. Tony had been able to move on without giving the girl much thought. His father had made the situation right, both for them and for the Black family.

'You know she was murdered six months ago?'

'Of course I know that. It was all over the news. What's that got to do with me or the construction industry? You were the one that was hung up on her.'

'We have reason to believe the murder of Rose Black is linked to the attacks on the properties in the city,' said Millar.

'You think an illegal immigrant killed her?' He gave another shrug of his shoulders. 'Makes sense if she was mixed up with those sorts of people. I still don't see what you want me to do about it.'

'I want to get the person that killed her,' said Cal.

'Of course you do,' Tony said to him. 'But that's her job.' He pointed at Millar.

Millar tried to steer the conversation back to the reason they had come to see Tony. 'You must know of people in the industry using illegal labour. A lot of them end up on construction sites. What about other companies?'

'You would need to talk to them about that.' It was clear Tony did not want to cooperate with them.

'I could come back with a warrant to look at your employment contracts. Start visiting some of your sites, see who we find there. Maybe bring some NCA officers with me. All linked to my current investigation. How does that sound?'

'Wait a second, wait a second. There's no need for threats.' There was sudden panic in Tony's voice. Any more police intervention in his business now would be the end of McArthur Construction, and they all knew it. 'I'm telling you I'm clean and what anyone else does is up to them.'

'But you know other firms use illegal labour.'

'Other people, right,' Tony agreed. 'Times are tough. Materials are expensive and the costs keep rising. Companies are going bust all the time. So some other firms might be looking to cut corners.'

Finally they were getting somewhere. 'And how would other companies find these people?'

'I'm just speculating here, you understand?' said Tony.

'Of course.'

'I imagine there would be a middle man, a gang leader who would go around and offer their services. A broker.'

'Okay, someone who would approach site bosses or company bosses and offer labour services.'

'Right, something like that.'

'Any of those kinds of people ever approached you?'

'Not me,' said Tony, a little too quickly. 'This is just what I heard.'

'Right, you're speculating,' said Millar, going along with Tony's game.

'Right. I mean these are nasty people, you know? Exploiting vulnerable people. I wouldn't get involved. My dad would never have worked with people like that.'

That much could be true, thought Millar. For all his criminal activity, Francis McArthur had had his own twisted integrity. 'Heard of any problems on any sites around the city in the last few days?'

'What sort of problems?'

'Anyone been short of labour? Anyone had workers stop showing up?'

Tony shook his head, but his eyes gave him away. He was debating how much he should say.

'If you know something, Tony, it really would help if you told us.'

'And after that you would guarantee not to look too closely at the past employment records of McArthur Construction?'

'I'm only interested in the attacks and Rose Black,' Millar reassured him.

'I might have heard something about a bunch of guys who disappeared from a job.'

'Keep going.'

'One of the sites out at the Mearns.' The area around Newton Mearns to the south of the city had been expanding for years, with several large housing estates being built on farmland. 'I'm not giving you any names, you understand? But a group of Albanians, or something like that, didn't show up one morning. I got a call to see if I had any spare labour that could go over and cover for them.'

'Albanians?' said Cal.

'Something like that. They're all the same though, right?'

Millar ignored the racist comment. 'Anything else you can tell us about them? Like the name of their broker?'

'Nothing to do with me. I sent some guys over to help them out. They said something about a guy letting them down – think they said his name was Constantine or Conrad, or something like that.'

'We get it, Tony, nothing to do with you.' Millar stood up to leave. 'Thanks for your time.' She walked to the door.

Tony remained seated behind his desk and watched her leave. He turned to Cal. 'You should call Marie. She wants to see you.'

'I'll think about it.'

'The kid should know her uncle.' Family had always been important to the McArthurs; that was how they had ended up in this mess in the first place.

'Tell her to call me sometime,' said Cal, and walked out of the room.

Tony slumped back in his chair. He turned round and looked out of the window, and saw Millar and Cal exit the building and cross into the park.

'What do you think?' asked Cal as they passed through the gate and joined the joggers and dog walkers.

'I think McArthur Construction uses illegal labour, or has done in the past.'

'He mentioned Albanians again.'

'Could just be a coincidence. He gave us a name though. We can start with that and ask around.' She looked at him as they walked. 'You never really got over this thing with Rose, did you?'

'I always felt like I owed her something.'

'You didn't get her killed.'

'I owe it to her to find out who did kill her, and why.'

They found Dykes sitting on a bench, his suit jacket on his lap and an ice-cream cone in his hand. 'Get anything from him?' he asked as they approached.

'Maybe something, maybe nothing. Heard anything about anyone called Constantine or Conrad?'

Dykes shook his head. 'I can ask Chopra at the NCA, see if it means anything to him.'

'Where's the car?'

'Parked at the museum.'

'Come on. There's one last thing I want to check out before we quit for the night.'

19

Dykes pulled up in front of the group of high-rise buildings as the sun dipped behind them, providing a fiery backdrop to the grey cuboids. The residential tower blocks had sprung up in the late 1960s, particularly across the north of the city. They were supposed to be the future, an answer to the ongoing housing shortage. A mixture of poor building fabric, poor management, high crime levels and high maintenance costs had brought down most of the original towers, including the famous Red Road Flats, but the Westercommon Road scheme still stood. For over half a century they had provided social housing to the less well-off. It remained to be seen how much longer they could last before regeneration plans brought in the demolition crews.

There were some signs that attempts had been made to make the tower blocks welcoming. The exteriors looked clean; the windows were double-glazed. Grass areas around the base of each tower were well-maintained and the streets were litter-free. There was no fly-tipping. Tell-tale signs still spoke of some social disquiet – patches of off-colour paint hid graffiti that had been covered while freshly sprayed tags marred the walls.

Groups of young children ran around on the grass areas and rode bikes around the car parks and streets. A group of older kids were having a game of football on the concrete, using the wheelie bins for goalposts. Teenagers hung around, vaping and chatting. Adults leant out of windows and occasionally a child was called in for bedtime. Despite the community atmosphere, the contrast to the leafy surroundings they had recently left in Kelvingrove Park was evident. No amount of community spirit could disguise the difference between poverty and prosperity.

Dykes stopped the car at the bottom of the tower numbered 151. The locals eyed them with suspicion. They had already been marked as strangers. 'Which tower does Charlie's mother stay in?'

'No idea,' answered Millar, looking up at the tall building. 'Let's have a wander round and see if we can see anything.' Millar got out of the passenger seat. Dykes turned off the engine and followed her.

Cal got out from the back seat and joined them. 'What are you looking for?'

'We got a tip off about a group of immigrants living in these blocks who are bussed in and out each day in a Transit van.'

They walked around the base of 151 and followed a path that led them to the next block, 187. The towers looked identical from a distance. It was only when they got closer that small differences gave each block an individuality. Watchful eyes followed them and children who had been happily playing paused and stood still until they passed. The group of strangers, two of them dressed smartly and obviously officials of some kind, brought with them a sense of tension, an atmosphere that was heightened by the recent riots. The community here was made up of the minorities that Fergus Bennett and his followers sought to demonise. The people out enjoying the last of the daylight were a diverse ethnic mix. Refugees and asylum seekers were housed amongst social welfare residents. The soundtrack was a harmonious swirl of different accents and languages. The only sour note was Millar, Dykes and Cal appearing amongst the tight community.

'How many of these people do you think are here illegally?' asked Cal, keeping his voice low.

'Maybe none of them.'

They circled round 187 and moved on to 231, the tower that marked the eastern border of the estate. Millar stopped and pointed to windows about halfway up, on the side facing away from the other towers. 'There,' she said.

Dykes and Cal looked in the direction she pointed. 'Boarded up,' Dykes said, when he spotted what had caught Millar's eye. Charlie the bartender's mother had mentioned boarded-up windows. It was on the eleventh floor of the tower.

'Boarded on the inside.'

'Could be for any number of reasons.'

'All the other windows on all the other towers are in good nick; a lot of them look fairly new. What happened to those ones?' The glass looked intact and the boarded-up windows covered at least two rooms of the flat.

Millar started walking towards the communal entrance. 'No harm in taking a closer look.'

Cal looked round and saw several residents watching Millar as she made her way to the door. He followed and felt their eyes on him.

An electronic entry system barred their way. There were two panels – a numeric keypad and a panel that listed every flat number with a buzzer next to it. Millar studied them and pressed the button marked "Building Supervisor". It made a ringing noise but no one answered. She tried it again with the same result.

A man with black hair, a moustache and dark brown skin approached them. He had been leaning against a wall, watching them impassively. Without saying a word, he entered a code into the numeric keypad. The sealed door popped open, accompanied by a short beep. He smiled at them and beckoned them to enter.

'Thanks,' said Millar. She pushed through the door, Dykes followed her and Cal brought up the rear, returning the man's smile. He presumed the man was the building supervisor, enjoying the sunshine rather than sitting at his station inside the building. The man turned away and went back to the spot he had occupied before, folding his arms as he resumed his watching brief. The door swung closed with a soft click as the locking mechanism fell back into place behind them.

Inside, the building was clean and well-maintained. What had Cal expected? Piles of litter? Junkies and homeless people wrapped in cardboard and dirty sleeping bags? Flickering lights and broken lifts and graffitied walls? The lift doors opened straight away and they stepped in. The lift looked new – a recent addition. Millar pressed number eleven and the doors closed.

'Shouldn't we have called for back-up or something like that?' Cal asked.

'We're only going to knock on a door.'

'I'm thinking about who might answer that door.'

'It'll probably be an elderly couple wondering what all the fuss is about.'

They reached the eleventh floor and stepped out into a vestibule. There were six flats on each floor, three to the right and three to the left. The flat with the boarded-up windows was to their right at the front of the building – flat 11/4. Millar chapped the red wooden door. She took out her police identification and held it open in front of the spyhole. There was no answer. She knocked again.

'No one home?'

'Maybe not.' Millar looked at the other doors. 'Try the neighbours.'

Dykes knocked on the doors marked 11/5 and 11/6. He got the same result. 'All out enjoying the sun.'

'We need to contact the housing association and find out who owns that flat.' Millar gave the door to 11/4 one last rap with her knuckles. The silence continued. Her instinct told her something wasn't right. It was too quiet, too silent, like someone was trying not to breathe. Her instinct wasn't enough to justify breaking down the door though, not without reasonable cause.

They turned and headed back towards the lift. When they stepped back into the evening air, the man who had let them in was still leaning against the wall.

Millar approached him. 'Who lives in flat 11/4?' she asked, flashing her identification.

The man continued to smile and shrugged in reply.

'Anyone called Constantine or Conrad or something similar live around here?'

The man did not seem to comprehend what he was being asked. He just kept smiling and nodding. Millar gave up and thanked him anyway.

They made their way back to the car.

'Thanks for agreeing to come with me to see Tony,' Millar said to Cal.

'I don't think he was too happy to see me.'

'Happy isn't the right word, that's for sure, but you're still his brother-in-law, so he had to hear you out.'

'Happy to help.'

'Maybe leave the detective work to us from now on, though. No more unscheduled visits to interview witnesses.'

'Understood.'

A group of older youths had gathered around the car, leaning on the side and resting on the bonnet. They backed up to let Millar, Dykes and Cal pass. There were a few muttered comments.

Dykes hit the starter button and the radio burst into life at the same time as the engine. Cal recognised the unmistakable tone of Fergus Bennett's voice. He was being interviewed, answering in loud, declarative statements. He denied playing any part in instigating the riot that took place in George Square. It was the action of a minority who had nothing to do with him or his political party. The interviewer pushed him – wasn't this just what he wanted? More unrest to capitalise on? Bennett ignored them and turned it back to his favourite attack line – too many immigrants, too many illegal immigrants. Governments in Edinburgh and Westminster that were too soft on the issue. He pronounced his policy of mass deportations. Globalisation had failed, integration had failed. These people threatened the very existence of a Scottish and British way of life.

Cal looked out of the window at the groups of young children of all nationalities playing together.

Millar clicked the radio off. 'They still give him airtime,' she sighed.

Dykes did a three-point turn and they drove away.

20

Konstandin watched the dark-blue car drive along Westercommon Road. At the junction it turned right and the tail-lights disappeared from view.

He looked at the photograph he had taken on his phone. He could see the two men and woman in clear detail. One man he did not recognise, but he would find out who he was. He was about six foot, with close-cropped dark hair that was starting to recede. He wore jeans and a plain t-shirt. *Not police,* thought Konstandin.

The other man was a cop, but he was not the one that worried Konstandin. He was obviously the junior partner, younger and still learning the ropes, and following the orders of his senior partner.

The woman, on the other hand, he knew all too well. Her presence was not good news. Konstandin had never seen Detective Simone Millar in the flesh before. She had been pointed out to him in pictures. Her movements had been monitored, but they had never taken any action against her. She had left the investigation into Rose Black's death when the trail had run cold. There had never been a need to intervene. That would change now.

He did not know how they had managed to find the flat. Someone must have spoken. Konstandin was confident it was no one from inside. The men were too scared to do anything so foolish. It was probably one of the other residents of the estate. He would have to report it. They would have to move the men now, they had no choice, and they would have to do it quickly before the police returned with more officers.

That would not be enough, though. Not for Konstandin and not for that idiot Riz. They had more to lose than the others. This would require direct action, and the fool Riz could do it. He had to make amends for his own mistakes.

Konstandin clicked his phone off and put it in his pocket. He stepped out from behind the corner of the building that had shielded him from the detectives and walked across to tower 231.

Dikran was leaning against the wall. They shared a look of relief. Konstandin had made a calculated risk when he had motioned Dikran to let the detective into the building. If she had discovered the men gathered in the room, it would have blown up in their faces. The men would have been arrested. One of them, probably that weak fool Erjon, would have talked. Konstandin would have had to get out of the country fast, and where would he run to? Albania would not be safe. His masters would be after him.

The alternative would have been to try to block them from entering the tower. That would only have increased their suspicion and shown them that they were on to something.

He had bought himself a bit of time. Enough time to take evasive action.

She was here only on a hunch. She could have no concrete evidence or she would have come with a search warrant and a team of officers. Back home the police could break down doors with no justification, but not here in the United Kingdom. Here they had to follow rules and procedures, the same as all citizens. She had brought no back-up with her, just her junior partner and this other man following her around.

'She asked if I knew anyone with your name,' Dikran told him.

Then it was worse than he thought, but not the end of the world. His name was not on any official document that could lead them to him.

He would move the men tonight, after darkness had fallen. Dikran would have another place they could move to before any police came back, and would cover their tracks with the paperwork. The lease on the property would not lead back to them; it would lead Detective Millar to a different name and a dead end. By the time she had figured that out, the flat would be empty.

He entered the security code on the keypad, went inside and got the lift up to the eleventh floor. Dikran would erase him from the CCTV footage as usual.

Konstandin was calm but he did not like seeing the police turn up at the high-rise. They were getting too close and he must put a stop to her before she found out anymore.

He unlocked the door to flat 11/4.

Riz heard the key enter the lock in the door. What was happening now? Erjon was next to him in the dark. Riz again put his finger to his lips and prayed no one would make a noise.

They were all awake now.

They had been slumbering in their sleeping bags, listening to the distant, muffled sounds of the children playing eleven storeys below. To Riz, the sound reminded him of children playing in the street below his own apartment in Durrës. He closed his eyes and saw Zerina running with her friends, her long dark hair billowing behind her.

Then someone had knocked at the door. It was not the usual sound of Konstandin arriving. Hushed conversations stopped, half-closed eyes sprung open, the men stared at one another. No one made a sound.

They could not have answered the door even if they had wanted to. They were locked into the rooms. But any one of them could have called out.

No one had knocked at the door before in all the months they had been kept here. Their masters all had keys and let themselves in and out. Was it a service man of some kind? A salesman? Or just a neighbour, finally curious enough about the strange comings and goings of the flat to make an enquiry?

Whoever it was knocked again. Each of them held their breath. Was it someone who could help them or someone who would bring more misery to them? Was it worth the risk to find out?

They knocked one last time and then there was only more silence.

Five minutes later, they heard the familiar sound of a key in the lock. The front door opened and closed. Footsteps came along the hall.

The door opened and light flooded in from the hallway. Before Riz's eyes had time to adjust to the brightness, he felt himself being hauled to his feet. It was Konstandin. He dragged Riz across the room and out into the hallway. The door to the room was slammed closed behind him.

Something had happened. Fear gripped Riz. He was on a final warning, Konstandin had made that clear. One more slip-up and Riz was done for. What had he done? They had not left the flat since the nightclub. He could not have made any further mistakes that would have infuriated Konstandin.

'I knew I should have killed you,' Konstandin pinned him up against the wall. 'Six months ago, I should have killed you.'

'Please, *zotëri*. I do not understand what I have done. You gave me one last chance; I will not fail you.'

'That is true. You have one last chance, and I will give you that chance now. You have another special mission. Like the one six months ago.'

Riz's stomach lurched. Not that again. He could not do that again. 'Another woman,' Konstandin continued, 'another woman who must disappear. This time it is your own fault. If you had done things properly, if you had not made mistakes, you would not be in this position.'

'I cannot do that again, *zotëri*, I beg you.'

'You have no choice. If you do not, this woman will find you and arrest you. That is, if she finds you in time. It is more likely that it is you who will disappear, you and your pretty wife and daughter.'

'Why must I kill another woman? Who is she?'

Konstandin gave him an evil smile. 'She is a police officer, a detective. She is on to us because of your incompetence. She knows about the woman you killed, she knows about the jobs you have done for me and she needs to be stopped.'

Konstandin released Riz from his grip. Riz leant against the wall. His life was crumbling around him once more. He could not kill a police officer. He would never get away with it, he would never get out of the country alive. There would be a manhunt for him, everyone would be looking for him. And he knew he could not go through with it, not after the last time. Konstandin had promised him he would be paid well and could return to Albania after the last time. It had never happened. This time he wasn't even pretending to promise him anything. This time Konstandin was using only threats.

Konstandin pulled out his phone and held up the screen for Riz to see. It was a photograph from outside the tower block. It was a woman with her hair tied up, wearing a black t-shirt and tight blue trousers.

'Her name is Detective Inspector Simone Millar,' said Konstandin, 'and either you kill her, or I will kill you and your family. Do you understand me?'

Riz could not stop the tears from falling as he assented with a nod of his head, 'Yes, *zotëri*.'

He had no choice. He would do anything to save Leandra and Zerina. He would do anything to get back to them. He would do anything so that they would never learn what sort of a monster he had become.

PART 3

CRY OF THE HUNTED

21

Jenny watched Cal wipe down the bar, put away the clean glasses and replace the empty optics. He could feel her watching him as he worked and tried to hide his emotions, but she knew the turmoil he had been through in the last few days.

Cal had done what Millar had told him to do. He had not pursued any private investigation; he had left it to the professionals. Millar had not been in touch and it was best to let her get on with her job. If she needed him for something, or had anything to tell him, Millar knew where to find him. Despite that, the fact they had been so close to discovering Rose's killer played on Cal's mind.

He had told Jenny about the visit to the high-rise flats and the theory that the group of illegal immigrants involved in the attacks on properties around the city were also linked to Rose Black's murder.

She told him, 'I'm worried about you getting involved with this Rose Black stuff again.'

She had seen him at his worst six months ago when he had found out that Rose had been killed, when he had slipped into the destructive mindset that was always within him, waiting for a reason to surface. After avoiding alcohol since leaving prison, Cal had reached for a bottle to shield himself from the pain and regret of his past, which was threatening to swamp him. The darkness that had eaten away at him for years after he had almost killed Rose, and his father had killed himself, had returned.

Two days later, Jenny had found him in a night shelter in the city centre. She took him back to her flat and sobered him up. Cal promised it was over with. The shock of Rose's violent death had caught him out and caused him to falter. It had sliced through the defences he had built up.

Jenny put him back on the right track and showed him how selfish he had been. She had no time for his self-pity. A woman had been murdered – Rose was the victim, not Cal. Over the next few weeks, Cal had pulled himself together and avoided descending back into the despair that had overwhelmed him for that moment.

Jenny remained vigilant and now she sensed something slipping within him. She cursed Millar for involving Cal again. She tried to talk him out of getting too close.

The evening had passed like most others in the Carnival. The crowd had peaked around eleven o'clock and it stayed busy until two, when people started to drift away. At three, Patrick closed and locked the doors behind the last customers to leave.

Cal had avoided Patrick. They had not spoken beyond a civil greeting in the shifts they had worked together. Small talk seemed out of the question. If Carmen felt he was necessary, Cal could only accept it or quit. If everything calmed down in the city, then Patrick would disappear.

Final duties completed, the staff moved downstairs to collect their belongings and leave via the staff entrance.

'My place tonight?' Jenny asked Cal in the staff room.

'Sure,' Cal answered.

'See you both tomorrow.' Lauryn picked up her bag and jacket and left with Georgia.

Carmen passed them in the corridor. 'Try being on time tomorrow, yeah?'

Patrick followed Cal, Jenny and Carmen along the corridor. A night security guard was due to arrive and would stay until morning, a new precaution that Patrick and Carmen had brought in on police advice.

'I'll wait behind until he shows up,' said Patrick.

'Who was meant to be on duty?' Carmen asked.

'Pete. He's reliable.'

Cal pushed the security bar to open the door. He let Jenny step out in front of him and bumped into her back as she stopped suddenly.

In front of her, Pete was lying on the ground, blood seeping from a head wound.

Lauryn and Georgia stood over his prone body. They were being held there by arms around their throats. Cal saw the terror in their eyes. They had all heard what happened to Nathan MacDonald. There were at least ten men, all dressed in dark clothes. They wore black balaclavas and carried weapons – baseball bats and sledgehammers.

'Let us all go back inside the club, yes?' one of the men said. The knife he held to Georgia's throat glinted under the glow from the security light.

***

Millar called it quits at three in the morning. The office was deserted. Dykes had gone home at ten o'clock. Even then, he knew he was in trouble with his wife. He had missed bedtime with the kids again.

Millar threw the latest folder on top of the pile and looked at the boxes of records they had spent the last two days wading through. So far, they resembled nothing more than a dead end.

She refreshed her email, even though she knew no one would be sending her an update at this time of night. Normal people were at home in bed and fast asleep, the clerks at the Home Office and the officers at the National Crime Agency included. She would chase them again in the morning.

She clicked on to the internet browser, still open at the city council internal records site, showing details of the Westercommon Road residents. They had been chasing an electronic trail of red tape that frustrated and confused. The housing association gave them the name of the resident in flat 11/4 as Miss Karolina Dabrowski, born in Łódź, Poland in 1993, who immigrated to Scotland in 2014 on a student visa and ended up staying when her course was completed. That much seemed to be true. She applied for accommodation with the housing association in 2018. Dykes had found her application form. Her reason for needing social housing was given as the breakdown of a relationship with an abusive partner with whom she had been living. After a six-month wait, she was housed in the flat at Westercommon Road. Since moving in, Karolina had been an exemplary resident. She paid her rent on time. She paid her gas and electricity bills. Her last payment was dated the previous month.

There was only one problem. When Dykes ran Karolina Dabrowski through the Home Office database, he found a standard exit check report stating she had flown back to Poland in the aftermath of the pandemic lockdown in 2022. There was no record of her ever having returned. Her visa had expired.

Dykes made calls to various departments in the Polish government. Eventually he found someone who confirmed that Karolina Dabrowski had returned to her home town of Łódź and was now living and working in the city of her birth. The National Crime Agency said they had never had anyone called Karolina Dabrowski on their radar. Their own police records came up blank.

'So who is paying the rent and staying in the flat?'

Millar contacted the housing association again. They claimed ignorance and assured her they would send a housing officer round, but budgets were tight and personnel stretched. As far as their records showed, Karolina Dabrowski continued to be a dependable and trouble-free resident.

It was obvious that someone was using Karolina Dabrowksi's identity in order to use the flat, but who? And for what reason? From what Charlie and Tacky McGee had told them, they had a good idea. They certainly had enough to get a search warrant and take a closer look at flat 11/4.

Dykes had filed the request that afternoon. Millar hoped they would be granted the warrant first thing in the morning. If they were right and a gang of illegal immigrants was living in that flat, they would not hang about now they knew the police were snooping around. They might already be too late.

Millar considered staying in the office. The sofa in the breakout area was comfortable enough – she had slept on it before. The temptation of her own bed, a shower and fresh clothes in the morning persuaded her to leave. There was nothing more she could do tonight.

She shut the computer down, then gathered up the files strewn across her desk and threw them back in the box they had come from. She pulled on her jacket and headed for the door. She paused in front of the evidence board. Various photographs of the damaged properties and their owners, with names and dates scrawled beneath them, were lined up in a row. There were blown-up images of the fingerprints that Pat Golightly had sent over – one taken from the bloody stain at The Shed nightclub, one from the sledgehammer recovered at the Peaceful Dove massage parlour, and the third one taken from the handle of the knife that had stabbed and killed Rose Black. There was a picture of the blood-stained knife next to it. It had been recovered not far from Rose's body, dropped in panic by her assailant as they fled. There was a photograph of the murder scene – Rose's body lying in a pool of blood on top of a thin layer of snow.

Millar felt that she was close to finding out what had happened to Rose that night. She was going to finally nail the bastard who had killed her. The net was closing.

She switched the light off and closed the office door, locking it behind her.

Only at the front reception was there any sign of the twenty-four-hour life of the station. Hugh Stapleton was on desk sergeant duty tonight. Millar liked him. They often bumped into each other at the vending machines in the middle of the night when everyone else had gone home. She asked him how his shift was going. So far, it had been a quiet night. The patrol cars were out, but no one had been brought to the station.

'Hope it stays that way,' Millar replied, and promised him she would get some rest before returning in the morning.

She stepped outside. The day had been warm, but the clear sky meant it was a cool night. She pulled her jacket close around her and fished her keys from her pocket. She hit the button to unlock her car. Indicator lights flashed on the far side of the car park. She started walking towards them.

Halfway across the car park a streetlight had gone out, creating a dark spot. As she passed through the gloom, she sensed him there. It was too late to turn and run back. He stepped out from behind the streetlight. Millar could see the large knife he held in front of him, pointed at her. It was identical to the one she had just looked at on the evidence board upstairs.

The man in the balaclava did not say anything. They stood still, facing each other.

Millar raised her hands, palms out, fingers pointing to the sky. 'You don't have to do this,' she said.

She looked into his eyes – wide, white orbs against the black cloth that surrounded them – showing him that she was just a person, a fellow human, a life that should not be taken.

She sensed his moment of indecision. Then he moved, suddenly and forcefully, thrusting forward, the knife out in front of him. Millar felt the cold steel slice through her skin.

22

The men ordered them to sit on the floor. Their wrists and ankles were bound with cable ties that bit into their skin. Then they were dragged across the floor and lined up against the main bar. Pete lay in front of them, still unconscious. Georgia and Lauryn huddled together and Jenny did her best to keep them calm. Cal was next to them. Carmen eyed their captors with determined venom; Patrick's expression remained neutral.

Around them, hell was breaking loose in the nightclub. The men swung their bats and hammers with abandon and trashed the bar. The tables and chairs were wrecked, the light fittings smashed. Behind them, glass shattered as the rows of optics were obliterated. Splinters of wood, shards of glass and a rain of alcohol swirled around them. One of the men had been ordered to watch over them. He continued to yell at them and threaten them with the baseball bat he held.

Carmen couldn't help herself. 'I'm going to kill you bastards for this,' she said, staring straight at the man in front of them.

He smashed the bat down on the bar above her head in reply. Carmen did not flinch.

They knew about the previous attacks on the other nightclubs and venues, but this was different. Those attacks had been about destroying property. The venues had been empty. There was never any intent to harm the people who worked in those places. This time they had taken the workers hostage. They could have waited until the place was empty. They had targeted not just the venue, but the people working there as well.

Cal had a bad feeling. These men were not here just to do damage to the club. They were here to do damage to the people as well.

They had murdered Nathan MacDonald at The Shed. They had killed one person, what did five or six more matter?

Cal looked across at Georgia, Lauryn and Jenny. Fear was written across their faces. It could not be them that the men were here for. It was possible that Patrick was still mixed up with these sort of people – he had history – but Cal had a sinking feeling that it was him and his actions that had put them all in danger. Millar had stirred the hornet's nest, and Cal had been with her.

A thunderous crash exploded next to him. A table was upended and broke into pieces. A splinter of wood broke free and caught him on the side of his face. He felt the warm blood run down his cheek.

'Are you okay?' Jenny asked.

Cal grimaced, righted himself and tried to give her a reassuring look. 'I'm fine.'

Then the noise stopped. The man in charge yelled new instructions. His English was broken and accented. It sounded like his second language.

He ordered them to be dragged behind the bar. Lauryn and Georgia screamed as they were manhandled across the broken glass. Patrick kicked out at the man who tried to move him and it took two of them to subdue him.

Cal was left on his own. The man giving the orders kneeled down next to him.

'You should have minded your own business, *piçka*.' Cal didn't know what the foreign word meant, or what language it was from, but he could tell it was an insult, and a vulgar one at that. 'You and those pigs.' Pigs. Police. Millar and Dykes. They had been right. Their investigation had been leading them in the right direction. He realised Millar was in danger too and he couldn't warn her. Cal had brought this on those that he cared about. They were trapped here and whatever happened to them, it was because of him.

'Now you have to pay the price for sticking your nose in where it was not wanted. Understand, my friend?'

'You can let the others go.'

'Too late, *miku im*.'

The world shrank around Cal, dissolving into a black abyss.

The man stood up and shouted more orders. Two men appeared with petrol cans. They started showering the destroyed bar with petrol. The fumes filled the air. Cal flinched as the liquid was doused over his head. He retched, swallowed a mouthful and spluttered it back up. Behind him, behind the bar, he heard the others scream as the petrol was poured over them. He heard Patrick and Carmen swear and struggle. The men laughed at them.

Rough hands grabbed Cal and hauled him to his feet. They took an arm each and dragged him across the floor to the middle of the room.

A hand yanked his head back and Cal thought they were about to slit his exposed throat. He felt a rope fall over his head and settle around his neck. The knot was pulled tight and he felt the coarse fibres against his skin. The leader of the men was back in front of him. Cal stared into the eyes that leered out from the holes in the black balaclava.

'I do not care if you strangle to death or burn to death first, you pig.'

Cal spat petrol in his face, causing the man to flinch backwards. It was an ineffective resistance, but it was all Cal had. The man stepped forwards and punched Cal in the stomach, knocking the wind out of him.

'Do it,' the man ordered the men holding Cal. He felt the rope go tight as he was pulled up. It bit into his neck. He struggled for breath, trying to draw in oxygen. Then the men let go of him and the rope took his weight, and with uneven jerks he was pulled further upwards. He strained to look up and saw the rope above him, looped around the light fitting that hung in the middle of the ceiling.

He gasped and choked as his feet left the ground. He was hanging in mid-air.

The rope began to spin as he jerked and struggled. He looked down and saw a flash of orange as a flame ignited. He watched the flame loop through the air and land on the prone body of Pete. There was a blast of heat and a rush of air as the petrol ignited.

Cal heard the piercing screams from behind the bar.

***

Instinct told Millar to run. So why wasn't she?

She felt blood running down her leg from the wound in her side. She had reacted just in time, moving to the left as her assailant thrust forwards with the point of the knife. The blade had slipped inside her open jacket and slashed through her top and skin. She felt the sharp pain, but it was not a deep cut.

She should have turned and gone back towards the station, but it was not in her nature. Millar always stood her ground, whether it was the right thing to do or not.

She grabbed at him, pulling herself close into him, not letting him get the space he needed to attempt another lunging stab. She held the wrist of his knife hand in hers. He was stronger than her, taller and with a longer reach, but he had not expected to miss, or for the woman to fight back.

Millar drove him back two paces before he recovered. Slowly, he pushed back and the knife edged closer to her chest.

Millar dropped her arm, dragging his knife arm down at the same time, and spun round as she stepped towards him. Now her back was against his chest. She swung her elbow back and connected with his gut. She did it again and hit his solar plexus. He grunted as the air was knocked out of his lungs.

She needed to get the knife out of his hand before he recovered.

She dug her elbow into his midriff again and then threw her head back as he bent over. The back of her head connected with his face.

The tension went out of his arms for a moment and Millar took her chance. She pulled his hand carrying the knife towards her mouth and bit into it as hard as she could. She felt his skin break under her teeth and she heard him scream out. His hand opened and the knife fell to the ground.

The man pushed her violently away from him. He swore in a foreign language Millar did not recognise. She spat a chunk of his flesh out of her mouth as she turned to face him.

The knife was on the ground somewhere between them, but in the dark neither of them could see it. They circled each other, both breathing hard.

He faked one way and then came the other, and before Millar could respond he had hit her hard on the side of her head. Millar felt her legs go weak, but she refused to go down. He had her in his grip now, a hand around her throat. He punched her again and Millar felt herself start to lose control. Now he had both hands on her throat and the pressure started to build.

No way, Millar told herself, *not like this, not like Rose Black.* Rose never stood a chance; she wasn't prepared or trained. Millar was.

She kicked out with her right foot, connecting with his shin. He didn't flinch. He kept squeezing and bearing down on her.

She kicked out again, a full swing with all the strength she could muster. This time she connected right between his wide-open legs.

Instinct brought his hands away from her neck as he cried out in pain. Millar followed it up with a barrage of blows to his face using the side and base of her hand, as she had been taught to.

Then there was a shout from behind her. It was Hugh Stapleton, running towards them.

The man in the balaclava stood up and looked from Millar to the onrushing sergeant. As he turned to run, Millar made a grab for him. She got a handful of balaclava and it came off his head as he ran away. In the glow of the streetlamp, Millar saw his dark-black hair and dark skin. By the time Stapleton reached her, her attacker had disappeared into the murky night.

'Are you alright?' Stapleton asked. 'Who the hell was that?'

'I'm fine.' Millar spat on the ground to try to get the taste of the man's flesh out of her mouth. She stood up and drew in breath and then folded over, her hands on her knees.

'You're bleeding.'

'He slashed me with a knife. It's on the ground somewhere around here.'

Stapleton took a quick scan of the ground around them and saw the blade. 'I'll get an evidence bag. You're sure you're okay? You need to get to a hospital.'

'I'll be fine.'

Stapleton took her arm and threw it over his shoulder, then helped her back towards the station. Once inside, he put her in one of the reception waiting chairs. 'Just wait there. I'm going to collect that knife.'

Millar slumped back in the chair. Her mind raced. It was him, she was sure of it. It had been the same scenario as Rose Black: the attacker waiting for his victim in the dark – a woman on her own – armed with a large knife. She was sure she had just met Rose's killer.

Stapleton came back with the knife in a sealed evidence bag. He put it on the desk then fetched a first aid kit and came back to Millar.

'Let me look at it. I've radioed for an ambulance; they'll be here as soon as they can. Might be a wait though. They've all been called to a nightclub – another attack in the city. I'll put a dressing on it that'll stem the bleeding until they get here.'

The words took a moment to register in Millar's drowsy brain. She sat up straight. 'A nightclub?'

'Yeah, another one. This time there are multiple victims though. It's getting worse, this gang war or whatever it is.'

Millar pushed his hands away from her. 'Which nightclub?'

'The Carnival in the west end, up at the university. The call came in over the radio about five minutes ago. That's why I came out to see if you were still there. I thought you would want to know.'

Millar grabbed the padding from Stapleton's hand and pressed it against her side. She knocked the chair over as she bolted out of the door.

'You can't drive in your condition, Millar,' Stapleton called after her.

The door swung closed with a soft bump.

23

Cal fought for every breath. He could feel the rope gripping his skin, closing his throat. Panic set in. He jerked and swung his legs and the rope constricted further. Every movement made it worse, made death come closer. He blacked out.

Adrenalin brought him back to the surface. He sucked in smoke and petrol fumes and choked on them. His chest felt like it would explode. Through the oxygen-deprived fog of his mind, he heard the others screaming.

There was nothing more he could do. He stopped fighting. He went limp and still. His eyes closed.

A sharp sting forced him to open his eyes again. He felt it again. A hand was slapping him across the face.

'Open your eyes,' Patrick screamed at him. 'Hang on.'

Other hands were pushing his legs and feet upwards. The tension in the rope slackened. Patrick's arms banged about Cal's head as he hacked at the rope.

'Catch him,' Patrick cried. Cal was falling downwards. Hands tried to grab him but failed to stop him hitting the hard floor.

Now he became aware of the intense heat. His skull throbbed. Over the pounding of his own pulse, he heard the roar of the fire.

'Get out of here,' Patrick shouted to whoever was with him. 'Get out of the main door.' He grabbed Cal and lifted him over his shoulder.

Cal was floating above a floor that was being eaten by flame. Patrick struggled to move but Cal was not a light man. *Put me down,* thought Cal, *save yourself,* but he did not have the strength to shout, and if he did try his voice would be swamped by the howling fire that surrounded them.

Patrick stumbled and they almost fell into an orange-red abyss, but he somehow righted himself and, with a final lunge, they burst through a black cloud of smoke and into the night air.

Patrick fell, his energy spent. He heaved Cal forward, throwing him to the ground. Cal hit the ground and rolled over. Other hands appeared and dragged him away from the building. The night was a swirling mass of blue lights. Sirens pulsed through the air.

A black void swept over him once more and Cal's eyes closed.

When he woke up the next time, it was Jenny's face he saw. She looked down at him, like an angel floating above him. There was something on his face, covering his mouth and nose. Cal raised a hand and pulled at it.

'Leave it, Cal. You need oxygen,' Jenny told him.

He clawed at it despite her objections, until a fit of coughing overtook him and forced him to relent. Jenny stroked his forehead and took his hand in hers.

'You're okay?' Cal asked weakly when the hacking cough had stopped.

'I'm okay.'

'The others?'

'They're all okay,' Jenny paused, 'apart from Pete, the security guard.'

'Patrick?' Cal asked.

'He saved you. Him and Carmen.'

'How?'

'They used the broken glass behind the bar to cut themselves free. They got the girls and me out, then went back for you.'

'But Pete?'

'They doused him with petrol and set him alight first.' Jenny's voice trailed off.

'You're okay?' Cal repeated.

'Just some smoke inhalation and cuts and bruises.'

Cal reached up and stroked her cheek, leaving a line of black soot running down her face.

He became aware of his surroundings. He was lying on a trolley and a paramedic was attaching a finger pulse monitor to his free hand. He saw Lauryn and Georgia sitting on the edge of the pavement, blankets wrapped around their shoulders, another paramedic crouched in front of them. Firefighters ran past. Jets of water sprayed up into the night sky, falling on the roof and walls of the Carnival.

Cal looked back at Jenny and saw the tears in her eyes. He managed to prop himself up and put his arms around her. He felt her heave and sob as the emotion came out. He found he was doing the same. He felt the cool wet tears trickle down his face as the shock wore off and the reality of what had just happened hit them both.

The paramedic interrupted them. 'We need to get you both to the hospital. You can come with him in the ambulance.'

Jenny broke away from him but kept hold of his hand. The trolley started to roll over the tarmac, the wheels juddering across the unsmooth surface.

The back door of an ambulance came into Cal's field of vision. Just as the paramedics prepared to lift him inside, they were stopped by an urgent shout.

It was Millar.

'Is he alright?' she asked the paramedic at the foot of the stretcher.

'He'll be fine. Smoke inhalation and minor burns. A few cuts and an abrasion around his neck.'

'What about the others?'

'One fatality that we know about. Everyone else made it out.'

Millar looked back down at Cal. 'This is my fault. I got you involved in this.'

'You're bloody right it's your fault,' Jenny cut in.

'I'm going to get the bastards that did this.'

Millar swayed above him. Cal thought he was losing consciousness again, or were the painkillers making him woozy? It wasn't that. It was Millar who was lurching back and forth. Then she fell backwards into the arms of the paramedic who had stepped towards her.

'What the hell?' the paramedic shouted and held up his hand. It was covered in fresh blood. 'She's injured! Get another team over here.'

'Millar?' Cal shouted, but she had disappeared from his view and all he could see when he turned to look for her were the backs of the paramedics as they laid her on the ground and started to work on her.

* * *

Riz had failed. He slapped himself on the side of his head.

'*Budallaqe.*' *Stupid*. When Konstandin found out, he would send word home to Albania – punish the woman and the girl. That was the price of failure. He'd had one task to do in order to protect them: kill the detective, and all his debts would have been forgiven. He would have been free to go wherever he wanted. He could have gone back to Durrës and this nightmare would have been over. All he'd had to do was make this one last sacrifice.

But he had failed. The cop had fought back, not like the other woman. The other woman had been surprised and did not fight back. She had frozen in shock. Once, twice, three times, he had stabbed the blade into her. He hated doing it, but he needed to do it. He needed to turn himself into a monster in order to survive.

This time it had been harder. Even if the cop had not fought back, he might have failed. He had no conviction, no heart. He did not like the monster within him. Before he left Albania, he had never been in a fight. He had never killed anything, not even a fly. He was not a monster by nature. He kept trying to convince himself of this.

He stumbled along the dark alley. He thought of Leandra and Zerina. He tried to convince himself that there was still a way back to them, that he could be with them again. But deep down he knew he would never see them again.

What had he become?

That poor girl. He saw her face, blanketed by the falling snow, startled as she saw him approach.

'Are you looking for help?' she had asked him. 'We can go inside and talk if you want?'

The panic showed in her eyes when he drew the knife from inside his jacket.

She had pleaded. 'I want to help you. Whatever it is that you have done, however you have ended up here, I can help you.'

He'd let the monster inside rise up. He heard Konstandin: *'Do this, or it will be your women that die.'*

As she lay on the white ground, he leant over her. He noticed a faded scar on the side of her face. 'I'm sorry,' he whispered.

She did not scream or speak.

He dropped the knife, tripped on the kerb and landed on his back. He crawled away.

'I'm sorry,' he said one last time.

He saw the pool of blood spread from under her body, like the wings of an angel growing from within her.

He turned and ran into the night.

Budallaqe.

Përbindësh. Monster.

He had become what they all called them. That man on the television who hated all of them, who said all the immigrants and refugees were evil monsters here to destroy his country. No one was interested in listening to them, to their story. Nothing Riz could have done would ever have changed their minds about him. No one wanted to help him. And now it was true. He was evil, he was a monster.

He had nowhere to go and no one to turn to. He had nothing. All that he had was this hell of his own making.

24

The broad sunlight beaming outside the front window did little to alter the interior ambience of the Cathcart Road Café. It failed to penetrate beyond the serving counter at the front, where Big Mags stood guard.

Only one table was occupied inside the café this morning, right at the back corner in the shadows.

Mags had not commented on Cal's appearance as she had delivered coffee to the table. She knew he worked at the nightclub that had burned down. It had been on the news a couple of days ago. One person had died. Cal had cuts and bruises around his face, his arms and hands were a patchwork of bandages and plasters, his hair looked dirty and singed. Mags could not imagine what could have happened to result in the angry, red abrasion around his neck, although she knew how such marks were formed.

The woman police officer sitting with him did not have any similar injuries, but she seemed paler, Mags thought, and when she reached forwards to pick up her cup of coffee, Mags had noticed her grimace.

It was none of Mags's business what they had got themselves into. She had no desire to mix herself up in other people's troubles.

Through the window, Mags saw a man in a suit approaching. Mags clocked him straight away – another police officer. He checked his stride at the doorway and looked at the sign above the window.

'They're waiting for you, at the back,' Mags shouted.

'How do you know who I'm looking for?'

'You're not the only one around here with ace detective skills, son.'

Dykes sat down next to Millar and put the manila file on the table. 'How are you both?'

'Just dandy,' Millar answered. 'So, the latest?'

'Technically, I shouldn't be talking to you. Forsyth was pretty clear on this, "to avoid any misunderstanding", as he put it. You are on rest and recuperation leave until further notice. A review board will determine when you are ready to return to active duty.'

'He said as much when he came to visit me at the hospital.'

'Boyle is taking over the investigation into the club attacks and it's officially being merged with the Rose Black murder investigation.'

Millar muttered a swear word under her breath. She hated the thought of Boyle and Scott going over everything they had so far, pulling it apart and arriving at the wrong conclusions.

Dykes jabbed the manila file with his index finger. 'The attempted murder on you is being rolled into the same investigation too.'

Millar picked up the file and opened it. Cal watched her reading the contents inside. He tried to judge her reaction.

'Sonovabitch.' Millar passed the single sheet of paper over to Cal for him to read.

There was a photocopy of fingerprints at the top of the sheet. Circles had been drawn around parts of it. He scanned the text underneath, and the conclusion was written in bold print.

'It's the same guy,' Cal said. 'He killed Rose and he tried to kill you.'

'I had him right in front of me and I let the bastard get away.'

'No one is blaming you for him getting away,' Dykes said, sticking up for his partner. 'You're lucky he didn't kill you. A few inches to the side and—'

'But he didn't, and I disarmed him. I should have been able to take him down. The whole case would be over by now and we would know who he is.'

'You told Forsyth you would recognise him if you saw him again?'

'I think so. When the balaclava came off, I got a glimpse of his face.'

'What did he look like?' Cal asked.

'Dark skin, black hair, dark stubble. I didn't notice any distinguishing features or marks, but I would know him if I saw him again.' She turned back to Dykes. 'Anything else?'

'The balaclava gave us hair samples and DNA; the knife gave us fingerprints. When we catch this guy, the evidence is there to link him to Rose Black's murder, the club attacks and your attempted murder.'

'Except,' Cal said, 'he couldn't have been at the Carnival when it was attacked because he was outside the police station waiting for you.'

They paused as Mags clattered three plates down on the table in front of them, each with a filled morning roll on it. 'I'll bring over fresh coffee.'

Once Mags had delivered fresh mugs of coffee and left the sugar sachets on the table for them, Dykes continued.

'They raided the flat at 231 Westercommon Road.'

'And?' asked Millar.

'Abandoned. Whoever was staying there has cleared out. The neighbours were reluctant to talk; not much trust in the authorities around there.'

'Not surprising.'

'But they did confirm that a group of men had been in that flat and had been seen going in and out at strange times.'

'Descriptions?'

'Only generic. All "Middle Eastern-type men". All aged between eighteen and thirty-five. No one admitted to having any contact with any of them.'

'White Transit van?'

Dykes nodded. 'Several sightings picking up and dropping off the men.'

'It's them,' said Millar. 'The fuckers were probably in there when we visited them. As soon as we left, they got the hell out of there. We tipped them off.'

'We didn't know that at the time.'

'Twice I've had these bastards right in front of me and let them get away, and now another person is dead and they've vanished, never to be seen again, if they've got any sense at all.'

Peter Jones's name had been added to the news reports, alongside Nathan MacDonald, as another victim of the spate of gang attacks sweeping across the city. So far Rose Black's name had been kept out of it. The media had yet to connect the attacks to illegal immigrants, only reporting it as gangland violence, the likes of which had not been seen in Glasgow for decades. When they did make the connection, the unrest in the city would reignite. The far-right would stoke the flames.

Yesterday, Jenny and Cal had gone to see what was left of the Carnival. They had found Carmen there, along with a group of officials – fire investigators and insurance agents. Uniformed police guarded the perimeter of the roped-off area. They refused to let Cal and Jenny through until Carmen saw them and came to speak to them. She lifted the police tape for them and they ducked underneath.

The walls of the building still stood. The windows were gaping holes, the paintwork around them stained black. The main door had burnt away. The air was acrid; the smell of burning hung around them. The ground around the building was littered with debris that had been dragged out of the building after the fire. Broken pieces of chairs and tables lay in heaps against the exterior walls. Broken shards of glass, light fittings, bottles, black ashes and lumps of charcoal painted the scene. The sign over the door had been ripped down and was lying on the grass verge, surprisingly unharmed and incongruously colourful.

'How bad is it?' asked Cal.

Carmen kicked at a charred brick on the pavement, her hands on her hips. 'Too early to say for definite. The roof is gone, but there is a chance the structure and some of the walls can be salvaged.'

'The insurance will cover it?' asked Jenny.

'Some of it, hopefully. I had criminal damage cover.' Carmen cast an eye over to the group of suited insurers. 'I'm sure they'll try to find a loophole to get out of paying up.'

'Anything we can do to help?'

Carmen shrugged. 'Maybe once this lot clear out and we're allowed to touch anything. It's going to take a lot of effort to clear up this mess and start rebuilding.'

They walked at a slow pace around the perimeter of the building, treading carefully to avoid the piles of discarded debris. Jenny, Georgia and Lauryn had been released from the hospital the day after the fire. They had suffered smoke inhalation and minor cuts and burns. Cal was kept in an extra night and released the following day. They were concerned about the damage to his throat from the hanging rope.

'Have you spoken to the police?' Cal and Jenny had been interviewed while they were at the hospital. Carmen and Patrick had checked themselves out almost as soon as the paramedics had dropped them off.

'I told them what I could, which wasn't much. A group of men in black clothes and masks broke in, tied us up, trashed the place and set it alight.'

'What about Patrick?'

'Peter was a friend from way back. Patrick is with his family just now. No kids, at least, but still.' Even though they had hardly known Pete, they still felt the loss was personal – and it could just as easily have been one of them.

'I thought we had seen the last of this kind of thing with Francis McArthur gone,' said Carmen.

They were at the side of the building. The staff entrance had lost its door, and the corridor inside was blocked by piles of rubbish. Puddles of water reflected the black walls and ceiling, and stretched away into the gloom inside.

'The thing I don't get,' continued Carmen, 'is why they wanted to kill us. From what I heard about the previous attacks, from what your detective pal told us, it was about putting the business out of action. A rival gang trying to muscle in. The poor lad at The Shed was just in the wrong place at the wrong time, but here, they wanted us dead as well as the club destroyed. And why you in particular, Cal? Why did they try to hang you?' Carmen looked at him. 'Why did they single you out from the rest of us?'

* * *

'Why you, Cal?' Millar asked him the same question, looking at him across the table at the rear of the café. 'Why did you get special treatment?'

Cal swallowed a mouthful of the hot roll, trying not to wince at the pain in his throat. 'Because they saw me with you.'

'Exactly. They didn't just happen to pick the Carnival. We know the same man who tried to kill me is part of the gang that is attacking nightclubs. At the same time, they burst into the Carnival and string you up to the ceiling.'

'You're saying it was coordinated?' asked Dykes.

'They have to be connected.'

'But how?'

'We got close to them, it panicked them, forced them to do something rash. Rose's killer has done it before, so he is sent to take care of me. The rest of the gang head to the Carnival. They want to make it look like another random attack on a property in the city, but the real reason is that they want to take care of Cal.'

'They would have killed everyone there just to get to Cal?'

'Makes it look like a random act rather than a targeted murder.'

'But they didn't come after me,' said Dykes. 'I was at the flat with you as well.'

'Not yet,' answered Millar. 'Perhaps they thought two cops in one night was too much of a risk.'

'But they're still out there.' A look of panic spread across Dykes's face as he realised what Millar was saying. 'Shit.'

'Where are Lucy and the kids?' asked Millar.

Dykes jumped up and sprinted to the door.

'I'll call it in,' Millar shouted after him. 'I'll get a unit over to your house right away.'

25

Jenny pleaded with Cal not to get involved. 'Let Millar go and get herself in trouble. She's not even supposed to be working the case. She's suspended.'

'She's not suspended. She's signed off on sick leave until she gets the all-clear to return to work.'

'Why can't you just leave it alone? None of this will bring Rose back to life. She's dead, Cal, and it wasn't your fault. Christ, you didn't even know her, you just stalked her.'

That stung, as Jenny knew it would.

Cal had told Jenny everything about Rose Black – the accident, the deal struck by Francis McArthur to keep Tony and Cal out of prison, the injuries Rose suffered, her recovery and his obsession with her. He tried to justify it to her. He wasn't a bad guy, he wasn't a creep. He wanted to make amends; he wanted to protect her.

Then it became obvious that Rose Black did not need his help or protection. Rose did not need to be saved.

Until that night last December.

By then, Cal had lost track of Rose. He had reined in his obsession, recognised its destructive nature, disciplined himself to move on and concentrate on fixing himself. He should have known the next disaster was waiting to trap him.

Jenny held him together. He let the police do their job. Millar was on the investigation and he trusted her to find out who had killed Rose. When the investigation hit a brick wall and Millar was reassigned, Cal carried on. Rose was gone, her killer had disappeared – what else could he do?

But that had changed now. They were closing in, and now the killer had made the wrong move.

Cal could feel the self-destructive thoughts returning – the mentality that had brought him to the brink of destroying his life, the anger, despair and the guilt. He had to harness them into something positive before they overwhelmed him.

It was too late to protect Rose, but he could get the man who had killed her.

Jenny had not signed up for any of this when she had decided to share her life with Cal. He had put her in danger. If Jenny was to be harmed, Cal knew he would never be able to recover, not this time, not again.

Jenny knew what he was going through, but she would not give up on him.

She tried a softer tack. 'Why can't you just leave it behind you and be happy with where you are now, with what you have now?'

She was right. Why couldn't he just be happy to be with Jenny and leave all the baggage behind?

'I need to do this,' was all Cal could say. 'If I do nothing, I will slip back into the person I was before. The person who ended up in prison. I have to see this through.'

Jenny had not said anything else after that. He left her sitting on his couch in his living room in his flat on Cumming Drive. She had not moved when he had leant over and kissed her on the top of her head and said goodbye.

Millar drove, Cal sat in the passenger seat. She got on the motorway at Tradeston and crossed the Kingston Bridge. The city rose up to greet them on the north side of the river before they dipped down and skirted the western edge of the ULEZ zone and re-emerged at Charing Cross.

'Dykes is with his family. Everyone is fine. Lucy and the kids are going to stay with his in-laws up north somewhere. Aberfeldy, Pitlochry, Auchtermuchty – one of those places – until this is over.'

The motorway disappeared below them as Millar took them along St George's Road and onto Maryhill Road. Firhill Stadium loomed up as the city buildings gave way to housing association homes and new-build flats. Behind those, in the skyline, the Westercommon Road high-rises stood tall.

'What do you think you'll find here? Dykes said they found nothing. They've bolted without a trace.'

'I want to take a look for myself.'

'You don't trust Boyle?'

'I wouldn't trust him to make a decent cup of builder's tea, but that's not the point. We need to start somewhere.' They crossed the Forth and Clyde Canal as it wound its way across the city. If the stitches in her side were causing Millar any pain, she was not showing it as she threw the car around the corner onto Panmure Street. Only when she turned into the Westercommon estate did Millar apply the brakes.

'Shouldn't we have back up with us?'

'I'm supposed to be resting up in bed. As far as Forsyth and Boyle are concerned, I am, so I don't think they're likely to support this course of action. Sure you're up for this? No turning back and all that.' She unclipped her seat belt and gave Cal one last chance to change his mind.

'I'm in,' said Cal. For once, he knew exactly what he needed to do.

'Then let's go.'

They rounded the corner of the tower at 231 Westercommon Road and saw the two uniformed constables standing at the main entrance.

'Bollocks,' swore Millar under her breath.

She put on a bold smile and a casual attitude, and flashed her Detective Inspector identity. Her colleagues already knew who she was; it was more to remind them where they stood in the police hierarchy. 'They got you on door duty, Nicolson? What a waste of your talent.'

The young constable returned Millar's winning smile with one of his own. 'Detective Millar, what a surprise. We were told to look out for you making an appearance.'

'You know me, can't stay off the job when there's a criminal to be caught.'

Constable Nicolson eyed her and looked across at his colleague, who only shrugged his shoulders.

Millar carried on. 'Going to pop up to the flat and have a nosey around for myself, see if the team missed anything. It was me that tracked down this place.'

'Afraid I can't let you do that,' said Nicolson. He cast his eye over Cal. 'Especially not accompanied by a civilian.'

'He's a material witness assisting the investigation,' tried Millar.

Nicolson shrugged. 'We've got our orders.'

'You're taking orders from Boyle now?' Millar tried to laugh it off.

'I always take my orders from Detective Inspectors seriously,' replied Nicolson. Millar took a step to the side to go round him and towards the door. Nicolson mirrored her and cut her off. 'But this isn't an order from DI Boyle.'

'Forsyth?'

'The superintendent told us you would likely turn up even though you were supposed to be recovering at home. What were his exact words?' Nicolson asked his partner.

The other officer theatrically pulled out his notebook, thumbed through a few pages until he found what he was looking for, cleared his throat and read from the page. '"If that bloody woman turns up, and I'm sure she will at some point, tell her to get back to her fucking bed and leave it alone".'

'You're paraphrasing?' said Millar.

'No, those were his exact words,' confirmed Nicolson. 'Seems he knows what you're like. There was something more about not making this a personal vendetta.'

'A bit bloody late for that. Someone comes at me with a sharp object, they better believe it's personal.'

'Either way,' Nicolson shrugged once more, 'we've got our orders from the top and we can't let you up there.'

Millar stared at the pair of them, although she knew she was defeated. It wouldn't do to let the rookies think she was taking orders from them. 'Keep up the good work, lads.'

'Will do, DI Millar.'

'I hope it pisses down on you all night.' Millar turned and left them with that final dig, pointing at the grey clouds gathering in the sky above the city. Cal gave them a sympathetic look and followed after her. The constables could only hope they had not made an enemy for life on the police force.

Riz watched the detective get back into her car. He knew he had not struck a fatal blow that night. By the looks of it, she was not even injured, even though he knew he had cut her. Only when she opened the car door did she pause and he saw her hand reach for her side. He waited, poised, until the man who was with her got into the car as well. When he closed the passenger door, Riz made his move. He knew this was crazy, but it was the only choice he had left.

26

'Bloody upstarts,' moaned Millar as she punched the starter button.

'You can't expect them to ignore orders.'

'They won't get anywhere in the force if they don't use a bit of initiative.'

Millar was going to carry on and say something more, but the back door opened behind her and brought her to a sudden stop. She looked in the rear-view mirror in time to see a blur as someone jumped into the back seat. The door slammed shut behind them. Cal spun round in his seat. The new arrival crouched in the rear footwell.

'Just drive,' the man hissed at them urgently, 'like I am not here, like nothing has happened.'

Millar saw the back of his head as he lay there. She froze for a split second. She recognised the sweep of dark hair and the brown skin of his neck. He still wore the same black clothes as he had been wearing that night under the streetlights of the car park when he came at her with a knife.

When the car did not move, he turned to face them and urged them again in a panicked whisper, 'Drive. If they see me here with you, I'm a dead man. Please.'

Millar looked him directly in the face. Cal looked between them both. Millar's expression suggested the man was dead whether they drove anywhere or not.

'It's him?'

Millar nodded. She put the car in gear and reversed, turned the car around and drove out of the car park at a normal pace.

Cal felt the anger swell up inside him. It was him. The man who had tried to kill Millar, which meant Rose Black's murderer was lying on the car floor behind him. Only the shock of his unexpected appearance and the uncertainty of the man's actions stopped Cal from getting out of the car, dragging the bastard out and beating him to a pulp right there and then.

'Keep an eye on the mirrors,' Millar said to Cal. Her response was cold and calm. If she could resist the impulse to lash out, so could Cal. She wanted to see how this played out.

No one spoke as Millar turned down Garscube Road, heading back towards the motorway and the centre of the city. She drove with exaggerated care. Cal looked in the passenger wing mirror and the rear-view mirror, and turned to look out of the rear window. There was no sign of anyone suspicious following them.

They stopped at a red light as the motorway loomed ahead of them. Millar checked the mirrors and looked to either side and ahead. There was no sign of a trap being set.

'Tell me why I shouldn't drive straight to the nearest police station and hand you over?' she asked over her shoulder, without taking her eyes away from the road in front of them. 'Or better yet, if no one saw you get into the car and no one knows you're with us, why I shouldn't find the nearest alley and give you the punishment you really deserve?'

'You must listen to me. I can help you,' the man answered. 'I can take you to the leaders. Me, I am just a nobody, you understand?'

'You expect me to trust you after you tried to kill me?'

'But it was not me, you understand? I had orders. I have to do what they tell me or they kill me and my family back home. You understand this?' He was pleading with them.

'Are you armed?' Millar asked.

'No, I have nothing.'

'You believe him?' asked Cal. Millar didn't respond, but the man was still crouched in the footwell and showed no sign he was about to attack. And if he was going to, now would be his best opportunity. They were defenceless and stuck in the car, with their backs to their enemy.

The lights changed to green and Millar pulled away at an even pace.

Cal spoke to Millar. 'We're taking him to the station, right? The guy who tried to stab you to death.' Millar did not answer him. 'Right, Millar?'

'I'm thinking,' she said.

They pulled up at the next junction. The turn left would take them across the top of the city centre, down through the Merchant City, around Glasgow Green and bring them to Dalmarnock Police Station. To the right was the on-ramp to the motorway that would take them back over the river to the south. Millar hesitated.

'Millar?' Cal asked.

The car behind sounded its horn.

'Fuck it,' said Millar. She punched the accelerator and spun the wheel hard right.

'Millar,' Cal shouted, 'what are you doing?'

'Following orders,' she replied. 'I'm on sick leave – best make the most of it and take a drive.'

Millar crunched through the gears and they re-joined the motorway. She swung them out into the fast lane and put her foot down.

Five minutes later they stopped outside a corrugated grey shutter, one entrance in a row of anonymous warehouses.

'Watch him,' Millar instructed and got out, the engine still running. Cal had not dared to take his eyes off the crouched figure in the back seat since he had got in to the car. Millar unlocked the padlock on the entrance, then lifted the shutter over her head and pushed it up. She got back into the car and rolled it forward, through the opening and inside. She killed the engine, got back out and pulled the shutter back down behind them. For a moment they were in darkness, until Millar turned a switch by the entrance and tube lights flickered on, revealing the interior. Two of the lights continued to flicker. Through the dim light, Cal could make out only some boxes in the far corner, a battered old couch and empty cans of lager discarded around it. The rest of the space was empty.

Millar opened the boot of the car. When she reappeared, she was holding the Taser in front of her and pointing it at the rear door.

'Get out of the car slowly.' The instruction was directed at the man in the back seat, but Cal took it as his cue to exit the vehicle. He stood next to Millar. There was no movement from inside the car. 'Open the door,' Millar told Cal.

He stepped forwards and pulled the door open.

The man was on the floor, his hands raised above his head. 'Please, don't shoot me. I can help you. I only want to help you.'

'Out now. Crawl forward.'

He did as instructed, pulling himself along, his hands coming out first and finding the floor. He crawled forwards and ended up lying face-down on the concrete. Millar watched him and gave Cal her handcuffs. 'Put these on him, hands behind his back.'

Cal went forwards and took the man's wrists. He pulled his arms behind his back and snapped the cuffs on.

'Sit him up, back against the car.'

Cal pulled him up and sat him against the closed door of the car, then stepped back and stood next to Millar. The man looked pitiful and defeated. He was malnourished, his beard and hair were greasy and unkempt, his skin was covered in a layer of dust and dirt and his clothes were shabby. Cal could smell his musty body odour as he leant over him.

'Who are you?' asked Millar.

'My name is Tariq Rizwan. Riz.'

'Okay, Riz. You have a lot of explaining to do.'

Cal could not restrain himself. 'Did you kill Rose Black?'

The man called Riz only looked up and Cal knew what the answer was. The look of guilt and shame in the man's face told him everything he needed to know. Cal took a step forwards and punched him across the face before Millar could stop him. Riz fell to the side. Cal followed up his punch with a kick to the man's midriff before Millar was able to grab him and pull him away.

'Not yet,' said Millar. 'I want some answers first. Then we can hand him over to Boyle. You aren't the only one who will be queueing up to take a shot at this piece of shit.'

Millar let him go. Riz cowered from Cal as he picked him back up and pushed him against the car door again.

Millar spoke to him again. 'Tell me why I shouldn't let him kill you?'

'Please, I did not want to kill anyone. I had no choice.'

'You'll have to do a whole lot better than that,' Millar threatened him with the raised Taser. 'Where are you from?'

'Albania.'

'And you came here illegally?'

'Yes.'

'When?'

'A year ago, I think. They do not let us keep time.'

'Who are "they"?'

'The men who held us. They will not let us go until we have paid off our debt.'

'The debt owed for getting you into the country?'

Riz nodded. 'Except we had paid them their money. Then they said prices had gone up. "Unexpected costs", they said. We had to work for them to make up the difference before we could earn the money for ourselves.'

'Rose Black was helping you. Why did you kill her?'

'No, she was not helping me. I did not know her. I did not see her until that night. Only after did I learn who she was.'

'Who told you to kill her?'

'The man who held me prisoner here. The men who brought me here. They had my family, you understand? Back in Albania. If I did not do what they asked, they would harm my child, my wife. You understand?'

'Who are these men? Who brought you over here?'

'I do not know names, only the faces I have seen.'

'If you don't know anything, then what good are you to me?' The Taser twitched again.

'No, no, wait. I can take you to them, yes? I can take you to the men who held me. They will know the big boss, yes? The gang leaders. It is them you want, yes?'

The man was so pathetic and defeated that Cal almost felt sorry for him. Then he reminded himself what this man had done. He had to switch off the humane side of himself. He had to revert back to the side of himself he had tried so hard to bury these past few months, the side of his personality that had put him in jail on assault charges.

'We should kill him and ditch him in the river,' Cal said in a level monotone.

'That's one option,' replied Millar.

Riz looked from one to the other, pleading with his eyes.

'You don't believe him, do you?'

'I want the people who run the operation. This waste of space is nothing.'

'Please, I can give them to you,' Riz pleaded again.

'Shut up,' said Cal. 'Not another word.'

'We need to talk,' Millar said. She lowered the Taser and went back to the boot of the car. She pulled out everything that was in there and dumped it on the ground. 'Put him in here.'

'What?' Riz's eyes widened.

Cal grabbed him and pulled him up on to his feet. He was light, underweight.

He pushed Riz and he tipped over the lip of the boot and fell inside. Cal grabbed his legs and tucked them in. Riz did not resist. Cal slammed the boot closed and turned to Millar. 'You believe him?'

Millar put the Taser back in its holster. 'Fuck.' She walked across the warehouse to the old couch and slumped down on it. Cal followed her.

'What?' he asked, standing next to her.

'Give me a can.' She pointed at a cardboard box at the side of the couch. Cal opened it up. There were two remaining cans of Tennent's Lager in the box. 'Have one for yourself if you want.'

'I don't drink.'

'I forgot. Good for you.' Millar pulled the ring tab and tossed it away. She took a long slug from the can.

'What do we do?' asked Cal.

'It's a trap, you get that, right?'

'What is?'

'He's been sent to bring us to the leaders. You think he would just hand himself over when he's wanted for murder and the attempted murder of a police officer?'

'You heard him, he has no choice. They have his wife and child.'

'Maybe they do, which is why he will do whatever they want him to do. He's already killed an innocent woman for them. He would kill a police officer for them – except that didn't work and so now he's screwed no matter what he does. He's a liability to his masters.'

'Unless they use him one last time to lure us in.'

'Exactly. I'm sure they'll have told him that if he does this, all will be well, but I bet once he's delivered us to them, we'll all end up in the same body bag together.' Millar took another slug from the can.

'So we take him in. Let Boyle arrest him and break him under questioning.'

'What are you, a boy scout?' Millar scolded him. 'You think he'll talk to Boyle? This guy doesn't know who the gang leaders are; that much was true. He's a nobody to them.'

'What then?'

'I want the people who run this gang, more than this nobody they sent to kill me. I want the guy who gave the order. The same guy who told him to murder Rose Black.'

Millar's thinking dawned on Cal. 'You're going to walk right into their trap, even though you know it's a trap?'

'It's the only shot we'll have to get to the ringleaders. I'm sick of dealing with the little guys.'

It had been the same with Francis McArthur. Millar had no interest in picking on the little waves caught up in the tide of crime that flooded across the city. She wanted to take out the guy who was behind it all, the guy who was really responsible. Then she could make an actual difference. She had no time for causing ripples; she had to unleash a tsunami.

'They will kill us as soon as they see us.'

'You don't have to come with me.'

Cal thought for a moment, then said the only word that he could think of to sum up their choice. 'Fuck.' He slumped on to the couch next to her. The smell of warm lager emanating from the open can in her hand made him nauseous. At least alcohol held no appeal for him anymore. 'What is this place anyway? Your own private interrogation facility?'

'It was a safe house. We used it during the McArthur investigation. If anyone needed to disappear for whatever reason, somewhere to bolt to in a hurry, they could come here. There used to be some gym equipment and a TV and fridge. After the investigation wound up the lease was handed back to the owners, but I kept a key, just in case.'

'McArthur would never have gone after a cop though.'

'Wouldn't he?'

They sat in silence. There was no sound from the boot of the car.

'Are you going to tell Dykes at least, or Boyle? Before we do this?'

'Boyle will stop us from doing anything. I'm on sick leave; you're a civilian – worse, an ex-convict. We're on our own or we do nothing and hand him over. That's our choice. But if we hand him over, I guarantee you we will never find the person who ordered Rose's death.'

Cal knew Millar was playing with his emotions. She knew he could not turn down the chance to get revenge for Rose.

He pointed at the car. 'You think he's okay in there?'

'Let's leave him a little bit longer. Make him think we're really in trouble.'

'We are really in trouble, Millar.'

Riz blinked when the car boot opened. The dim flickering light of the warehouse was still bright enough to require his eyes a moment to adapt from the pitch black. The police officer and the man looked down on him.

'Alright, we'll bite,' said the police officer. 'You give us the ringleaders, we won't throw you in the river.'

Riz breathed an internal sigh of relief. There was still a chance for Leandra and Zerina. There was no hope for him, he knew this. He had given up on ever seeing them again when Konstandin had given him the knife and told him his mission was to kill the policewoman. What he did now, he did to save them, to keep them safe and let them escape the danger he had put them in. All he could do was pray it would be enough.

'Jimmy Koçi's Boxing Club,' Riz told them, as he had been instructed to.

27

Jimmy Koçi's Boxing Club was in Ibrox, in the shadow of the football stadium. Millar pulled up outside the address. The building, like much of the area, had seen better days. On one side was a Turkish barber's, on the other a kebab shop. Sandwiched between them was an inauspicious doorway with the shutter pulled down, covered by graffiti and flyposting. The gym was on the upper floor, above the retail units. Across blacked-out windows, the dilapidated sign with missing letters read: "Jim Ko's oxing Cub".

'This the place?' Millar asked Riz, peering up at the windows.

'Yes, this is the place,' he answered from the back seat.

'A gym that's not open on a Saturday morning?' Cal said to Millar.

'Doesn't look like it's been open for a while.'

'The gym is not open just now, but they have an office here, behind the gym.'

There were a few people on the street. A young man lounged at the front of the barber shop. Cal could see one customer getting a haircut. The kebab place was not open yet – even in Glasgow, it was still too early for that.

Cal turned to look at the man in the back seat. Riz was about the same age as him, maybe a couple of years younger. His dark hair was naturally curled, his stubble dark across his deep-olive-coloured skin. If he hadn't been underweight and dishevelled, he would have been handsome. He slumped on the back seat, defeated and broken.

'How did you end up here, Riz?' Cal asked.

Riz paused, unsure how to answer. 'That is a long story.'

Cal could not hide his hate for him – he knew what Riz had done – but he now knew it was not as simple as he had imagined it to be. Rose's killer was not a maniac or a deranged psychopath. He spoke softly; his manner was respectful, even timid. It was hard to imagine him as a knife-wielding attacker. Yet that was what he was, what he had become. He had killed Rose, and he had attempted to kill Millar.

'I'm going to have a look.' Millar opened her door and handed her Taser to Cal. 'You stay here with him.'

They watched her walk around the corner of the building.

'Why did you kill Rose?' Cal asked, without turning to face Riz.

'They told me to.'

'Why you?'

Riz gave a pathetic sigh. 'I came here for my family, you understand? To make a better life for us back home in Albania. They promised us money. Back home there was nothing for me, no opportunities. I worked at the port when they needed extra workers. I worked at a tobacco factory, making cigarettes. Neither of these paid me enough to live on, to support my family. Here, I could work for a year or two on building sites and then return home and we would be set for life, yes?'

Cal didn't respond.

Riz continued, 'Once I got here, what was promised did not happen. We were kept together in a dark room, all of us. No phone. Up at daybreak, driven to work on a construction site. Fed on bread and water and your porridge, yes? Not enough food or water. Sleeping on a floor. We put up with it because we thought of the money, of the better life for our families back home. Then we realised, there is no money. They say they will look after it for us, or they have sent it back home already, but I think there is no money and there never will be. Then it is not a construction site we are driven to. It is other things we must do.'

'Trashing nightclubs?'

'Trashing, yes. Destroy them – but no choice for us. We have no rights; we do not exist. We have no one to help us. We must do what they tell us.'

'Including killing innocent women?' Cal spun round in his seat, fighting to contain his anger. 'Rose Black was trying to help people like you.'

Riz cowered back, shrinking away. 'One moment,' he said and held out his hands to placate Cal. Then he slowly moved one hand to his trouser pocket and took out a small piece of paper. It was a photograph, crumpled and creased. He held it up to show Cal.

'My family. You understand. For them.'

Cal looked at the picture. A woman and a child, a girl with the same dark features as Riz, the same dark, naturally curled hair and olive skin, but healthy and smiling. The woman held the girl in her arms, their cheeks pressed together, the small girl's thin arms wrapped around her mother's neck. They smiled out from the photograph.

'My wife, my daughter. You see.'

It didn't make sense. How could this man, a loving husband and father, turn into a murderer?

'You killed for them?' Cal asked.

'To protect them, yes? The men who hold us here, they threaten them. They tell us if we don't do what is asked of us, then our families back home in Albania, they will be harmed or killed, yes?'

Cal said nothing. Riz turned the photograph around and looked at Leandra and Zerina. 'To protect them,' he said to himself, trying to justify his action, when he knew there was no justification for what he had done. 'And now, I think I shall never see them again. It is too late.'

Cal's anger faded, replaced by pity. This poor fool, trapped in a desperate situation by the decisions he had made with no escape, resigned to his fate.

'They sent you to get us, didn't they?' Cal asked. 'Millar and me.'

Riz nodded as he put the photograph back in his trouser pocket. 'They said I had to make amends for my mistakes, but I am not stupid. I think they will get rid of me as well as you and your detective friend. It is too late, but I cannot stop trying. For them.' He pointed at his pocket with the photograph in it. 'You have family?'

'Not like yours,' said Cal, thinking of Marie and his mum and the newborn niece he had never met. 'Not the way you do.' Maybe Jenny would be that for him one day, but would he ever kill another person for her?

'Then perhaps you cannot understand. They sent me to bring you to them, so I did it. No choice now. I could ask you and the detective woman to help me, but I think after what I have done, you would not. You see? It is too late for me, but for my wife and daughter, I try.' Riz trailed off into a moment of silent reflection. 'I wish you could see Durrës, my city. It has places like this, yes. Rough places, you would say. But it is beautiful, not like here. It is not all grey and depressing. When the sun shines, we go to the beach. The sun shining down on the sea, the sand on the beach. Zerina loves to play on the sand and in the sea.'

Cal realised how far this man was from home, how far away he was from the things he loved.

Millar reappeared and made her way back to the car. Cal got out to meet her.

'There's a door onto a lane at the back. No sign of anyone, but the door is unlocked.'

'He admitted it was a trap. He was told to bring us here.'

'So they will be waiting for us. They've probably seen us already.'

'Do we go in?'

'If you want to find out who ordered Rose's killing, this is how we find out.'

'This is going to hurt, isn't it?'

'Every chance.'

'You don't think we should let Boyle handle it?'

'I think if we don't go in here now, we probably lose any chance we'll ever have of getting to the real people behind this.'

Cal knew Millar would go into the gym whether he went with her or not. He couldn't let her go on her own.

Millar could see his hesitation and took out her phone. 'I'll message Dykes and tell him where we are. That do you?'

Cal wanted to get the people who killed Rose and tried to kill him and Jenny and Millar. He opened the back door of the car.

'Out,' he ordered Riz. 'Let's go.'

The back of the club was even less salubrious than the street-facing public entrance. The lane was covered in overgrown weeds and grass; broken glass and litter covered the ground. There was a narrow path that led to a door made of solid wood. Like the front of the building, it was covered in graffiti.

Millar led the way, followed by Riz. Cal brought up the rear, pushing the Albanian in front of him. Millar opened the door and stepped inside.

It opened onto a gloomy box hallway that led to a narrow flight of stairs. The smell of musty sweat and disinfectant mixed together. They made their way up the stairs in single file, moving as quietly as possible. Cal could hear only their breathing and the tread of their footsteps.

At the top of the stairway was another square landing and another wooden door. Millar waited for them to join her on the landing, then opened the door.

They stepped into an old-fashioned boxing gym. Bare light bulbs burned from the ceiling, hanging from electric wires. There were no white walls or neon signs, there was no fresh paint, no pandering to the part-time casual customer who came to make themselves look good in a mirror. This was spit and sawdust – a place to come and train hard, without compromise. Punching bags and speedballs hung from the ceiling, skipping ropes hung on the wall next to wall-length mirrors and in the centre of the wooden floor was a full-size boxing ring.

They were alone, and the gym was empty. The door swung closed behind them with a soft click.

'I am glad you came,' said a man's voice. 'We have a lot to talk about.'

He stepped out from behind a door at the far side of the gym. He wore a slim-fitting, fashionable suit. He was not a tall man; he held himself upright and straight, but he did not have the frame of a boxer, he had not spent much time working out at the gym. He had the same dark features as Riz, but his hair was cropped close to his head, his stubble was styled. As he walked around the boxing ring towards them, four larger men appeared and followed him.

Rather than greeting Millar and Cal, the man first went to Riz and stood in front of him. Riz was taller than the man, yet in his presence Riz became smaller in comparison.

'You did well, Tariq.' He placed a hand on Riz's shoulder, then moved it up and cupped the back of his head. He smiled at Riz, who tried to raise a smile in reply. Cal saw the flicker of hope in Riz's face. Despite what he had said in the car, he still believed these men would treat him fairly. He still clung on to some quantum of hope.

The man's head shot forwards in an instant and Riz was on the floor, his nose burst open by the man's forehead and blood trickling down his face.

The man left Riz there and turned to Millar and Cal. 'I apologise for the violence,' he said. His accent was similar to Riz's.

Another Albanian, Cal thought.

'My name is Konstandin.'

Millar watched him as he paced in front of them. This was him – the Constantine or Conrad that Tony McArthur had heard about. She knew instantly what sort of man he was. Mid-level – one step up the ladder from Riz, but not a leader. He liked to think he held the power, that he was in charge – but he was just another worker. He wasn't the one calling the shots.

'We want to talk to your boss,' said Millar.

'You can talk to me. I am in charge here.'

'You might like to think you are, but we're not interested in talking to mid-level management. We want your boss.'

Cal could see the man called Konstandin bristle. Millar was antagonising him on purpose, trying to get a reaction. Cal wished Millar would not do that.

'This is how you want it to be?' smiled Konstandin, before shrugging. 'Very well.' He turned to the men behind him. 'String them up,' he instructed them.

Before they could react, two of the men pulled handguns from behind their backs. They aimed them at Cal and Millar while the other men came towards them.

28

The punching bags had been taken down to make way for Cal and Millar. Their wrists were bound together with rope and they were hung from the hooks on the ceiling. They dangled side by side now, like pig carcasses at a slaughterhouse. Konstandin paced back and forth across the boxing ring in front of them. The men who had entered with Konstandin stood on either side awaiting instructions. Riz sat on a bench at the side.

'You have no idea what you are in the middle of,' Konstandin said.

'I've got a fair idea,' replied Millar.

Cal groaned. Millar did not know when to quit.

'You really don't.' Konstandin laughed. 'What do you think you can do? The city police officer, and her little sidekick. You really think you can succeed where international crime agencies have failed?'

'You really think you can make us stop coming after you?'

Konstandin held the top rope of the ring and leant against it. 'I don't think you want to know the answer to that question. My only mistake was sending this fool,' he pointed at Riz, 'to take care of you. I should have done it myself, or sent one of my professional boys here.'

Cal had to admit, the professionals looked like they could take care of business.

'But before I show you what they are capable of, I have some questions for you. I might be lenient with you if you answer them. Give you a quick death instead of a slow, painful one.'

Cal could feel the ropes cutting through his skin. His arms and shoulders ached under the stress. His injuries from the nightclub fire burned.

'You have brought this on yourselves, you understand?' Konstandin continued, resuming his pacing back and forth. 'You could have looked the other way. We were doing you a favour, really, you and your police colleagues. We were clearing away some of the bad people from your city. You should have been grateful. A little upheaval and once we had control of the city, you would have seen a drop in crime. The people I work for are serious business people. All they want to do is make money, not create havoc and violence.'

'You could have fooled me,' cut in Millar, interrupting Konstandin's flow.

He glared at her. 'You have a big mouth for a small woman. In my country, you would not be tolerated like you are here.' He turned to look at Cal. 'You do not control your women like you should.'

Cal tried his best to shrug in reply.

'Why do you need to take over all of the city? Why so greedy?' Millar asked.

'It is not about greed, it is about control. Unless we control all of the trade, then there will always be factions, arguments, conflicts. Once we take care of any dissenting competition, we can set prices, control flow and volume. This is how business is done. This is not the first city that we have chosen to help.'

'You picked the wrong city this time,' said Millar.

That drew another deep laugh from the Albanian. 'Still the big talk from the little woman.' Again, he addressed Cal. 'You let your women talk like this to men?'

'You're welcome to try to control her if you want.'

'I know how to deal with women like this, and weak men. In my country we do not have to put up with this behaviour. We do not have the same laws that get in the way. So tell me, what exactly do you think you know about us and what we are doing here?'

'We know you traffic your own countrymen and use them as slaves when they get here,' said Millar. 'We know you use them to do your dirty work for you – destroying property, and the odd murder on the side.'

'The boy was an unfortunate accident, I agree.'

'I'll be sure to share your regret with Nathan MacDonald's family.'

'But not one that I can take responsibility for. My mistake was relying on these weak boys to do a man's work. You can be assured that the man responsible for the boy's death has been punished.'

Cal grunted as his arm muscles spasmed. Another murder, this time one of their own. They had no compunction about killing anyone who stood in their way.

'So you take over the nightclubs, bars, restaurants, massage parlours – and then flood the city with your own product. Drugs, people trafficking.'

'Oversimplified, but essentially true.'

'A cartel. But you're not smart enough to do that on your own. You're nothing but a soldier,' Millar antagonised him. 'I'm not interested in you. I want the people you work for. Give me their names and I'll take it into account when I come for you.'

Cal tried to swivel round to look at Millar. What was she doing? Threatening him when they were about to be used as punching bags?

Konstandin saw the funny side of her threat. 'I admire you in a way, Detective – your stubbornness, your refusal to accept defeat. You have told me all I need to know, which is that you know nothing. Just like your colleagues at Interpol and the National Crime Agency, you are floundering in the dark. All my people need to know is that you do not know anything that might hurt us. Now we can dispose of you and we are perfectly safe. Boys, you can do what you like with these two, just make sure there are no traces of them. Dump them where they won't be found.'

'You think you can kill a police officer and no one will come after you?'

'You think we haven't done it before?' He pulled the lower rope of the boxing ring down, stepped through it and jumped down to the floor in front of them. 'I'm sorry our acquaintance was so short. Goodbye, Detective, and your little lapdog.' He walked past them.

'What about Rose Black?' Cal called after him. 'Why did she have to be killed? Did she find out who your masters were?'

Konstandin stopped at the door. He looked back at Cal, and at Riz, who still sat cowering on the bench.

'Ah yes, Rose Black. You failed to find her killer, didn't you?' He pointed at Riz. 'Well, there he is.'

'We know you had Riz kill her.' Cal carried on. 'Why? You say killing is a last resort for your people. You say you want to avoid conflict and run a smooth business. Why kill a human rights lawyer helping innocent refugees?'

Konstandin again looked around the room at Riz, at his men, at Millar and Cal. Cal followed his gaze and looked at the men next to him. He saw something in their faces he had not seen before now. They were confused and uncertain. They had no idea who Rose Black was or what they were talking about.

'And what was Rose Black to you, lapdog? A girlfriend? Your lover? Is that why you are involved with this policewoman? How quaint.'

Cal jerked his body and strained his wrists, his anger triggered. He wanted to get a hold of Konstandin and beat the truth out of him, but his efforts were pathetic and futile. Millar was motionless.

Konstandin looked at Riz. 'You see what happens when you make mistakes, Tariq? This is what I warned you about.' Then he turned back to Cal. 'He is like you, my friend – a weak man. It is best you forget all about Rose Black. If you think you are in trouble for interfering with our business in a few nightclubs and massage parlours, then you have no idea what awaits you if you meddle in this other business. This is why it is best for everybody that you disappear now.'

Cal realised that this was the end for them. These were serious people and they would not let them go. No one was coming to rescue them. They would kill them for getting too close, and Riz for making one too many mistakes. And no one would find their remains.

29

They started with Millar.

Cal could only look on as one of the men held her to stop her swinging on the hook while another of the men swung his fist back and launched it into Millar's stomach. She jerked as the impact doubled her up. The air was knocked out of her lungs and left her gasping for breath. She felt the stitches in her side split and the knife wound open up again. She lurched, struggling to break free from the hook, but the man holding her grabbed her and held her still. The man swung again, aiming higher with an uppercut that went into her ribs. Cal heard the crack of bone as his meaty fist crunched into her body.

'You are sure there is nothing more you need to tell us?' said Konstandin, watching on with indifference. 'This could be over much quicker and less painfully for you.'

'Fuck you,' spat Millar, gulping air into her lungs. Blood seeped down her side from the open wound.

The Albanian turned to Cal. 'You could help your friend out. Tell me what you know about Rose Black, what the police know, and I will not leave her in the hands of my men here. They can be very disrespectful to women.'

Millar's look told Cal what he already knew her answer would be – don't tell them anything. She would not do it to save him; she expected the same from him.

'I've got nothing to tell you. She's the police detective. I'm just a concerned citizen.'

Konstandin did not appreciate the excuse. He realised he had misjudged the power dynamic between the man and the woman. Typical of this meek Western country. The woman was the strong one, the man was the weak one.

'Get him down,' he ordered. One of his men handed Konstandin their handgun and then lifted Cal by his waist until the rope looped off the hook. Cal's feet hit the wooden floor and he was pushed forwards and down on to his knees in front of Konstandin. 'Let's see how much your police friend really cares about you. In my experience, police officers make the worst friends. You should never trust them.'

The click of the hammer being pulled back echoed around the gymnasium. Cal felt the hard, cool metal press against the side of his forehead.

'I will spare him if you tell me what the police know,' Konstandin said to Millar. His voice was level and calm, like he dealt with torture and killing every day. 'It is too late for you, but this piece of shit I do not fear. Will you talk to spare his life?'

Cal already knew the answer, but there was no harm in hoping Millar had a soft and caring side.

'Fuck you,' she repeated.

Cal waited for the gunshot. Would he even hear it, or would the bullet have bulldozed through his brain and killed him before the sound even registered? He stared at the wooden floor in front of him. There was no gunshot. Instead, the metal left his forehead and in one swift motion, Cal felt a rush of air before the butt of the pistol cracked into his skull and the wooden floor came up to meet him.

'Last chance,' he heard Konstandin say through the haze that clouded his senses. 'Talk or I put a bullet in him first and then you. But only after I've let my boys have their fun with you.'

Cal tried to get up, but his head throbbed and his limbs felt heavy and immovable. He was going to die on the dirty floor of a broken-down gym, and he did not want to think about what would happen to Millar next.

He looked up and saw the gun pointing at his face.

Then a loud howl rang out. At first Cal thought it was just him who could hear it, like it was some internal scream against imminent death from his brain, but then he saw the gun barrel swing away from him, reacting to the same noise.

And then Konstandin disappeared from his view as a man barged into him and tackled him to the floor. Cal pulled himself up and saw Riz sprawled on top of Konstandin. They wrestled for the gun and Riz hit him about the head, his arms flailing wildly. The other men were caught off-guard. They had almost forgotten Riz was there, cowering on the bench in the corner. They stared as their boss grappled on the floor with him.

Millar was the first to react. She had been waiting for her chance; a moment was all she needed. The man in front of her, the one who had punched her, had turned away from her to watch the fight on the floor. Millar swung her leg round and her boot connected with his head with enough force to send him spinning across the room and into the side of the boxing ring.

'Move, Cal,' she screamed.

Cal snapped into action at her command. He got to his feet. The room was still spinning and he could feel blood running down the side of his face, but this was their chance and adrenalin kicked in.

The man behind Millar was too slow. Caught unaware, he suddenly found Millar's legs wrapped around his neck, gripping him in a vice. Another of the men finally came to Konstandin's aid and rushed in to try to pull Riz away.

Cal faced the remaining man, the one who had given his handgun to Konstandin. Up against five armed Albanians, Cal knew he didn't stand a chance, but facing one of them in a fist fight was a different matter. The man may have been trained in combat, but Cal had not spent a year in prison without learning a thing or two, the first thing being to forget about fighting fair – this was about survival.

He rushed forwards and locked the man in an ungainly cuddle. He got his hand into the man's face and tried to drag him down. He pulled at his thick hair and when that failed, Cal raised his knee and smashed it into the man's crotch, right between his legs. The man doubled over and released his grip on Cal. Cal looked about for a weapon, anything that he could use to hit the man with. Nothing presented itself but his head was at a good height. Cal took a step back and kicked as hard as he could. The man toppled to the side and landed on the floor in a dead heap.

Cal spun around. Riz was still sprawled on top of Konstandin as the other man tried to pull him off.

'A little help, Cal,' shouted Millar. She still had her legs wrapped around the head of the man, who was desperately trying to prise himself free.

Cal sprinted across the gym floor and dived at the man, catching him in a rugby tackle. The man was knocked off his feet, Cal's momentum sending them into a wall mirror. The man's head thumped against it, shattering the glass. Cal felt him go limp.

Then he became aware of the strange creaking sound as he got back to his feet. So did Konstandin and Riz. They paused their scuffle on the floor and turned to look up at the ceiling, along with Cal.

'Shit,' muttered Millar as she looked above her head. Fault lines were appearing in the plaster ceiling around the hook from which she was suspended. It had not been built for the strain it had been subjected to in the last few minutes. With a final loud crack, the plaster gave way, along with the roof beam it was attached to, and Millar and a pile of debris plummeted to the floor.

There was a deafening thud and a cloud of dust engulfed the gym. Konstandin and Riz were caught by the falling debris. In the confusion, Riz rolled free from him and bolted for the exit.

Cal coughed and spluttered as he breathed in the dust. He cleared rubble with his hands, trying to get to Millar. He got hold of the heavy wooden beam and lifted it, expecting to find Millar lying underneath it, but she wasn't there.

'Too late,' said Konstandin. Cal stopped and looked up. Konstandin, with a bloodied nose and lip, covered in white dust, was standing by the door. 'Enough of the silly games.'

The man who had been wrestling with Riz and Konstandin stood holding Millar, propping her up with an arm around her throat. She was semi-conscious, her eyes were unfocused and she swayed on her feet. The man held a gun to her head.

'I should have just shot you in the first place. Now I will have to waste time hunting down that coward Tariq. No matter. He won't get far,' said Konstandin.

Cal made a motion to go towards Millar.

'No, no, lapdog. You stay where you are. This is over.' Konstandin's voice had lost its calm politeness. Now he sounded bitter and angry.

He raised a handgun and aimed it at Cal. 'Now you both can go together, at the same time.' He looked to his man who was holding Millar. They nodded agreement.

Cal was frozen. There was nothing he could do. He wasn't sure if Millar was even aware of what was happening. He waited for the double gunshot.

The sharp click of the hammer next to Konstandin's ear stopped them in their tracks.

'You're right,' whispered Dykes as he pressed the barrel of the gun he had picked up from the floor into the back of the Albanian's head. 'This is over. Tell your man to drop the gun, and drop yours too, or I'll blow your fucking brains out right where you stand.'

PART 4

THEY MADE ME A KILLER

30

'Enough.' Superintendent Forsyth raised his voice to silence the room.

Marcus Boyle and Simone Millar broke off their argument in frustration.

Forsyth dared one of them to break ranks and start again. When he was sure they had both finished, he gave them his final decision.

'It's Boyle's case,' the superintendent turned to Millar, 'and you are not even supposed to be here, you're on compassionate leave. Boyle does the interview.'

'If it wasn't for me, you wouldn't have anyone in custody and the case would still be cold.'

It was one argument too many for Forsyth. 'Need I remind you, Detective Millar, that you had the main suspect in two murder inquiries in your custody and you let him get away. The same man that also tried to kill you. I now have to divert significant resources towards apprehending him, even though he was sitting in the back of your car not three hours ago.'

'He's a pawn; he led us to the next level up in the organisation.'

'He's a desperate man who has killed and he's loose on the streets of my city!'

Millar opened her mouth to say something, Forsyth shut it for her with a look and a raised finger.

'I will allow you to stay and observe if you want, and Boyle can come to you for advice if he needs to, but that's as close as you will get to this. You're a victim in this case. You know it's a conflict of interest to have you anywhere near it.'

'But Nathan MacDonald's death is my case and so are the property break-ins. He's as much my suspect as he is his,' Millar jerked her thumb in the direction of Boyle.

'Wrong, Millar. Your cases were moved over to Boyle and rolled into the Rose Black investigation, as you well know. Now, have I made myself clear? Any more from you, any stepping over the line, and I will officially suspend you, never mind compassionate leave.'

Millar backed down. There was nothing more she could do.

There was a knock on the door and Forsyth's assistant stuck her head in. 'The public service defender is here. She's waiting downstairs.'

'Better get on with it.' Forsyth dismissed Boyle. 'Marcus, make sure you do this right.'

'Yes, sir. You know you can rely on me.'

Millar rolled her eyes and stood up to follow him. If she couldn't be the one to question Konstandin, she would make damn sure Boyle didn't mess the whole thing up.

'We'll have another discussion about what happened today when this is over, Millar. I will want a full explanation about how you managed to endanger yourself and a civilian. An explanation that doesn't result in your immediate dismissal. Do I make myself clear?'

Crystal-clear. Millar was being given time to come up with a believable story that her boss could use to cover her ass. She was grateful that Forsyth gave her this much leeway. Another superintendent might have dismissed her already.

Dykes was waiting for her at the door. Forsyth picked up a file from his desk and pointed at Millar's partner. 'And make sure you buy him a pint this evening. You owe him.'

The door closed and Forsyth sat down behind the mountain of paperwork on his desk. It would only grow taller after today, but he allowed himself a smile. Boyle was a pain in the ass – he would much rather have let Millar lead the investigation again – but his hands were tied by bureaucracy. He was mad at her for letting her own attacker get away, but she was right. He was only a pawn in this case. He needed to be apprehended and stopped, but so did the people who were trafficking these men into the country and taking advantage of them.

The important thing was that they had finally caught a break, both in the recent case of city disorder, and in the stalled investigation into Rose Black's murder. If the interview went well in the next hour, he could be calling the chief constable with good news, closing two high-profile cases in one day. And Forsyth knew how much the chief constable valued delivering good news to their political masters in an election year.

Cal sat in the holding cell. He had been in a similar cell before – right before he had been sent to prison for a year. He was confident that wouldn't happen to him this time, although he was still wary when it came to dealing with the police. He was merely a concerned citizen who happened to stumble into the middle of a police investigation involving a people-trafficking gang. He was only trying to assist the police with their inquiries and ended up in the wrong place at the wrong time. Due to his actions, a major suspect was in custody. Police Scotland should be awarding him some sort of civilian commendation at the moment. Plus, he had Millar to back him up.

He lay down on the hard bench, the only furniture in the holding cell, and waited for someone to come and talk to him. He might as well get comfortable; he would be waiting a while. They would question Konstandin before they got round to him. With luck, Konstandin would confess everything and all Cal would need to do would be provide a witness statement and be sent on his way.

Of course, it would not be that straightforward. Konstandin did not strike Cal as the sort of person who was going to be a voluble suspect, and Cal's experience with the police had never been straightforward in the past.

He put his hands behind his head and closed his eyes. Outside the cell, he heard footsteps hurrying up and down the corridor.

Millar sat down in front of the monitors, her arms folded, her brow furrowed. Her hair was still damp after her shower. She wore an old t-shirt, gym leggings and trainers – the only change of clothes she had in her locker. The police medic had checked her over and told her she should go to the hospital. She may have suffered a slight concussion and she required stitches in her side. Millar had patched herself up with a bandage from the first aid kit.

This was her case, they had Konstandin because of her, and it was her who had put her life on the line to get him. Not only that, the bastard she was watching now on the live feed from the interview room had ordered her to be killed. But she had to sit here and watch Boyle either take the credit for closing the case, or monumentally screw it up. It was fifty-fifty which way it would go with Boyle. She was tempted to say it was the old boys' network at play again, but she had fought against that and overcome it. She knew if there was any way Forsyth could have let her into the interview room, he would have done it, but his hands were tied.

The door opened and Dykes entered, took the seat next to her and handed her a cup of warm coffee.

'At least it's in HD now,' said Dykes, pointing at the monitor. Only recently had the internal cameras been upgraded from murky black-and-white CCTV to modern, colour high definition.

One camera was situated in front of Konstandin, showing his face in crisp detail as he stared blankly at the wall in front of him. The other camera was behind Konstandin's head, looking over his shoulder at two empty chairs.

The speakers clicked into life as they registered the sound of a door unlocking, followed by footsteps, and on the screens in front of Millar and Dykes they saw Detective Inspector Boyle and Detective Scott enter the room. In unison they pulled out the chairs opposite Konstandin and sat down. They were followed by a woman who sat next to the suspect.

Millar sipped her coffee and leant forwards in anticipation. As much as she resented Boyle, she wanted to hear what Konstandin had to say.

Boyle went through the mandatory introduction for the recording, stating the time and date and giving the names of those present. The suspect's full name was Konstandin Sula and the woman sitting next to him was the public defender assigned to represent him. Boyle reiterated the Miranda rights to the suspect, and the accusations he faced after the disturbance involving a police officer at Jimmy Koçi's Boxing Gym, which had led to his arrest. Konstandin stared at Boyle as he said all this and did not react in any way.

'Do you understand everything that has been said to you so far?' asked Boyle.

Konstandin still stared at him and said nothing. Boyle repeated the question.

The public defender leant over and whispered something in Konstandin's ear, which the microphones did not pick up. Konstandin whispered something back to her. Millar could see the frustration building in Boyle's face.

The public defender spoke in an educated Edinburgh accent. 'My client requests an interpreter be present to translate everything into his native language, to make sure he fully understands the details of what has been said.'

'We'll do everything in our power to get an Albanian translator here as soon as possible.' It was a familiar delaying tactic. Everyone in the room knew that Konstandin had a grasp of the English language that was better than half of the adult population of Glasgow. The smart criminals knew the police only had a certain amount of time to question a suspect before they had to be either charged or set free. By the time Police Scotland had rustled up an Albanian translator, half of Konstandin's time would be gone. 'In the meantime, Mr Sula, do you object to me asking you a few simple questions?'

The public defender and her client once again had a hushed consultation. She spoke on behalf of him again. 'He has no objection, although he reiterates that if he does not fully understand the question, he may refuse to answer.'

'Very well. Thank you, Mr Sula.' Boyle looked him straight in the eyes across the table. 'Let's start with a simple one. Are you, Konstandin Sula, involved in illegal people trafficking from your home country of Albania into the United Kingdom?'

Might as well be blunt, thought Millar. There was something to be said for the direct approach rather than wasting time.

Konstandin kept looking at Boyle, holding his stare. Then he turned and said something to his public defender, who relayed the message to Boyle.

'My client refuses to answer on the basis that he cannot fully understand the question being asked. He will be happy to provide an answer once a translator is available to explain the question fully.'

Boyle leant back in his chair; Millar mirrored his movements in the monitor room. The tone had been set. Konstandin Sula was not going to talk.

31

The lights were on behind the large window. Riz could see shadows milling about behind the net curtain. Every so often someone would arrive at the front door to the imposing sandstone building and go inside. There was a meeting going on about something in there. Was it about him? Was he that important? Riz did not feel that he was.

The sun had gone down at the end of that long, nightmarish day and he was no better off than when dawn had broken. He welcomed the return of the lengthening shadows and the dark spaces, which allowed him to shrink back and become invisible once more. His survival depended on his ability to stay hidden now.

Konstandin had betrayed him. Riz was not surprised by this. He already knew he could not trust the evil man who had enslaved him, but he had no other allies in this country, no one else he could turn to. He thought Konstandin might have protected him as a useful soldier, someone he could control and who would carry out his dirty deeds for him. Riz had obeyed Konstandin's orders. He had killed for Konstandin. He had delivered the policewoman and the man to him. Konstandin owed him.

And yet Riz had seen it with his own eyes at the gym club that afternoon. Konstandin had ordered Riz to be killed along with the policewoman and the other man. Even when he had done as he had been ordered.

He knew he would be punished after he had failed to kill the policewoman, but he had held on to the hope that he could somehow redeem himself; if not himself, then at least he could earn a reprieve for Leandra and Zerina – even though they would never know what he had sacrificed in order to keep them safe, thousands of miles away.

That was the moment Riz understood he had to fight for himself instead of relying on anyone else – slumped on the bench in the gym, cowering with fear and watching the woman and the man be beaten before they were to be executed. The policewoman did not deserve to die. She was doing her job, trying to protect the vulnerable from people like Konstandin. Neither did the other man deserve to die, though Riz had no idea how he was involved in this mess.

Something inside Riz had snapped. He had charged across the gym floor and crashed into Konstandin. All hell had broken loose. The ceiling of the gym had collapsed on top of them, stunning Konstandin and his bodyguard. Riz had made his escape, getting out of the door before anyone could stop him. He had bolted down the stairs and into the lane. He kept running. He had risked a look back and had seen the white man – the colleague of the policewoman – running towards the gym. Sirens echoed around the streets and he slowed to a walk, kept his head down, looked at the ground and made himself anonymous. He had walked away and crossed the river, and kept going until he found himself in Kelvingrove Park.

He had spent the early evening walking around the park, aimless and lost. He did not know the city well. He had seen little of it, despite having been trapped here for the last year. But he knew this park and he knew the house that overlooked it at the top of the hill. Konstandin had brought him there once before, the previous winter, the day before he had become a killer.

Konstandin had allowed him to sit in the front of the car with him when he had brought him to the house. For once, he was treated with something like respect instead of like an animal. The heater in the car was turned up full to keep out the cold December air. Konstandin told him he had been selected for a special assignment because he was a smart man and a hard worker, and because Konstandin knew Riz wanted to do his best for his wife and daughter back home. Riz heard the implied threat.

They had not been allowed inside the house at the top of the hill. Instead, Konstandin had parked on the street a few hundred metres away and sent a text message. Two minutes later, a white man had come out of the front door, walked over to the car and got in the back seat. He spoke with an educated Scottish accent. He told Riz to keep facing forwards and not to turn around.

'This is our man?' he had asked Konstandin.

'This is him. A good man, reliable. He will do what is asked of him.'

'You are sure?'

'I am sure. He knows what will happen to him and his loved ones if he fails.'

The man in the back seat had no interest in Riz's loved ones or his motives. Riz could tell the man did not want to be there, did not want to talk to them and did not want to deal with them. He was there through necessity.

He passed a photograph forward. Konstandin took it and held it up. Riz looked at it. It was a young white woman. The photo had been taken from a distance with a telephoto lens.

'This is her?' asked Konstandin.

'It is. This is where you will find her.' The man passed forwards a slip of paper. 'Tomorrow night.'

'Yes, tomorrow night.'

'You know what will happen if this goes badly, or if anything makes its way back to us.'

'Do not worry. You have our word.'

'I don't trust words. I trust actions.'

'Then you shall see by our actions that we can be relied upon.'

Riz saw the hand appear again, this time holding a padded envelope. Konstandin took it and looked inside. Riz saw the rolls of banknotes.

'Half now, half when we are sure it has been done properly.'

'As agreed.'

The white man opened the back door. 'And you have told no one about our approach?'

'No one.'

'Not even your boss?'

'No one at all. This is separate business. How do you say? Free market economy.'

The man shook his head in distaste and got out of the car. Riz turned around and looked out of the rear-view window. He saw the man in profile crossing the road behind them and watched him return to the house. He saw an expensive, tailored suit, a firm stride, a military bearing and neat brown hair.

'Who was this man?' he asked Konstandin.

Konstandin was too busy rifling through the contents of the padded envelope. 'Never mind who he was. The important thing is that you do not fuck up this deal for me, you understand?'

'We are not working for the usual people, the people who brought me here?'

'No, this is extra work, a bonus. It pays much better. You must not mention this job to anyone, you understand? None of your stupid friends back at the flat must find out, or you know what will happen to your family.'

'But who is this woman?' Riz pointed at the photograph that Konstandin had put on the dashboard.

'She is the woman you must kill tomorrow evening.'

Riz shivered in the cool summer night. Rain was in the air. It never stopped raining in this miserable country. Not like the rain back home, when it came as a welcome relief during the dry, scorched days. Here, the rain was constant and depressing, eroding away joy and colour every day.

He crouched in the undergrowth and watched the bright window. A streetlight provided a pool of white at the foot of the short set of stone stairs that led to the wide front door. More people came and more people left. They were busy, whoever they were, the people inside this house.

He did not know what to do. He had come here because it was the only place he knew in the city, apart from the high-rise flat, and because this place was where things had gone from bad to worse for him. It was here that he had started along the path to destruction that had been laid out for him.

Riz did not know what he would do until he saw him crossing the street – the firm stride, the military bearing and the neat brown hair. The man passed through the halo of streetlight and jogged up the stairs to the door. He recognised the man who had sat in the car with Konstandin and handed over the money and the photograph. Konstandin had kept the money; Riz had been given the photograph.

The man who had ordered the death of the young lawyer went into the house and joined the busy people behind the net curtains.

Riz had no one else to turn to, but he knew the man in the expensive suit would recognise him. Riz had done as he had been ordered by this man, and he had done it well and not been caught. Maybe this man would be fair and help him – or maybe he would also want Riz dead.

Riz had nothing to lose, and there was only one way to find out.

He left the shelter of the tree line and crossed the road.

32

'My client refuses to answer on the basis that he cannot fully understand the question being asked. He will be happy to provide an answer once a translator is available to explain the question fully.'

It had gone on for forty-five minutes now. Boyle had persistence, Millar would give him that, in the face of this futile exercise. It was a battle of wills between the two men, the detective and the suspect. Given long enough, perhaps Boyle might have got somewhere, but this was not some off-grid black op beyond legal boundaries. This was a police station in Govan and the European Convention on Human Rights was already twitching around the edges of this interrogation.

Dykes returned with two fresh cups of coffee from the staff canteen. 'Any change?'

'Not a single word.'

She focused on the Albanian man's face. There was no sign of fatigue or weakness, or of an imminent collapse of his resolve. He had probably been through a lot worse in his past. Everyday dealings with people traffickers, drug traffickers and desperate illegal immigrants probably made Detective Marcus Boyle's questioning seem like a walk in the park. She half-suspected Konstandin was enjoying this behind those dark eyes. Was that a fleeting smirk as Boyle launched into his next question?

'Let's talk about something else, shall we? Did you order the killing of a human rights lawyer named Rose Black in December last year?'

The fleeting smirk disappeared. Millar leant forwards in her chair. The change of subject had got a reaction. Just a small one, a brief ripple of panic that crossed the calm waters of Konstandin Sula's face. Then it was gone and he turned again to the patient public defender who sat next to him and nodded.

'My client refuses to answer on the basis that he cannot fully understand the question being asked. He will be happy to provide an answer once a translator is available to explain the question fully.'

It was something, though, thought Millar, and she was sure Boyle would have seen it too. Unlike the people trafficking and the property damage, the murder of Rose Black worried Konstandin for some reason. He was scared of that one. He feared that particular crime. Why that one in particular?

Before Boyle could follow up with another question, the door to the interview room opened. Millar couldn't see it on either of the camera angles, but she heard the sound and saw the people at the table react.

'This is a live interview,' said Scott, who had not spoken a word since the questioning had begun. 'You can't just barge in here.'

Scott was cut off by a thundering reply, 'I most certainly can when my client's rights are being abused in this manner. This interview is over as of right now. I demand to speak to my client alone.'

The hairs on the back of Millar's neck stood on end. She recognised that voice. She had dealt with him on several occasions. She watched the monitor, waiting for visual confirmation of what her hearing was telling her.

'Your client?' Boyle asked the man off screen, his voice full of incredulity.

'As of half an hour ago, I am Mr Sula's legal representative, and all matters pertaining to his police caution, custody, questioning and anything you may be considering charging him with should be directed through me. You are already on thin ice, Detective, and you know it. I could have this dismissed for gross misconduct in a minute.'

'Mr Sula, do you even know this man?' Boyle asked the Albanian, who looked as bemused as the detectives.

'Mr Sula, do you wish me to represent you?' asked the newcomer to the room.

Konstandin looked from one to the other, then spoke as a smile spread across his face. 'Yes, I think I would like you to represent me very much, sir.'

'Oh, you understood that question just fine. You don't want to wait for your interpreter for that one?'

'That's quite enough, Detective, or I'll have you on harassment charges.' The newcomer stepped across the room to the table and came into view on the monitor in front of Millar and Dykes.

'Jesus Christ.' Dykes had not picked up the identity of the lawyer from his voice alone.

'Not quite,' said Millar, 'but close enough.'

Alan Cox KC put his briefcase on the table and addressed the public service defender sitting next to Konstandin. 'Thank you, Fiona. Lovely to see you. You're free to go. I trust my client has not answered anything he shouldn't have before I could get here?'

'He hasn't said a bloody thing,' cut in Boyle.

Fiona stood and gathered up her notepad. 'Nothing at all. An Albanian translator was requested but has not been provided so far.'

'And yet the interview proceeded anyway? Dear me, Detective, you should know better than that. Now, if we could have the room, please, and if you could make sure the cameras and microphones are switched off.'

Boyle and Scott followed the public defender out of the door with a look of disgust but not another word. There was nothing else they could say.

Millar watched Cox take a seat opposite his new client and sit with his hands together on the table. Konstandin started to say something. Alan Cox raised a finger to his lips and stopped him.

There was an audible click and the monitors in front of Millar went black. The speakers crackled and then gave off nothing more than a low electrical hum.

'What the hell is he doing here?' asked Dykes.

Alan Cox was one of the top defence lawyers in the country. He was a King's Counsel, a legal representative of the great and rich. They had encountered him on various cases but they had crossed paths most recently last summer, when his long-term client Francis McArthur had been arrested on a number of corruption and fraud charges.

Dykes is asking the wrong question, thought Millar. Alan Cox was there for two reasons. The most obvious was easy – to represent his client. The second was just as straightforward – Alan Cox was there because he was being paid to be there. But Cox did not deal with immigration cases. He did not take on charity cases. He did not work pro bono. And there was not a chance in hell that Konstandin could afford his fees.

The correct question, given how much Cox billed per hour for his services, was *who* was paying Alan Cox KC to represent this lowlife immigrant? Konstandin was not penniless by any means, but neither was he even remotely close to being able to afford someone like Alan Cox as his lawyer.

The door to the holding cell sprang open. Cal glanced over from his bunk without getting up.

'Come on, I'm springing you,' Millar said as she appeared in the doorway.

'I haven't given my statement yet.'

'Don't worry, you can come back and do it later. You're in my custody now.'

Cal picked up the urgency in Millar's tone. 'What's happened?'

'Things have taken an unexpected turn.'

'Don't they always.' They invariably seemed to when Millar was involved, Cal had found to his own cost.

'Your old lawyer has turned up to represent our Albanian friend.'

Cal skipped through the various legal representatives he had had the pleasure of being represented by in the past. Most recently they had been provided by the public defender's office, but none of them would have caused Millar any qualms. He went back further and came to the obvious answer. 'Cox?'

'Ten out of ten. Get your belongings at the front desk.'

Alan Cox had represented Cal after the car accident. He was McArthur's lawyer and legal fixer, a keeper of all the dirty secrets. He had kept Cal out of prison and persuaded the judge to give a lenient sentence. In exchange, Cox had brokered a private deal between McArthur and the Black family, to provide them with adequate financial damages and to prevent them from pursuing the matter further.

Millar met him at the front reception. Dykes was with her.

They walked out of the station and onto Helen Street, then turned to cross over the motorway. Cars passed underneath them, their headlights beaming in the fading light. Millar did not talk as they turned into the retail park and into the fast food restaurant. Cal could tell she was processing the latest development, trying to make the connections that would lead to an understanding.

She ordered three coffees and they took a seat next to the window. They were the only people sitting in the restaurant. A steady stream of cars passed through the drive-thru outside, and delivery drivers came in and out collecting orders.

'Something's not right here,' she said.

It wasn't the revelation Cal had been hoping for. He could have told Millar that himself. He took a sip of the lukewarm coffee and waited.

'Alan Cox only works two types of cases – ones that pay well and ones that are high profile. This is neither. This is people trafficking. These are poor and destitute people. Ever since the McArthur case blew up, Cox has been quiet. He's kept a low profile for the last year and tried to rebuild his reputation, waiting for the next big murder trial or corporate payday to come along in order to redeem himself. He's kept away from organised crime and the city gangs. Now he appears – and not only is this organised crime, it's dirty and squalid.

'Nathan MacDonald has all the public support and Konstandin Sula has zero money and even less public sympathy, especially given the atmosphere and politics around immigration at the moment. Alan Cox gains nothing by representing Konstandin Sula.'

'So why is he doing it?' asked Cal, teeing Millar up to continue.

She tapped the plastic lid of her coffee cup but did not go on.

'There was only one thing that caused Konstandin even a hint of anxiety when Boyle was questioning him,' Dykes said.

Millar agreed. 'You noticed it as well. The only time Konstandin looked scared was when Boyle mentioned Rose Black. Just for a second, Konstandin was worried. A murder case that is certainly high profile and would certainly grip the public. A case that would perhaps attract someone with the deep pockets required to pay for Alan Cox's services.'

'Cox is here to make sure Konstandin doesn't talk about Rose's murder?' asked Cal.

Millar took the lid off her cup. 'Has to be. Konstandin is not worried about taking the rap for the people trafficking or smashing up a few premises around the city, but when Rose Black was mentioned, he looked scared. He knows something about it, and he's frightened of the repercussions.

'We've been assuming that the people trafficking and the property attacks and Rose's murder are all linked, but I think we're wrong. Rose Black's murder is separate from the rest of this in some way.'

Dykes followed his partner's thoughts and the penny dropped. 'He's been playing around.'

'I think so. Two-timing his Albanian boss, no doubt for a significant bit of extra money.'

'Someone else hired Konstandin specifically to kill Rose Black.'

Millar nodded. 'A job on the side of his main income. Someone who knew who Konstandin was. And Konstandin goes to his group of men, Albanian immigrants who he trusts to do his dirty work for him because he doesn't have the stomach to kill an unarmed woman himself. He has a hold over these men already. He picks Riz because he knows Riz will do whatever he is forced to do.'

'Because he is threatening Riz's wife and daughter back home,' chimed in Dykes.

'Right. So whoever paid Konstandin to have Rose Black killed by Riz…'

'…is also paying Alan Cox to keep Konstandin quiet about it.'

'Which leaves just one question.'

'Who would pay Konstandin to have Rose Black killed?'

Cal sat and watched them bounce the ideas between them. They sat in silence and digested what they had just figured out.

'So Rose wasn't killed because she was defending illegal immigrants?' Cal asked.

'Maybe she was. The point is, whoever had enough money to persuade Alan Cox to come down to the station and shut Konstandin Sula up, also has enough money to have someone killed.'

'You're saying Rose was killed in an organised hit now?'

'We've always assumed it was either a random attack, or an attack by an immigrant she had come into contact with through her work, but it was neither. She was targeted deliberately.'

'For what reason?'

'If we knew that, we would know who ordered her dead.' Millar stood up to leave. Cal and Dykes followed her and tossed their half-finished coffees in the bin.

Cal pushed open the door and they exited back into the night. It was after eleven and the sun had fully set now.

They walked back towards the station. 'If Konstandin won't talk, how do we get anywhere?' asked Dykes.

'There is one other person who might know who paid to have Rose killed,' said Millar.

'Our friend Riz,' said Cal.

'We need to find him before they do.'

'They?'

'The people who paid Alan Cox to come down to the station and silence our friend Konstandin, and who paid to have Rose Black killed. Probably.'

'Someone with money,' continued Dykes.

'Isn't it always?'

'But how do we find Riz? He could be miles away by now.'

'Patrols are out on the streets looking for him. So far nothing. He hasn't been seen back at the high-rise flat either.'

'We're going to have to hope we get lucky. He will resurface at some point. There's CCTV all over the city. It will pick him up eventually. We just have to hope it's not too late.'

33

Walking up to the front door of the rich house was not an option. Riz had no doubt he would not be admitted, and he did not know who to ask for when someone answered the door. He had no name for the man he was looking for.

There would be a side entrance or a back door that would be used by servants or workmen.

Riz skirted along the low railings that bordered the front of the property. It was the end house of the terraced row. He turned the corner and made his way up the side street, ducking behind the row of parked cars in case anyone should happen to see him. The house was as long as it was wide, and there was a large garden, but eventually he came to an opening that turned into a narrow, cobbled lane that ran along the back of the properties. Each had a small outhouse that backed onto the lane. Small was a comparative term – they were small in relation to the main houses they served; to many they would be an adequate family home.

He approached the first of these outhouses. There was a narrow door in the wall. He could still make out the sound of the gathering in the large house. Muffled voices floated through the night, made indistinguishable by thick sandstone walls. There was an intercom system next to the door, one that no doubt linked to a security system. His face had probably already been recorded. If that was the case, he may as well give it a shot. He had nowhere else to turn to. He pushed the buzzer and waited for a response.

For five minutes, nothing happened. He tried pushing the buzzer a couple more times during that wait, with the same result. Maybe they had recognised his face and were debating what to do with him. Maybe they had already called the police to have him removed. Maybe they were not expecting anyone to turn up at the workmen's entrance at this time of night and no one was monitoring the intercom. The longer he waited, the more nervous Riz became.

He gave the buzzer one more try. If no one answered this time, he would leave.

Still nothing. There was not much else he could do. There was no way he could force his way into the house, no obvious way to break through or climb over the exterior wall. Perhaps he should have tried the front door after all.

He turned and retraced his steps back up the cobbled lane, his footsteps echoing between the walls of the narrow space in the quiet night.

There was no moonlight; it was swallowed up by the blanket of cloud that suffocated the city. Riz kept close to the side of the building, sticking to the shadows. He was a fugitive, after all, a wanted man.

As he approached the corner of the house, he heard the front door open. For a moment the chatter from inside the house increased in volume before the door swung closed and it faded away again. He heard footsteps coming down the stone set of stairs. At the same time, a new noise entered the scene – a car engine coming along the road, travelling up the steep hill that separated these exclusive residences from the crowded city below.

It took Riz too long to put the concurrence of the two events together – the approaching car and the descending man. They converged upon him before he could react. The man who had left the house swept Riz up in a bear hug as the car came to a controlled stop opposite them. The back door swung open and Riz was bundled inside the car, pushed down onto the back seat. He had no chance to escape as the person who had manhandled him into the car followed him inside and closed the door behind them. The engine accelerated smoothly and they moved away from the house. It had all happened in less than five seconds and even a clear-sighted and sober-eyed witness would have struggled to recall if Riz had ever been there; it might have been a trick of the dim light and the dark shadows. All they would have been able to swear to was that a man had left the house and was picked up by an arriving car. It was as though Riz had never existed.

As Riz came to his senses in the back of the car, he realised his problems, as bad as they had already been, had just got a whole lot worse.

'What the hell are you doing here?' asked the man who had pushed him into the car.

Riz felt the pressure ease and he was allowed to sit up on the back seat. He took in his new surroundings. The upholstery was black leather, the interior of the doors, black plastic. The glass windows were blacked out. He could not see out of them. The vehicle was divided by a glass partition, also blacked out, so that the driver in the front of the car could not be seen or heard. In effect, Riz was trapped in a moving blackout cell, his senses disorientated, starved of light and sound.

He looked at the man sitting next to him who had asked the question. He was only an outline, a deeper shade of black in their surroundings. He did not turn to look at Riz, but kept looking forward. His silhouette was enough for Riz to be able to identify him. It was the man he had been looking for, the man who had sat in the back of the car behind Konstandin and Riz seven months ago and handed them the picture of the woman.

'You know about Konstandin?' Riz said. 'The police have him.'

'And should that concern me?'

'If he tells them what he knows.'

The man turned and faced him. Even in the dark, Riz did not like the look of menace he could make out on the man's face.

'He knows the price of breaking his silence, and he is not a stupid man.'

'They know about Rose Black. They know I killed her.'

The man sighed. 'You, on the other hand, are a very foolish man, Tariq.'

How did this man know his name? Konstandin must have told them who he was.

'Perhaps we should have taken better care of you at the time, but we didn't want to risk getting ourselves involved more than we needed to be.' He made "taken better care" sound like a death sentence. 'You would have been more useful if you had been caught. Or, better yet, if the police had taken care of you in their usual heavy-handed way. Everyone likes a nice, tidy dead-end to a murder investigation. Saves all the tedious legal wrangling and expense. Then the public would have had a face to direct their anger towards. Not some nameless illegal immigrant, but a figurehead to hate. Confirmation bias would kick in – "all these immigrants coming over here are murdering thieves and rapists, destroying our way of life". As it turned out, we had to make do with a vague witness account of an Eastern European suspect. Fortunately, that was all we needed to get the public on our side.'

The car had reached the open road now. Riz felt the pace pick up and they no longer slowed for corners. They were on a motorway or an expressway.

'Unfortunately, the way things have developed, it's too risky to have you identified now. Too risky to have you say anything we might regret to the police. I'm afraid we're going to have to make you disappear in a more subtle and quiet manner. You have outlived your usefulness, Tariq. Coming to the house tonight was your last fatal error of judgement in a lifetime of missteps.'

Riz didn't notice the man move. He didn't feel the air shift or hear the leather upholstery creak. He only felt the sharp prick of the needle as it entered the side of his neck and then withdrew a split second later.

'Just relax,' the man said.

Riz felt drowsy. His muscles, which had been tight and taut for months, began to relax. The anxiety seeped away from his brain. He slumped down into the black seat and the black world grew deeper and darker until it overwhelmed him completely.

34

The musty scent of dampness was not what Riz expected when he came round. He had not expected to come round at all after the first wave of narcotics had washed over him. He had fallen into the black hole and did not expect to resurface. The fact he was still alive should have been a source of joy, but as he regained consciousness, Riz feared it may not be the best outcome.

He was on his stomach, staring at a hard floor covered by dry strands of hay. He rolled over and took in his surroundings. It was a farm barn of some kind, with wooden walls and roof, and horse stalls running along one side. There was no sign of any animals in the stalls and no fresh hay, although the faint smell of animals still hung in the air. A barn that was out of use. He expected to find his wrists and ankles bound but they were free. He clambered to his feet and leant against a wooden pillar, stamping his feet and rubbing his hands together to get his blood circulating.

He did not know how long they had driven for, or what distance they had covered, or how long he had been asleep. He did not remember being lifted from the car and dumped on the floor of the barn. He did remember that it had been night time when he had been bundled into the vehicle. Now he glimpsed the rays of sunlight glinting through the slats of the wooden walls, and above him blue sky peeked through the roof beams. The sun seemed to be directly overhead. Whether it was the middle of the next day or a week later, Riz could not tell.

There was no one else in the barn with him. There was a trough, but it was dry. The thought of water made him thirsty and then he realised how hungry he was.

He staggered over to a small door that was inset into the wide barn doors. He was surprised when it swung open without any resistance. Maybe he was not being held prisoner. He was unbound, the door was unlocked and there was no guard on duty. Had he been set free? Had something else happened while he was unconscious? Perhaps his captors had been ordered to leave him alone. Or had they been caught by the authorities and even now there was a search party looking for him, not knowing yet if he was alive or dead? Riz walked around the corner of the barn, which turned out to be bigger on the outside than he had thought it was. The ground was wet, a recent downpour had left puddles in the uneven gravel, and his unsteady feet slipped on patches of mud.

The barn formed one side of a rectangular courtyard. On the other side was a low, whitewashed farmhouse, a single-storey building with a slate roof, pock-marked with holes, with a crooked chimney with a bush growing out of it. At the top end of the courtyard was a gate and a rough track that led off across open land until it disappeared into a wood. At the bottom end, the land sloped away and ran into a pebbled stone bay, beyond which was an expanse of clear blue water, with ripples twinkling in the sunlight. As the water stretched away to the horizon, it was bordered by steep-sided hills, coloured deep purple, lush green and rock grey. The sheer sides plunged straight into the surface of the lake, or loch, Riz corrected himself – that was what they called them in this country. Assuming he was still in Scotland.

In the middle of the courtyard stood a black SUV.

He looked inside the blacked-out windows, shielding his eyes from the sun. He could not see anyone inside.

He tried the doors, but they were locked.

He caught the faint smell of smoke in the air, the ashy aftermath of a fire that had been allowed to die down and had recently been extinguished.

Then he heard footsteps – crunching, heavy steps on loose stone and shingle. He looked towards the bay and saw the man's head first, the neat, brown hair rising from the wild grass, followed by the tall, lean torso dressed in an expensive shirt. The clothes looked out of place against the wilderness of the backdrop from which they emerged. Riz recognised the man from the house, the man he had been looking for who had bundled him into the car.

A second man of similar bearing followed him. He was dressed in black jeans and a black top and had shaved black hair. Riz guessed he had been the driver.

They followed a well-trodden path through the wild grass between farmhouse and lochside and appeared to be in no hurry. At first, Riz wasn't sure if they had spotted him and he was tempted to turn and get back to the barn, but the man in front looked up as he reached the courtyard and smiled at him.

'You're awake.'

Riz felt like he was expected to reply but could not think of an appropriate response and instead settled for an uncomfortable half-hearted wave at his captors. Then he felt like a fool for doing it.

The man seemed not to notice his unease. 'You missed breakfast. We cooked it on the beach over an open fire. Breakfast with a view. It's worth putting up with the rubbish weather for scenery like that. No other country in the world like it.'

Riz guessed he was still in Scotland. He had not had a chance to see much beyond Glasgow and the central belt of the country. This could be his first glimpse of the Highlands.

'Come in and get some coffee.' The two men turned away from him and walked to the low doorway that led inside the farmhouse. Riz looked around and tried to figure out what might happen next and what options he had to do anything about it. There were not many choices. He followed them inside the house.

The low door led into a basic, old-fashioned country kitchen. It was large compared to modern standards and in the middle was an oak table surrounded by dining chairs. Along one wall was a huge wooden larder, but the shelves were empty and covered in a layer of dust and cobwebs. The floor was made of broken ceramic tiles. A freestanding iron oven and hob sat in the corner, looking solid and unmoveable. A gas canister was hooked up to it via a rubber hose. The driver sparked a match and turned the gas on, then lit a hob and placed a metal kettle above the flames.

'A bit basic, I'm afraid,' the man in charge said. 'Doesn't get used much anymore. A shame. Someone could do the place up and make a small fortune selling it. Take a seat.' He pulled out a chair for Riz to sit on. The man pulled out another chair opposite him and also sat down. The driver remained standing by the cooker. Despite the show of civility and small talk, Riz felt unease creep over him.

'Tell me, Tariq Rizwan, do you know who I am?'

Riz looked from his questioner to the man standing by the kettle and back again. 'No, sir. Only that I saw you at the big house before.'

'And that's why you went there? To look for me?'

'Yes, sir. You see, I am in trouble.' Riz looked between them again. The standing man showed no emotion or reaction on his face; his features stayed set and uncompromised. 'The police, they have Konstandin. I managed to get away.'

'And you had nowhere else you could go, so you found the house you had been to before with Konstandin?'

'Exactly, yes. I thought you would understand, that you might help me after I helped you.'

The water in the kettle began to boil and a sharp whistle began to grow, filling the air in the kitchen. Riz began to feel the temperature rise, and not because of the gas flame in the corner.

'I am glad, in a way, that you chose to come and find me, Tariq. It makes my life easier. If you had not, I would have had to send someone out to find you.'

The kettle started to rattle on the metal hob as the water boiled. The clattering sounded like an alarm in Riz's head.

'You can trust me, sir. About Rose Black. I will not say anything to anyone. I haven't. I just want to get back to my own country, to my family. Once I am there you will never hear from me or see me again.'

'I believe you, Tariq. After all, you murdered the poor girl, so it is in your interests to not get caught. It is good that you have not mentioned me to the police. That makes things easier. Konstandin won't talk about me, we will make sure of that. The trouble for you is the police now have evidence linking you to the girl's murder. They know that it was you who killed her.'

'But I could disappear in Albania. They would never—'

The kettle reached the peak of its scream and the other man removed it from the hob and placed it on the table. The sudden silence was deafening.

'But they might, Tariq, and "might" is not something we can afford to live with.' He reached for the kettle, picked it up and threw it at Riz.

Riz managed to raise his hands in time to block the scalding kettle. He felt the burning metal on his hands. A split second later, the boiling water that flew from it hit his face and he screamed in sharp pain. His hands instinctively went to his face to wipe away the scalding water.

The driver was now behind Riz. He grabbed him around his shoulders and pushed his hands down onto the table. Riz felt the rope slip over his head and go tight around his neck. His skin crawled as the boiling water burned into him, and then he lost consciousness again.

The jerk of the rope jolted Riz back to life. His face and hands stung with pain. The rope jerked again and pulled him backwards and upwards so that he was standing on his feet, supported by the rope around his neck. If the rope had not been there, he would have fallen back to the floor.

He was able to open his eyes. He was back inside the barn. The sunlight filtered through the cracks in the walls and roof. The sun had moved round and the shadows had lengthened and spread across the dusty floor. Dust motes danced in the shafts of light. The man who had been speaking to him appeared in front of him in a hazy mirage. He did not talk now, he only watched.

The rope bit into Riz's neck again and hauled him upwards until his feet were no longer on the ground. Panic overwhelmed him. His scalded hands clawed at the rough rope that was digging into his burnt neck. He thrashed his feet, trying to find some purchase. He gasped and found he could not force air back into his lungs as his throat was restricted tighter and tighter. Another jerk and the roof of the barn came closer to him. His struggling made the rope spin and as he turned, he saw the man tying the other end of the rope around the wooden pillar. Riz spun a half-circle again and saw the two men standing together, watching him from below.

He managed a weak, pathetic cry as he realised that this was the end. Going to the house had been his final, fatal mistake.

He should not have killed the girl. He should not have left Durrës or Leandra or Zerina. He should not have believed the lies of the criminals who had brought him to this country.

He would never see his home again. He would never see Leandra or Zerina again. He would never see his daughter grow up. Would they ever find out what had happened to him? He hoped they would never learn the truth about what he had done.

The final breath of air left his lungs and he could not pull any more back in. Seconds now. He stopped thrashing and struggling and hung in the air. His eyes flickered and he saw the two white men turn their backs on him and walk away.

He saw the woman he had stabbed lying on the street and the pool of dark, red blood spreading beneath her against the white ground. He tried to say he was sorry. He tried to tell her, *They made me a killer.* He tried to take it back, but it was too late. He was not an evil man, he thought, but he had lost his way and done an evil thing. This ending was all that he deserved.

His final thought was of his love, her blonde-brown hair flowing behind her as she stood on the rocks in front of the blue sky and the blue water of the Adriatic Sea. He hoped his spirit would go back to her. He hoped there was something beyond this miserable life, a way that he could go back to her and Zerina and wait for them to join him, years from now, on this dark side that was calling to him now.

Leandra's smile lit up the brilliant sky around her and there was a white flash that filled his vision, then it collapsed into blackness and she was gone, and so was he.

Later that night, the sparrow who had made a nest in the roof of the barn returned to find the new addition to its home. It had been used to the quiet solitude of the barn. It circled around the object that hung from the roof and caught the smell of the human. It landed on the wooden beam and hopped along it to the rope. It could sense the decay of death that was radiating from the hanging body. When it was certain that the new arrival posed no threat to it or its newborn chicks, it returned to the nest and the demanding call of its young.

The body swung gently in the gasps of wind that breezed through the gaps in the walls of the barn.

35

A week later, the sparrow was disturbed again. It had grown used to the thing that hung from the end of the rope in the barn, but when it returned after another expedition to find food for its hungry chicks, it found its space had been invaded by more human bodies. These ones were alive.

The man and woman who arrived at the farmhouse in the early evening had looked at the house and decided it would be more romantic to spend the night in the old barn. They had hiked down from the hills and managed to miss the bothy that was marked on the map. The barn was a more than acceptable alternative. They opened the door, expecting to find hay bales to lie on, rusting farm equipment and a space to dry out their tent and clothes after the afternoon's unexpected downpour. Instead, the woman stepped through the door, stared up at the body hanging from the rafter and screamed. The man followed her in and grabbed her, and they turned away from the ugly sight.

They went back outside and called the police. It took the response car an hour to arrive from the nearest police station in Fort

William. It was another two hours before the Major Investigations Team had gathered at the location.

Superintendent Douglas Forsyth had mixed feelings when he left the joint meeting with the Chair of the Scottish Police Authority and Scottish Government Cabinet Secretary for Justice and Home Affairs. He had told them what they wanted to hear.

It had been a frustrating week after the arrest of Konstandin Sula. Once Alan Cox had turned up to represent him, the Albanian had refused to answer a single question or utter a single word. Although a judge had agreed to extend the time Konstandin could be held – thanks to the irrefutable evidence that he had assaulted a police detective – and Marcus Boyle had continued to probe and question, there had been no progress. They had no physical evidence that Konstandin had been present at any of the properties that had been attacked, or that he was involved in the murders of Rose Black, Nathan MacDonald or Peter Jones.

They had not found any sign of Konstandin in the security camera footage from the high-rise flat, where they suspected the gang of illegal immigrant men had been housed – and the men had disappeared. It was circumstantial at best.

The pressure from above was growing as his political masters looked for a breakthrough that would bolster public support in the current government before the election, and also public faith that the mainstream politicians had a grip on the immigration issues that had been stirred up in the recent campaign. An illegal immigrant who was now known to have committed murder was loose on the streets of Scotland. That was the sort of headline that bolstered the fanatical far-right and boosted the profile of the likes of the Scottish First Freedom Party and Fergus Bennett.

Then a husband and wife, visiting from England on a hiking holiday through the Scottish Highlands, had got a nasty shock when they stumbled upon the body of Tariq Rizwan, also known as

Riz, swinging from the ceiling of an abandoned barn in the middle of nowhere. A holiday adventure the couple would remember for a long time, if not the advert for Scotland that the Tourist Board would want to shout about.

Marcus Boyle and Finlay Scott had dashed up to Ranochan, on the edge of Loch Eilt, half an hour west of Fort William on the A road that led to Mallaig. How the hell had an Albanian immigrant wanted for murder managed to find himself there? Had he made his own way there in a desperate bid to evade capture?

Boyle and Scott overnighted in Fort William before returning and being summoned to report by Forsyth.

'Definitely him. Fingerprints match those from the Rose Black murder scene, the hammer from the massage parlour and the wall of the nightclub. Hung from a rope, dangling four feet off the ground. Been dead for a week or so, according to Dr Golightly,' Boyle had informed him.

'Suicide?' Forsyth asked in a hopeful voice.

'Unlikely. He must have had help to be that high up. There was no stool or chair underneath him.'

'He could have tied it from a higher platform in the barn and jumped?'

Boyle thought back to the layout of the barn. There were stalls and raised wooden dividers that Tariq Rizwan could have balanced on. 'I'd need to get someone to check the distances involved. I think it unlikely though.'

'But not impossible?'

Boyle paused and tried to infer what his superior was angling at. 'Perhaps not.' That answer seemed to satisfy the superintendent. 'But there was also something else.'

Forsyth sighed. It was never straightforward.

Boyle continued. 'Burn marks on his hands, face and neck.'

'He'd been set on fire?'

Boyle shook his head. 'Not from fire. Scalded by boiling water.

An old iron kettle was found in the farmhouse kitchen next to the barn. Looks like maybe someone tortured him first.'

'Unless it was an accident.'

'An accident?'

'Spilled boiling water over himself.'

'Over his face?' Boyle was incredulous.

'It's possible.'

'And then while he's in pain, he takes himself to the barn and rigs up the rope, hauls himself up a piece of wood, balances on it and jumps to his death?'

Forsyth's detective was not making this easy for him. 'I'm only asking if it could be possible that he killed himself. A desperate criminal, wanted for murder, facing life in prison in a foreign country. Who knows what his mental state was?'

'The evidence strongly points to another person being involved and this being another murder,' Boyle tried one last time.

'I'm only asking that you include the possibility in your report that this could have been a suicide by a desperate man, guilt-ridden by his past crimes, with no future to turn to. I will speak to the procurator fiscal on the case too and make sure he includes a similar theory in his report.'

Finlay Scott, sitting silent in the corner of the office, was younger and less experienced than his senior partner. He had yet to learn the diplomacy required to advance his career in the force. 'You want it to be a suicide. You're going to cover up the murder.'

Forsyth had dealt with enough principled detectives over the years to shut them down with one hard stare. 'I said no such thing, Detective Scott, and you'd do well to remember who you are talking to.'

'But that's what you're saying.'

'Do you fancy plodding the streets as a constable again, Detective?'

Scott turned to his partner. 'You're not going to let him do this, are you? This is murder and you know it.'

Marcus Boyle was caught between his partner and his boss. He knew the right thing to do. He also knew what career suicide was.

'Calm down, Finlay. The superintendent is only asking about the possibility. We can include that in our crime scene report, while speculating that it was more likely a murder.' Boyle did not turn to see the look of disgust on Finlay Scott's face. Instead, he held Douglas Forsyth in a hard stare. 'That suit you well enough, sir?'

'I'm glad you can be pragmatic about this, Marcus. Should any new information come to light, we can always look at the case with fresh eyes.'

'When should that be, sir? After the upcoming election, by any chance?'

Forsyth managed to hold his fury inside while maintaining a calm demeanour in front of his officers. 'Political events cannot interfere with live investigations, as you well know, Detective.'

He dismissed them from his office and had his personal assistant put through a call to the procurator fiscal's office.

News of the discovery of Tariq Rizwan's body had another knock-on effect that put Superintendent Forsyth in an even better mood – Konstandin Sula suddenly started to talk. With the approval of his lawyer, Konstandin admitted to organising the property attacks around Glasgow. He told them he had used a gang of illegal immigrants to carry out the attacks. He refused to give the names of the men; he would only confirm that they were all from Albania and had entered the country illegally. When pressed to tell the police where these men were now, he said he did not know.

'Which of these men killed Nathan MacDonald?' asked Boyle.

'Tariq Rizwan,' Konstandin answered without hesitation.

'Peter Jones?'

'Tariq Rizwan,' Konstandin answered without hesitation.

'Tariq Rizwan was assaulting Detective Simone Millar at the time of the attack on the Carnival nightclub.'

'You must be mistaken.'

Boyle shook his head. 'And who were you working for?'

'Sorry, I do not understand.'

'Who did you take your orders from?'

'Nobody.'

'You expect us to believe you weren't working for someone?'

Alan Cox cut in, 'Asked and answered, Detective. He has told you he was working alone.'

'You ran the whole thing?'

Konstandin looked at his lawyer for guidance. Alan Cox nodded.

'Yes, that is right.'

'So you could do what? Take over all the organised crime in the city?'

'Yes, exactly.'

Boyle shook his head.

'Move on, Detective.'

Boyle glared at Cox, then turned back to the suspect. 'What about Rose Black?'

'Who?'

'Tariq Rizwan murdered Rose Black last December. Did you order him to do that as well?'

Alan Cox again interrupted on behalf of his client. 'The deal was a full confession to people trafficking and the property attacks, and the matter of Rose Black would be dropped.'

'Who is this Rose Black you speak of? I know nothing about this Rose Black.'

Boyle had got all he was ever going to get from Konstandin Sula.

Forsyth had told the government justice secretary what he wanted to hear – a dangerous criminal, a double murderer, a violent illegal immigrant who had also tried to kill a serving police officer, had been found dead. He had taken his own life. Case closed.

The attacks on properties in Glasgow had been stopped, and the main perpetrator, the man behind the gang who had committed these acts, was in police custody and had admitted organising the crimes. Unfortunately, the immigrants had disappeared – scattered across the country or on their way back to Albania, Forsyth could not say which. They would work in conjunction with the National Crime Agency to track down these men if it was possible. The main thing to focus on, the headline to give to the media and the public, was that Police Scotland had cracked the people-trafficking gang.

'Everything wrapped up in a neat bow three weeks out from the election.' The Justice Secretary beamed at Forsyth. 'Great work, Douglas. The First Minister will be greatly appreciative of your efforts.'

'I hope he will bear that in mind when the budget negotiations come around again,' Forsyth replied.

'He has an election to survive before that, Douglas, but this will certainly not do our chances any harm. Well done.'

They shook hands and Forsyth departed.

He had mixed feelings. He knew the real bad guys were still out there. He had not lied. Tariq Rizwan had killed Rose Black and now he was dead and could cause no more harm. If Konstandin could be believed, Rizwan had also killed Nathan MacDonald at The Shed nightclub. The cases were closed. Konstandin was taking the fall for the attacks and he would not give up anyone else. The Peter Jones murder bothered Forsyth the most because he knew Tariq Rizwan could not have been there – but the file would be closed and it would appear as a solved crime on the records and in the statistics. The attacks would stop, at least for the moment, at least until after the election. They could always reopen the case if something further happened.

Cases closed, perpetrators dead or in prison, a police force that was showing the public that they were on top of illegal immigration. The people could have faith in the authorities and the politicians. They were taking immigration seriously; they were being tough on illegal immigrants and the gangs that trafficked them. They did not need to turn to the fringe lunatics like Fergus Bennett.

All in all, Forsyth thought, as he got into his car and his driver whisked him away from the government building, *things could not have turned out much better.*

And yet there was still the nagging thought in the back of his mind. That part of him that had once been a detective like Boyle and Millar, that part of him that still had a moral compass and refused to give in to the dance that he had to negotiate as a superintendent. The nagging thought that somewhere out there, on the streets of his city, there was a guilty man, a bad man, who had got away with it.

That would have to wait for another day.

Millar's phone rang just as she was getting out of the shower. She had been to the local gym as an excuse to get out of the house. She was not good at doing nothing. She had realised in this past week that without her work to keep her occupied, she had very little else in her life. It was a depressing realisation.

Forsyth had insisted on her taking the recommended leave. She had been shut out of the investigation and the hunt for Riz. Dykes had kept her informed, which had been a succession of messages to tell her that no progress had been made. The killer had vanished.

Until he had shown up dead in a barn somewhere up north, discovered by accident by members of the public. The man who had tried to kill her, and had killed Rose Black. But Millar did not feel joy at his death. Millar was upset – not because he did not deserve to be punished, but because the trail that could have led them further up the chain had died with him. She wanted to get the people who had orchestrated this, not the puppets but their masters.

Dykes had called her again last night. They were calling it suicide. Case closed. Konstandin had taken the rap for the nightclub attacks. It was over.

Millar had not slept. She lay in the dark until daylight broke. She took some of her anger out on the treadmill and the weights at the gym, but she was still angry when her mobile rang. The caller display read "Boyle". Strange. They were not on friendly terms, and after the mess he had made of both the Rose Black case and the property attack case, Millar was in no mood to talk to him.

'Boyle,' she said into the handset after swiping up to answer the call.

'You heard?'

'I heard. All very neat. Congratulations, I guess.'

'Don't give me that tone. I know it's bullshit as well as you do.'

'But you're going along with it.'

'My hands are tied. Forsyth is pushing it for the paymasters. There's an election in less than a month and they want good headlines, especially ones that make them look good on immigration.'

'Thanks for phoning to tell me that.'

'Christ, Millar, give me a break. I'm saying I know it's bullshit, but there's nothing I can do here. The case is closed.'

'So why are you phoning me? Looking for moral support?'

'You still have some time off?'

'Another month before they'll even consider putting me back behind a desk.'

'Want to spend your time doing something useful?'

Millar sensed Boyle was reaching out to her with something. 'You mean something more than sitting around my house eating junk food and watching daytime TV?'

'I'm sending you a file. It's from an encrypted server. It can't be traced back to me and I'll deny this call ever took place if you try to sell me out.'

'What are you sending me?'

'Just look at it. Then it's up to you what you do with it.'

'What's it about?'

'You want to catch whoever ordered Riz to kill Rose Black?'

'Of course I do. They made him kill her. Don't you?'

'Millar,' Boyle's voice was serious, 'be careful with this. It goes into deeper water than we are used to treading in.'

The line went dead. Millar stared at her phone. What the hell was he talking about? And why all the cloak-and-dagger stuff?

The screen in her hand lit up and there was a ping as an email arrived in her inbox. The sender was not marked as Boyle, but was instead an obscure long line of numbers and letters.

Millar opened up the email app and clicked the message, hoping it was not a spam message riddled with malware. There was no text in the body of the message. A video file was attached to the message. The subject said only "Surveillance Camera Footage".

PART 5

THE PUBLIC ENEMY

36

The flat was sparse and minimal. There were no home comforts, no pictures of family or loved ones on the walls, no personal stamp of colour or personality. The décor had remained untouched since the builders and decorators had applied the finishing touches to it. The carpets were silver-grey and the walls covered in white paint. A cream rug lay in the middle of the room with a clear glass coffee table on it. A large black television was on the main wall, and on the opposite side French windows opened out onto a small balcony. The living space was open plan, with a breakfast bar dividing lounge and kitchen. The kitchen had white cupboards and worktops, and white flooring. The place was spotless. Cal could smell the cleaning bleach. The small pile of used plates and glasses next to the sink were the only sign that Simone Millar had inhabited her apartment in the last few days. On the breakfast bar, a laptop was open.

Cal had never been in Millar's flat before. He had never glimpsed much of her life outside of her police work. He had expected her flat to be more of a mess – nothing more than a stopping-off point for her between shifts of the work that she lived for. Maybe it had been like that a week ago until Millar was forced to stay at home and she had spent the last few days giving the place a deep clean. It was more likely that this was what her place was always like. Cal wondered if she suffered from an obsessive-compulsive disorder. She had tunnel vision when it came to her work. Maybe this was how it manifested itself in her home.

'Coffee?' Millar offered him as she started prepping an expensive-looking espresso machine. Her reliance on coffee extended from work into her home life.

'Just water, thanks.'

Millar took a clean glass from the cupboard, filled it from the tap and placed it on the breakfast bar. 'Grab a seat.'

While the coffee machine went through various stages of operation, each accompanied by a distinct noise, Millar tapped the keyboard of the laptop.

'You said you had something to show me?' Cal asked, watching the screen.

The coffee machine made one final strangled gurgle and spat out liquid into the cup Millar had placed underneath its nozzle.

Cal had read the headlines: *Tariq Rizwan, wanted killer of Rose Black and Nathan MacDonald, found dead.* The police suspected suicide, the last act of a desperate criminal who had been hunted to his end. Further detail in the body of the articles that followed described the confession of Konstandin Sula, admitting to being the ringleader of the immigrant gang who had attacked a number of business premises around Glasgow. He had been charged. His lawyer, Alan Cox KC, had read out a statement in which Mr Sula expressed his sorrow and regret for the harm he had caused. There had been quotes from the lead detective on the case, Marcus Boyle, and Superintendent Douglas Forsyth. Both praised the hard work and dedication of their team, and the commitment and resources that had been properly utilised to bring to an end the crime spree that had gripped the city. The government's justice secretary was quoted as saying this showed how his political party could be trusted to keep the people of Scotland safe in a way that no other party could. The government was tough but fair when it came to immigration and crime. The message to the electorate heading to the ballot box was clear. A smaller byline focussed on Fergus Bennett's response to these events – a diatribe explaining the horrific results of allowing uncontrolled mass immigration and illegal immigration, and the continued corruption of British society and culture.

Millar had called Cal and asked him to come over to her flat. He was surprised by the invite, especially as Millar refused to tell him over the phone why she needed to see him.

With the Carnival closed for the foreseeable future, Jenny and Cal had been forced to start looking for other work. Jenny had an interview that afternoon for a bar manager position in the city centre.

'Please don't let her get you into more trouble,' Jenny had warned him when he told her he had been summoned by Millar.

'I can't promise anything,' Cal replied as he kissed her and headed out of the door.

'Just be careful,' Jenny called after him, but the door had already closed.

Millar sipped her fresh coffee and clicked on a video file on the desktop of the laptop. A password box appeared. Millar tapped a combination of letters and numbers and the video player opened on the screen.

It was surveillance camera footage, showing a city street. It looked like the camera was situated on a streetlight. It showed the front of a building opposite, the road that ran in front of it and part of the T-junction with a side street.

'What is it?' Cal asked.

'Watch it first,' said Millar.

Cal watched the screen. The footage was grainy due to the low level of light. It was evening; a streetlight provided a halo of light in the middle of the image. At first Cal thought the image was frozen as nothing moved. Then he saw a man emerge from beneath the camera view and cross the street. He seemed to stare at the building before disappearing up the side street into the darkness.

Millar used the cursor to drag the timeline of the video forward, skipping ahead ten minutes.

It was the same still scene, only the daylight had dimmed a little more. Again, there was no movement until a man appeared. It looked like the same man coming back down the side street, this time towards the camera.

Cal felt a cold chill run down his spine as he recognised the figure. He was wearing the same clothes he had been wearing when they had last seen him as he was fleeing Jimmy Koçi's Boxing Club. 'Riz?'

Millar nodded. 'Now watch what happens.'

As Riz reached the corner of the street, another man appeared beside him, coming down the stairs from the building on the corner. Then there was a blur of action. A new light source from the side of the camera appeared and grew in size and a car pulled up at the corner. Cal almost missed what happened next in the murky darkness. Millar scrolled back and let him watch it again. The back door of the car swung open, the man appeared to grab Riz and bundle him into the car and then the car was gone, accelerating away along the street and out of the camera's field of vision.

'He was abducted?'

'Looks that way.' Millar dragged the timeline back and stepped through the images a few frames at a time to let Cal see it in more detail.

'When was this taken?'

'The same day Riz bolted from the boxing club, while you were locked up in a holding cell and I was watching Konstandin being questioned.'

'A week before Riz turned up dead having hung himself?'

'You still think he committed suicide?'

'I read what was in the news. You know something different?'

'It wasn't suicide.'

'Says who?'

'Boyle.'

'He spoke to you?'

'It suits everyone for the case to be neatly packaged up and swept away. Good work all round and an outcome that pleases everyone.'

'Except anyone looking for the truth, right?' Cal took a sip of the lukewarm water and played the clip of footage again. 'Boyle sent you this?'

'I'm not going to answer that. You don't want to know where this came from if someone asks you about it in the future.'

'Why are you showing it to me?' Cal asked.

'We're off the books here. The case is closed, I'm on forced absence and there are no resources to pursue a closed case. If we want to do anything with this, it's you and me on our own. If you want to find out why Rose was killed and who ordered Riz to kill her, this is it.'

Cal was being offered a choice – walk away now and stay out of trouble, but never know what really happened to Rose, or follow Millar wherever it may take them. He knew what Jenny would tell him to do. He should walk out of the door now and tell Millar he wasn't interested. Rose was gone, the man who killed her was dead. What more did he need to know?

He watched the clip again. 'What are you saying? Whoever put Riz in the car killed him?'

'There's a fair chance – or at least knows exactly what happened to him.'

'You can't make out the licence plate, it's too dark.'

'We don't need the licence plate. Look at the building.'

Cal clicked on the video again and paused it. He had not been paying much attention to the building in the background. The man who appeared and grabbed Riz seemed to come out of the door and down the steps. It was an old sandstone building with a low railing in front of it and a short set of stairs leading up to a double front door. It looked like the sort of terraced building that was common enough around Glasgow. They had once been houses for the great and good. Most of them had been converted into office space now; some still housed the richer residents of the city. 'Should I recognise it?'

'It's on the corner of Park Terrace and Park Street, at the top of Kelvingrove Park.'

The address meant nothing to Cal.

'Why would a homeless, illegal immigrant, a wanted murderer with nowhere else to go, decide to hang around this particular house?'

Cal waited for Millar to enlighten him.

'He must have been there before, right? He's desperate, he has no one to turn to, so he goes to a place in the city that he has been to before. He must know someone in this house.'

'I guess so.' It made sense.

'He's not going to wander up to a stranger's door in the night and look for help. He must have a connection to this building. And the man coming out of the building throws him in a car and takes him away. Whoever is in that building doesn't want anything to do with Riz.'

Cal caught on. 'So whoever is in the building must have known who Riz was and arranged to have him taken away.'

'Exactly.'

'I buy that. So we should go to this house and find out who lives there.'

'No need to go there to find that out. The police are well aware of who lives in that particular house.'

Millar was toying with him, deliberately building up the suspense, drawing him back into her world. Cal knew he could not back away now – he would follow Millar to the end. He wanted to find out the truth about Rose's death.

Millar made him ask before she told him.

'Who lives there?'

'Everyone's favourite far-right politician, Fergus Bennett.'

37

Cal's mouth hung open, caught in disbelief. Riz had gone to the home of Fergus Bennett. That could not be a coincidence. An illegal immigrant wanted for murder seeking out the man who incited hatred towards immigrants and refugees.

It took him a moment to process the revelation. His mind turned over the possible scenarios. Millar was a step ahead of him and had already been through them. She waited patiently for him to think through the possibilities.

'Was he going there to attack Bennett? Riz blames Bennett for what has happened to him, so he goes there to try to get some sort of revenge?'

'It's possible,' Millar conceded, 'but I don't think so. We met Riz. Sure, he lied to us about some things, but he also told us some things that I believed, like wanting to get home to be with his family, his guilt and regret about what he did to Rose, and to me. He did those things because he was blackmailed to do them. He thought he had to do them to save his family. I don't think he would set out to kill for himself. He had had enough of killing.'

'He could have snapped, under all the strain.'

'True, but that still doesn't explain what we see in the footage. They knew who he was and they got him away from the house before he did anything threatening that we can see. And even if they did take him away to protect Bennett, they still have to explain how Riz came to turn up dead, hanging on the end of a rope a week later in the middle of nowhere.'

'We should go and talk to Bennett.'

Millar gave him one last chance to back out. 'If we do this, there is no going back. Bennett will file a complaint. He will kick up a fuss. It's what he likes to do. He'll claim harassment and you will get dragged into it. He will welcome the publicity; he thrives on it like oxygen. He will drag us down and try to ruin us.'

'I need to know why Rose was killed.'

Millar left the motorway at Charing Cross and turned onto Woodlands Road. Then she turned left and headed up the slope. The tyres juddered along the cobbled street before they swung onto Woodlands Terrace, which led onto Park Terrace. On the corner stood the three-storey end-terrace house, solid and imposing, adorned with cornices above the large bay windows and along the edge of the roof. Wide chimneys and a dormer window decorated the slate-black roof.

Millar pulled up opposite the front of the house and turned the engine off. She pointed up, out of the windscreen. 'That's the camera.'

Cal looked at the Victorian-style streetlight they had parked underneath. Just beneath the light fixture, a closed-circuit camera pointed towards the junction and the corner house.

'The election is in two weeks. You're sure about this?'

'You think we should wait until after the election? He might be a member of parliament by then. You think it will be easier then?'

The latest polls had Bennett's Scottish First Freedom Party holding at around five percent. Their relentless progress had stalled in the last few days, but thanks to the Scottish election's use of proportional representation, five percent of the vote would be enough for Bennett and one or two others to be elected into the parliament. They had always been a fringe party. At the last election they had polled less than one percent. They were dismissed as racists and not taken seriously. Even when vast swathes of England turned to parties considered to be far-right, in Scotland they barely registered a ripple. Bennett and his like were still not welcome in Scotland.

Then Rose Black had been murdered by an immigrant.

In the aftermath of her murder and the unrest that followed, Bennett had found a more receptive audience.

'I still can't believe they would do something like this,' said Cal.

'It's straight from their playbook. Stoke up division and hate of the "other". Capitalise on people's fear and prejudice. Turn the majority into the victims.'

'Sure, on social media. But orchestrating an actual murder – that's a bit extreme.'

'Haven't you heard? Fergus Bennett is an extremist.' Millar opened her door, got out of the car and crossed the street.

The heavy black door was opened by a broad white man with close-cropped hair, one of the identikit group who seemed to accompany Fergus Bennett wherever he appeared. Millar had seen them on the stage in George Square, right before the riot kicked off.

'Can I help you?' he asked, sizing them up to see if they posed a threat.

'We'd like a word with Mr Bennett, please,' said Millar, and flashed her police identification.

The man looked at it as if it was a piece of shit on the pavement. 'Do you have an appointment? I am sure you can appreciate that Mr Bennett is a very busy man at the moment. His campaign schedule is full for the next few weeks.'

'Just tell him Detective Simone Millar and Cal Jackson would appreciate a word. He will have heard of us both, I'm sure.'

'And if he says no?'

'Tell him it's about our mutual friend, Tariq.'

If Millar was hoping that Riz's name would provoke a reaction from the man, she was disappointed. He only looked confused, probably because it was unlikely Fergus Bennett had any friends called Tariq. The man eyed them both up once more and then closed the door on them and disappeared inside.

'You think he will know who we are?'

'If he has done what we think he has, then he will have heard of us. If I had to give Fergus Bennett credit for anything, it would be being fully briefed on anything he was getting himself into.'

Their answer came two minutes later when the door reopened and the same man stood to the side and bade them to enter. 'Mr Bennett can make time over his lunch break to see you. Follow me.'

He led them through a hallway. The interior of the house matched the exterior. The ceilings were high and the hall was lit by a chandelier. Touches of wealth adorned the fittings; watercolour art hung on the wall in elaborate frames and they walked across plush, deep carpets. A wide staircase took them up one floor. The man knocked on a door and then showed them into a drawing room. Cal could not remember ever having been in a house that had a drawing room before. What would Bennett's followers think if they could see how their working-class hero actually lived?

Fergus Bennett sat on a comfortable sofa, holding a teacup and saucer, with a selection of newspapers open next to him. His own face beamed back at him from the pages of the tabloids. His grey hair was neatly parted to the side. He wore a plain shirt and suit trousers – expensive but not ostentatious, part of his carefully cultivated persona.

'Do come in, Detective,' he greeted them without standing, 'and your friend.' He smiled at Cal. 'Take a seat. Can I get you a tea? Coffee?'

'No, thanks,' said Millar. She remained standing, filling the room with an awkward tension.

'Thank you, David.' Bennett dismissed the man who had shown them into the room. David closed the door behind him as he left. Bennett made them wait a moment more before breaking the silence. 'I was just taking a moment to keep across the media coverage. I don't get much time to myself these days. Crucial few days ahead.'

'It seems to be going well,' said Cal. He moved round the room and leant against the sill of the bay window. Millar remained standing just inside the door.

Bennett looked from one to the other. 'Quietly confident, but there is still time for things to change. One final push before polling day.' Millar and Cal did not respond. They waited for Bennett to lead the conversation. 'You wanted to see me about something. Someone called Tariq? I'm afraid I don't know anyone of that name.'

'You must have read about him in your newspapers, or on social media. He's been all over the news in the last couple of days.'

'You mean the man who was found dead? The murderer? Of course I've heard of him, but what has that got to do with me?'

Millar walked around the sofa and sat down opposite Bennett, who watched her all the way. Cal remained at the window.

'Did you know Tariq Rizwan?'

'Of course not. He is exactly the sort of person I want to see removed from this country.'

'A Muslim?'

'An illegal immigrant.'

'A man of colour.'

'I resent the implication you are trying to make, Detective. If this is all you came to say, then I suggest you can leave. I've got plenty of others who like to cast these aspersions about me – although few have the gall to turn up at my front door to do so.'

Cal spoke. 'Why did Tariq Rizwan turn up at your front door a week before he was found dead?'

'That is ridiculous. I told you, I have never met Tariq Rizwan, nor would I want to associate with such a person. Tariq Rizwan was a vile murderer who came to this country illegally and killed an innocent young woman – and I believe he also tried to kill you, Detective.'

Cal watched Bennett closely. He almost believed him. Then he remembered who Bennett was: a man who spread lies for a living, a man who lied until people believed he was telling the truth. He was a politician. Lying came as second nature to him.

Millar took out her phone and tapped the screen.

'What are you doing?' asked Bennett.

Millar held her phone screen out for Bennett to see. 'This was taken from the camera across the street on the night Konstandin Sula was arrested and Tariq Rizwan fled.' He watched the clip of the man coming out of his house and bundling Riz into a car.

'You can't tell who that is. That could be anyone. It could be a fake video. They make those so easily now.'

'You would know about fake news,' said Millar.

Bennett ignored her remark. 'Is this really all that you have? This is why you came here? A grainy clip in the dark that doesn't show anything?'

'It shows Tariq Rizwan being forced into a car outside your home, by a man who has just left your house,' said Cal.

'I disagree. It shows nothing of the sort.'

It was a familiar tactic of populist leaders around the world – deny true facts.

'Tariq Rizwan killed Rose Black,' said Millar.

'I am well aware of that.'

'In the days and weeks after her death, you organised a series of demonstrations and protests. You stoked up tensions between communities; it led to rioting. Your poll ratings took a big jump.'

'I was merely reflecting the legitimate concerns of the population and highlighting the serious problem we have with illegal immigration in this country.'

'Save it,' snapped Millar, 'you're not on the campaign trail just now. We both know exactly what you were doing.'

Bennett smiled. It was not a nice sight. It was a smug, self-satisfied smile that grew across his toad-like features.

'Cal and I spoke with Tariq before he died. He was not a deranged killer. He held no grudge against Rose Black or any other person. He was ordered to kill Rose Black. The question is, by who? We thought at first it was the people traffickers who had smuggled him into the country, but they did not gain anything from her death – if anything, it made their lives more difficult. The investigation went cold because we could not find any motive for anyone to kill Rose Black.'

'But you benefited from her death,' Cal took over from Millar. 'You took advantage of her death at the hands of Tariq to further your own cause, to spread your hate-filled lies.'

'From what I have learnt, it was *you* who almost killed Rose Black, Mr Jackson. I would be careful what aspersions you cast on to others. You're stepping over a line. Remember you are in my home.'

'You've stepped over a few lines yourself. Don't expect us to respect your boundaries now,' said Millar. 'What was the problem? Not enough genuine crimes committed by immigrants for your cause to feed off?'

'Let me get this straight. Are you suggesting I had Rose Black killed for political gain?'

'Did you?'

Bennett laughed. Cal recognised the smug guffaw from his television interviews. It annoyed him even more in real life. 'This is absurd. I think you had both better leave now.'

'I believe you, Mr Bennett,' said Millar. For a second Cal wondered what she meant. 'I don't think you did know Tariq Rizwan. I don't think you ever met him. I don't think you would be stupid enough to put yourself in that position.

'Let me tell you what I think happened. I think someone who works for you had an idea. A way to speed things up for your political message. They came up with a plan, or maybe you suggested it to them. Maybe you innocently speculated that a killing by an illegal immigrant would be of benefit to you, especially if the victim was an innocent, white, Scottish woman. Even better, a woman who was dedicating her life to helping the people you despise.

'Maybe you set things in motion; maybe one of your people decided to take the initiative for you, do something that would make you proud of them. Your followers do treat you like you are some sort of god.

'Somehow, they got in touch with Konstandin Sula, a known associate of people traffickers and illegal immigrants. They offered him a business deal – a lot of money. They paid him to organise a murder. Maybe your man suggested Rose Black to them. Maybe Konstandin picked her out. She would be known to him as a human rights lawyer who helped some of the people he had illegally smuggled into the country. It would benefit Konstandin if Rose Black was out of the way too.'

Bennett let Millar talk. His face was fixed in quizzical thought, like he was tolerating her mad ramblings, allowing her to get her ridiculous story out. His expression gave nothing away, but Cal could see beneath the fixed stare. There was panic there, he was sure of it.

'Konstandin picked one of his workers for the task, a man he knew would do it out of desperation and love for his own family. Tariq Rizwan was blackmailed into killing Rose Black because if he did not do it, his own wife and daughter in Albania would be killed.'

'This is preposterous.' Bennett threw his arms up in the air and stood up. His teacup and saucer fell from his lap on to the carpet. 'I would like you both to leave this house right now, before I call my lawyer and have you done for harassment. As I understand it, you are on enforced leave as it is, Detective. I do hope you are recovering from your ordeal.'

'I worked on the investigation into Rose Black's death,' Millar continued, unabated. 'It was an anonymous witness who told us they had seen a man of Middle Eastern or Eastern European ethnicity fleeing the crime scene. We never did trace the source of that information. Within hours of the tip-off, you were all over social media, telling everyone that an illegal immigrant had murdered Rose Black.'

'Well, it was true,' stuttered Bennett. His veneer was slowly starting to crumble.

'Who gave you that information about the suspect? Did someone in the police leak it to you, or was it you who started the rumour because you knew fine well it was an illegal immigrant who had killed Rose Black? That was what you wanted the world to know.

'You thought you had got away with it until Tariq Rizwan resurfaced last week, wanted by police for the murder of Rose Black and another man, Nathan MacDonald. But it was okay, you had the situation under control. Konstandin and Tariq had never spoken to you directly. You could deny ever having met either of them. Until Tariq showed up at your house one night. Then you were forced to take drastic action.'

'David!' Bennett shouted. The door flew open instantly. David must have been outside the room the whole time. 'Detective Millar and Mr Jackson are leaving now. Be so kind as to escort them off the property, and in the future, they are not to be admitted under any circumstances. Good day to you both.'

38

'Guilty as hell,' said Millar as they got back in the car.

Cal punched the dashboard with the ball of his hand. 'He had her killed. It was all over his smug face.'

'Or he knew all about it,' Millar agreed. 'But we'll never get him for it.'

'What do you mean? We can't just let him get away with it.'

'Nothing sticks to Fergus Bennett. He's got convictions already. He associates with known criminals and far-right thugs. Somehow he always comes up smelling of roses. Even when you think he has finally disappeared from our lives, he resurfaces.'

'So we don't do anything?'

'What can we do? Our best hope is that we've rattled him enough that he reacts, and then when he reacts, he makes a mistake that can lead us back to him, that somehow connects him to Rose Black. But I think he's too smart an operator to make that big a mistake.'

Millar started the engine.

'Fuck!' shouted Cal as they pulled away.

Fergus Bennett stood at the window of his drawing room and watched the car leave from behind the net curtain. He waited until the car's tail-lights braked at the corner and disappeared from view. Then he left the drawing room, walked out to the landing and proceeded up the staircase. He passed his bedroom on the third floor and crossed to the narrow stairs that led up to the converted room in the attic of the house.

He knocked on the door at the top of the staircase before entering. Alex MacKinnon stood at the dormer window, looking out over Kelvingrove Park and the west end beyond. His broad frame blocked out the sunlight.

'They've gone,' said Bennett.

'I saw,' replied MacKinnon, without turning round. 'What do they have?'

Bennett sighed. 'How could you be so careless after all this time? Honestly, the security camera right outside my house?'

MacKinnon turned to face him, then turned back to look at the view from the window. 'We wiped it the next day, when we got back.'

'Well, someone got a hold of the footage before you managed to wipe it.'

'What does it show?'

'You leaving the front door and throwing that idiot Tariq into the car and then speeding off.'

'Do they have anything else?'

'They didn't say, but they've made the connection to the lawyer. They're speculating, but they have the right idea. They know that this Konstandin was involved and that someone paid him, they just don't have the evidence to link it to us. But they will keep digging. They won't let it drop.' Bennett ran his hands through his grey hair and paced across the room. 'This is bad. Bad enough to undo all the good work we have done, all the progress we have made. Right before it was going to pay off at the election, just as we finally have a foothold on some real power.'

'Relax,' said MacKinnon. This time he turned away from the window, walked across the room and stood in front of his boss, forcing him to stop his anxious movement. 'They haven't gone public with anything, because they know they don't have anything to back it up. They have one video clip that proves nothing and no other evidence. So we have time.'

Bennett looked at his friend. MacKinnon had been with him from the start. He was the first person he had hired to be on his staff when he had set out along this path. He took him on as his head of security. Bennett knew he would need security before he embarked on his crusade to take on the establishment. He knew he would become a target for the left-wingers, the political class and the wealthy people whose social circles he had once moved in. He was setting himself up as an outsider, a man of the people, a disrupter. There would be a reaction and people would come after him. Alex MacKinnon had kept him safe. He'd brought in some of his ex-army colleagues. There had been the odd egg thrown; a couple of milkshakes had ended up down his front. That was the price Bennett paid for walking the streets to prove he was just like Joe Public. But he had never felt in danger because he knew Alex was there by his side. Now, just as they were about to finally achieve something truly noteworthy, Bennett knew he would have to do it without his most trusted friend, a man who would do anything for him and their cause. Anything Bennett asked him to do. Even kill.

'Not this time, Alex.'

'What do you mean?'

'The election is two weeks away. It's too much of a risk. We do nothing until after the election unless we are forced to.'

Alex nodded in reluctant agreement. 'Very well, perhaps you are right. But afterwards, once you have been elected, we can clean all this up.'

'She's a police officer, for God's sake, Alex. We can't touch her. That idiot Konstandin and whoever his boss is tried to kill her once already and failed miserably. The police will stop at nothing to track down a killer of one of their own. Besides, Millar has to play by the rules. Once I'm elected, we can use our position to get her to back off, claim she is harassing a member of parliament.'

'And him?'

'He's a nobody. A nobody with a weird obsession about Rose Black.' Bennett paused, 'Perhaps he is more of a danger to us. He's got a criminal record. He used to be tied up with Francis McArthur; his sister married into the family.'

'I could take care of him. It would be a warning to the cop as well.'

Bennett shook his head. 'Not until after the election. It's too close to the immigrant being found dead. We ride it out. I'm sure they won't do anything. They can't.'

'If you're sure.' MacKinnon shrugged and sat down in the only armchair in the room.

'But just in case they do decide to do something stupid…' Bennett hesitated and MacKinnon swivelled round to look at him.

'What?'

'It might be best if you weren't around for a little while. At least until this blows over.'

'You aren't being serious?' MacKinnon was on his feet again.

'If that footage gets out into the wider public, I need deniability. I have to be ahead of the story. You know that. I need to be able to say you left my employ some time ago, that I have nothing to do with you anymore. You know the drill. I can't do that if you're standing next to me every time I appear in public.'

MacKinnon had a fearsome temper. Bennett had seen it on more than one occasion, directed most often at the immigrants and counter-protestors they confronted at rallies. Bennett was glad it had never been directed towards him – he could see MacKinnon was fighting to stop himself from exploding. Bennett knew this would hurt his friend, but he also knew he could trust Alex not to betray him. MacKinnon knew all of the skeletons in Bennett's closet, but he believed in their cause. If anything, Bennett had often thought MacKinnon believed in ridding the country of the immigrants more than Bennett himself. For Bennett it was a means to an end, a strategy to obtain power and overthrow the normal order of things. For Alex MacKinnon, getting rid of the immigrants who had overrun his country was an end in itself. Bennett recalled the ecstatic look that had been on Alex's face when he told him what they had done to Tariq Rizwan. Alex wanted to hang them all.

MacKinnon's fists were clenched, his knuckles white with rage, but then they relented. 'Will you take me back on after the election?'

'Perhaps. We'll need to see how things pan out. Once it's all died down, I'm sure we can find a use for you.' Bennett was an accomplished liar. He had no idea if Alex believed him or not. Now that the detective was on to him, Alex MacKinnon was dead weight that Bennett needed to get rid of with as little fuss as possible. 'You understand, don't you? For the greater cause, we can't risk anything now.'

MacKinnon relented. His shoulders slumped. He would do what Bennett asked, he was a good soldier and a loyal friend. He had made a mistake, and he would have to take his punishment. He could disappear for a few weeks, lie low until this all blew over. Then, with Fergus safely elected, MacKinnon would return and take his revenge. He would do anything to protect his boss, he would do anything to protect their common cause. He could not have people out there who could cause Bennett – or their cause – harm.

When they were least expecting it, Alex MacKinnon would get rid of the policewoman and her friend. They would be the last hurdle that they needed to remove. After that, nothing would be able to stop the rise of Fergus Bennett and the Scottish First Freedom Party.

Bennett saw the acceptance in MacKinnon's face. 'Good lad, Alex. Take yourself away for a few days. Have a holiday. There will be plenty of hard work to do after the election.'

The two men shook hands. Bennett felt the tight grip and stifled a yelp. Did MacKinnon know that he was out for good?

Bennett left the room.

MacKinnon wasted no time in picking up his rucksack and started to pack away the few belongings he kept in the attic room.

He cursed the incompetent immigrants that had put him in this position. He should have killed the lawyer himself. But then that was not part of the plan. The plan had worked – the unrest that followed her murder by an immigrant, the platform it gave Fergus for lift-off. And now he was on the verge of claiming victory at the elections. Their time was coming, Alex just had to be patient.

He thought of the policewoman and her friend. Their time would come too.

39

Jenny made herself busy in the kitchen. She had seen enough of the coverage and she did not like what it was doing to Cal. He could not take his eyes off the news. He had stayed up through the night to see the election results coming in. Jenny suggested he should get some sleep. She had given up at three in the morning, before most of the results had been declared. Cal could not tear himself away from the horror that was unfolding.

To a dispassionate observer, the election could have been seen as a disappointment for the Scottish First Freedom Party and their populist leader. The huge breakthrough that some polls had predicted in the few days leading up to the election had failed to materialise. The wave of far-right support had crashed on the shore and caused barely a ripple. In the end, the common sense of the majority of the Scottish public had come to the fore. The two centre-left parties had led the way again and the incumbent government had clung on to power, albeit with a reduced margin of the popular vote and with a minority government. The centre-right party had made no gain, although it still surprised Cal that one in five of his fellow citizens would vote for them. The far-right had faltered. Scotland had rejected them.

And yet, despite that, there was one bit of consolation for Fergus Bennett. Thanks to the convoluted voting system of the parliament, in the Lothian list, Fergus Bennett's party had secured enough votes – just – to get their leader elected as a regional member of the Scottish parliament. He had made it. The veneer of respectability and acceptability that came with it was what he had craved. The party had not made the huge breakthrough they had hoped for this time, but by the time the next election came round, they would be ready. It disgusted Cal that some people had been fooled by Bennett's ideology and his lies. It worried him even more that some of those who voted for him truly believed in the hatred Fergus Bennett spewed into the world. What made it worse for Cal was knowing how truly evil the man was.

The rolling coverage kept repeating the same shot of Fergus Bennett, his fist raised in smug victory, surrounded by his supporters, camera flashes flickering in a wave of explosive light. They kept playing the same quote, without questioning the spin Bennett was managing to put on the result.

'The people have spoken. They have had enough of the status quo, of the corrupt leaders who are selling our proud country down the river, who are allowing it to be overrun by foreigners who do not share our values or way of life. Let me assure everyone who has voted for me, and those who perhaps thought about voting for me but decided to give the main parties one last chance to fix the mess they have created – I will hold our leaders to account. I will fight for the people of this country who have the right to feel safe in our streets.'

The clip cut off at the same point each time. Cal had seen the full interview when it was live and unfiltered. They did not repeat his accusations about refugees and illegal immigrants being killers and rapists and benefit scroungers. They did not repeat his misleading figures about the number of immigrants in the country.

The smell of food came through from the kitchen as Jenny

came through the door. She grabbed the remote and switched the television off.

'Enough. Let's eat without thinking about that man.'

The last fortnight had crawled past for Cal. After confronting Fergus Bennett in his home, he had expected more, but there had been nothing. No fallout, no reaction, no further inquiry into Riz's supposed suicide.

Millar's hands were tied. After two weeks she was back at work, covering desk duties while others safeguarded the streets and ensured a smooth democratic election took place. She messaged Cal, but only to tell him there was nothing more they could do for now. She promised him she would get Bennett eventually. She was a patient investigator. She would keep her ear to the ground; she would build a case. She had been after Francis McArthur for years before they had charged him. She could do the same with Fergus Bennett.

But it was different this time. She did not have the support of the police force. There was no active investigation into Fergus Bennett.

Carmen Carmichael had promised Cal and Jenny and the rest of her staff that their jobs would be there for them when the Carnival reopened, but the prospect of that was months away. Jenny had secured another job, working as a bar manager in the city centre. She had offered to give Cal some shifts behind the bar on a casual basis. Cal said he would think about it. It was one thing to meet at work and start a relationship, but he had to stand on his own two feet at some point, and as much as Jenny insisted she wanted him there, Cal felt he was a burden to her, that she was offering him work because she felt obliged to.

The last fortnight had strained their relationship. Cal had brooded from the moment Millar drove them away from Fergus Bennett's house. His anger simmered and his temper was on a hair trigger.

He told Jenny everything. She understood his anger, she shared his frustration, but there was nothing she could do to release him from the helplessness he felt. She knew how much he blamed himself for hurting Rose Black. Even now he had learnt the truth, Cal still carried the weight of responsibility.

Cal wanted to punish Fergus Bennett. In his darkest moments, lying in bed, unable to sleep, he thought about taking the most extreme form of revenge. He was not a killer, but he knew part of him – the part that he had learnt to bury inside himself – would be capable of doing it if forced to act. If he did go that far though, Cal knew he would not just be ending Fergus Bennett's life. He would be destroying his own as well.

He thought about going to the media, or leaking something online, but he had no experience of playing that game, and Fergus Bennett was the master of manipulating the media, both the traditional press, who fawned over his every word, and social media, where his army of followers bolstered his ego and pushed whichever narrative he wanted them to believe in.

Cal was tempted to give in to his previous vices. He had managed to resist the pull of alcohol because he knew what lay at the bottom of that slippery slope if he chose to begin the descent. He had compromised and had bought his first packet of cigarettes in over a year.

Jenny did not approve and told him so. He promised her it was only one packet, just to get him through the difficult days as he came to terms with what Millar and he had learnt. Jenny decided to believe him, although he could tell she did not think he was telling the truth.

Cal was in a slump, and he was not sure how he would dig himself out of it. The hysteria and wall-to-wall daily press coverage that Bennett garnered in the days leading up to the election did not help. Everywhere he turned, he saw that smug grin, and Cal was one of the very few who understood the real evil that lay behind it.

And now the man who had killed Rose was a member of the Scottish parliament. Fergus Bennett was untouchable.

Alex MacKinnon listened to the news on the car radio. He had only got back to the city that morning. He had watched the election coverage last night in the bed and breakfast he had been staying in. When the results had come in, he packed up his rucksack, got in his car and drove back to his house. He had promised Fergus he would disappear until after the election. Now the election was over, he would go back.

He felt a swell of pride watching Fergus raise his fist, being hailed a hero by his supporters. Alex wished he could have been there to share the historic moment with him.

They had done it. Perhaps it was not the huge breakthrough that some had predicted and they had all wanted, but it was still a breakthrough. It was the only story that anyone was talking about on social media and on the news – Fergus Bennett elected to parliament. The Scottish First Freedom Party was no longer a fringe group of far-right extremists, they were a serious political movement. This was just the first step. This was the foothold they needed to build on. More people would flock to their cause, especially when they saw how effective Fergus would be as a Member of Parliament.

In a few days, he would return to Fergus and be welcomed with open arms. Nothing could stop them now.

Nothing, thought Alex, except the people who knew the real truth about Fergus Bennett and what he'd had to do in order to earn his legitimate place at the top.

They were a danger now more than ever, the policewoman and her friend. They could ruin everything for them at any time. Alex had been concerned that they would try something before the election, but they were being smart, playing the long game. He begrudgingly admired them for it. They had a hold over Bennett and they were saving it until the moment it would have the greatest impact. It might be months or years from now, when Fergus would be close to taking power away from the elite, that they would strike against him.

And it was partly Alex's fault. He had been careless. He had done it to protect Fergus, but he should have been ruthless. Was he going soft, spending too much time around the political class? He should have taken care of Konstandin and Riz after they had killed the lawyer. No one would have missed them if MacKinnon had made them disappear – and none of this mess would be happening now.

He would not make the same mistake again. Bennett needed to be free to manoeuvre without his enemies holding a gun to his head, waiting to pounce on him. Alex MacKinnon had helped Fergus get to where he was today. It was time to help him once more.

'I'll be late home, I'm closing up,' said Jenny as she stacked the dishes in the washer. 'Will you be here when I get back?'

'Do you want me to be here?'

Jenny did not answer him. The frostiness between them had yet to fully thaw.

'I might go for a walk then drive over to my flat and pick up a few things, then come back over.'

Jenny picked up her coat and bag. 'Okay.' She leant over the table and kissed him on the lips. The frost receded a little more. 'I would like it if you were here when I got back.'

She headed to the door.

'Jenny,' Cal called after her. She looked back at him from the doorway. 'I'll do better. I just need a bit of time.'

'I know you will do better. I'll see you later on.' She stepped out of the door and then stopped and turned back. 'Turn the TV off and get some fresh air, clear your head.' She closed the front door behind her.

Alex watched the woman leave the flat. She was attractive, in her early thirties, lean and healthy-looking with long black hair. Too good for Cal Jackson. How had she ended up with such a loser? She was dressed smartly. He knew from his research that Jennifer Doherty had worked at the Carnival with Cal. She had been there on the night it had burned down too. Now she had a new job managing a different bar. She was on her way to work a shift.

A thought flickered in his mind. Should he take her instead? Chances were Cal Jackson had shared what he knew with her anyway. She could still cause trouble for Fergus. There would be other benefits to taking her as well. She was certainly nicer to look at than Cal Jackson.

He smiled at the thought. He had been with a woman while he had been away, but it wasn't the same when you paid for it.

No, concentrate on the job in hand, he told himself. He could always come back for Jenny later. She would need a shoulder to cry on.

He watched her as she passed and walked along the pavement. She turned at the end of the street and disappeared from his rear-view mirror.

He turned back to the house.

Cal Jackson was alone in the flat.

Alex thought how delighted Fergus would be when he told him that all his problems had disappeared.

40

One cigarette left. Cal stared at the lone stick in the packet. This would be his last one. One final moment of weakness and then he would turn things around again. He had been through it before and come out the other side. He had sunk lower and pulled himself back up. That was what scared him now and made him resolve to put a stop to his descent – he knew how far he could fall before he hit rock bottom. He did not want to be back down there.

Jenny had, inevitably, barred any smoking inside her flat. Cal looked out of the window. It was the end of summer and a fair evening, without being either warm or sunny. A fair evening for a stroll down to the river, where he would enjoy his last cigarette overlooking the water.

He picked up his coat and headed out of the door.

MacKinnon was about to step out of his car and head towards the row of flats when the door opened and Cal Jackson stepped outside, pulling on his coat as he shut the door behind him. Alex stopped himself from exiting the car and slowly shrank back into the seat, hoping that Cal would not notice the movement across the street.

Cal kept walking, heading south along Gardner Street. Alex watched him until he had reached Dumbarton Road and crossed the busy main street. Then he got out of the car. He double-checked that the knife was secure inside his jacket and set off after his target.

The swing bridge that spanned the River Clyde and linked Govan and Partick was still new enough to provide a fresh perspective to those who had lived on either side of the river for many years. After ten minutes of walking, Cal crossed the footbridge over the expressway and the white pointed tower of the swing span structure was visible above the grey metallic roof of the Riverside Museum.

The museum was closed, but around the skatepark a group of teenagers were milling around, taking it in turns to ride the curbs and banks. The tall ship Glenlee was anchored next to the museum, sitting high in the water, which was at high tide. The new bridge had increased the footfall around the wide esplanade and on this pleasant end-of-summer evening, the residents of Govan and Partick had taken the opportunity to enjoy the fading sunset. Given the inclement weather that autumn would bring, along with the lengthening nights, it might be months before they were able to experience an evening stroll again.

Cal stepped on to the bridge and walked until he was at the halfway point across the river. He stood at the railing. The thick steel cable ran from the sides of the bridge up to the pointed tower. He took the packet of cigarettes and the cheap plastic lighter he had bought at the same time from his coat pocket. The breeze blew out the flickering flame and he had to cup his hands around the lighter to protect it and light the cigarette in his mouth. He inhaled a large breath and felt the smoke fill his lungs and the nicotine and tobacco rush through him. He faced out over the dark expanse of water and took in the old docks and the shipyard warehouses, and the new flats opposite them. From here the river flowed out to the Firth of Clyde and beyond that into the Atlantic Ocean.

MacKinnon followed at a sensible distance. He took precautions to make sure Cal would not see him, but his target never stopped or turned or looked behind him. He was unguarded and had no suspicion that he was being followed. Alex let him walk on to the bridge but did not follow him. The bridge was not a good spot. It was too exposed; there was no cover, nowhere to hide once the act had been committed, and there were too many civilians around. He walked to the tall glass front of the museum and took a seat on the shiny black bench. He was not in a rush. He would let Cal Jackson enjoy his cigarette in the fresh air – his final moments on this earth.

The water calmed Cal. It always had this effect on him. It gave him space away from the built-up city to stop and think.

Tonight, he thought about Rose Black.

The anger he felt towards Fergus Bennett would not subside. Somehow, Cal had to find a way to let the bitterness go before it ate him up inside. He could not believe Bennett could get away with what he had done. And yet Cal knew how the world worked, how the rich and the privileged were protected. Fergus Bennett would get away with it because he was in a position where he *could* get away with it. Not like Riz. The man who had killed Rose had himself been killed. There was no excuse for what Riz had done, and yet Cal was not satisfied. Riz may have wielded the knife that killed Rose, but he was not the instigator, it was not his decision, and the guilt lay beyond him. It was shared by Bennett and whoever else on his team knew the dark secret of his success.

The cigarette burned down to a small remaining stub. Cal took one last draw and flicked the remaining dout over the side of the bridge. He watched it spiral down and land in the still water, causing barely a ripple on the surface. The ritual completed, he vowed that it would be his last smoke. It was time to move on. Tomorrow, Jenny would lie in after her late shift at work. When she did get up, Cal would be ready to mend the damage he had done to their relationship over the last few days.

He put his hands in his pockets, turned away from the river and walked back towards the museum.

Alex saw his opportunity as Cal began walking towards him. There was a lull in the foot traffic around the corner of the museum. The teenagers at the skatepark did not have an eyeline to the corner of the bridge. At that moment, no one else was between him and Cal Jackson. Fate had decided this was the perfect moment for him to strike. Fate had decreed that Fergus Bennett was the chosen one who could not be stopped.

Alex stood up and walked forwards until he was next to the tall ship. All he needed now was for Cal to turn in his direction. He visualised the moment, he saw it happen in front of him. He would let Cal step past him, he would draw the knife. He would step behind Cal and thrust the knife up into his side, entering below the rib cage and slanting upwards into his lung and heart. He would hold him and prevent him from falling and he would look him in the eye. Cal would know who had killed him. Then he would lift him over the railing and drop him into the water, between the side of the tall ship and the dock wall. By the time daylight rose tomorrow morning and Cal's woman noticed he was missing, his body would be well on its way downriver and out to sea. The chances of the body ever being found were slim.

Cal decided to loop around the front of the museum and cross the expressway at the second footbridge further along the riverfront. It would be a longer walk back to the flat, but he was not in a rush to get back and he felt like extending his walk in the last of the fading evening light.

He saw the man leaning against the railing next to the tall ship. He noticed the short crew cut and the powerful build. Only when he drew level with the man did his memory and instinct combine to warn him that this man was dangerous.

The haircut or the build or the black jacket, or a combination of all those elements, registered as he took one step past the man. The video clip from the security camera outside Fergus Bennett's house played in his mind. He saw Riz on the street and he saw the man coming down the steps from the house ready to sweep Riz away. He saw the crew cut, the black jacket and the military gait of the man and he knew it was the same man who stood close to him now.

He took another pace and he sensed the man move away from the railing and step behind him.

Cal spun round and faced the man, who was caught by surprise for a fraction of a second. Cal saw that the man's hand was inside his jacket and was pulling out a metal blade. Before he could free the knife, Cal grabbed his arm and the two men were locked together, their faces inches apart.

The man tried to free the knife. Cal resisted.

'You will not destroy everything Fergus Bennett stands for.' The man's spittle hit Cal in the face.

They were locked together and Cal knew that if he let go, if he released his grip on this man, then he was dead.

'What did that stupid lawyer mean to you anyway? Was she really worth dying for? It won't bring her back. You should have just left it alone.'

Cal felt the anger and rage swell up inside him. He felt that part of him he'd worked so hard to bury resurface, the part of him that he knew was violent and uncontrollable unless he fought against his instinct. But now was not the time to fight that instinct. That instinct would be what saved him. It was part of him and always would be, and in this moment, he was glad that this part of him existed.

He did not speak, but the man who had attacked him saw the change in his face. He saw the look of venom that came over Cal.

Alex regretted opening his mouth. He knew he had unleashed some primitive evil within Cal Jackson and in that moment, Alex MacKinnon knew he had picked the wrong target.

They were no longer evenly matched. Now Cal pushed the man back until he hit the railing with force. The man buckled forward. His hand came free from the inside of his coat but he lost his grip on the knife and it fell to the ground. Cal ignored it. He had never liked knives. He grabbed the man, lifted him off the ground and pushed him backwards, and the man began to tip over the top of the metal railing.

He spoke again, but now he was panicking and pleading for his life.

The civilised part of Cal's mind told him to stop. The man was right. This would not stop Fergus Bennett. It would not stop his supporters. It would not dampen the far-right movement that was growing in the country.

None of that mattered at this moment. All that Cal could think of was Rose Black lying on the pavement and the blood pouring from the wounds in her chest. And then he saw Rose Black again, younger, lying on a different road, bruised and broken. And he saw the car windscreen and heard the sickening thud and the car brakes and the screams.

And then the man was screaming as he fell over the railing and Cal found he was no longer holding on to his attacker. He heard a heavy thud and saw the man's head smash into the giant metal chain that moored the tall ship to the river wall. Then there was a splash of water. Cal looked down and saw the man struggling briefly as he broke the surface of the river. He had fallen into the water in a gap between the dock wall and the side of the tall ship. His arm came up again, then his head, and there was a choked cry for help. Cal watched as the surface of the water folded over the man's head for a final time. The green-brown water was still and calm.

He stood and leant over the railings. The ship swayed back and forth. The surface of the water did not break. There was no sound.

Cal looked around and saw that he was alone. No one had seen the attack or the man going over the side.

The animal that lurked inside Cal receded and he turned and carried on walking the way he had intended to go.

Later he would wonder if it had actually happened, or if it had just been his imagination. Had it just been a revenge dream, the closest he would get to avenging Rose Black's death?

He did not tell Jenny about what had happened when she woke up late the next morning. He would never tell anyone, not even Millar. It was his own private moment, his own private demon, his own futile act of revenge.

PART 6

WALK SOFTLY, STRANGER

41

It was Jenny's idea to contact Rose Black's family and tell them what had happened, even if Cal wanted to keep Fergus Bennett's name out of it. Rose's parents had a right to know what had happened to their daughter.

But Cal could not bring himself to contact her parents. He knew they would not welcome him. He thought instead of the friend Rose had been at university with, who she had worked with at the law firm. He would tell Juliet and let her pass on the information to the Black family. They would be more receptive to her than they would be to him.

He called the office where he had met Juliet and arranged to meet. He told her it was about Rose and the investigation into her death. Juliet agreed to see him and suggested meeting at Rose's grave.

Cal had not visited her resting place before. He found Juliet amongst a row of clean, new gravestones, all recently installed in the Western Necropolis. Jenny had insisted Cal bring flowers to leave by the graveside. He placed them beside the plain gravestone that bore Rose's name and the dates of her birth and death.

They did not speak to one another at the graveside. Each had their own thoughts of Rose. Juliet turned away first and Cal followed her to the bench by the main path that cut through the large cemetery from east to west. In the shade of a large oak tree, its branches rustling in the breeze and its leaves turning golden, Cal told her about Tariq Rizwan.

'He was an illegal immigrant from Albania. He left his family over there and came here to try to make a better life for them.' Juliet had read as much in the press coverage after Riz had been found dead. 'He got mixed up with the wrong people.'

Cal told her about a man called Alex MacKinnon and the plan to gain support for his far-right cause by having an illegal immigrant murder an innocent lawyer.

The bloated and rotting corpse of a man had been found by a dog walker on the banks of the River Clyde near the village of Bowling. The authorities could only guess where the man had entered the water and roughly estimate how long he had been in the river before washing up on the shore. When Cal saw the news, he calculated the distance downriver from the Riverside Museum and the tall ship Glenlee. Only he knew the exact date and time three weeks earlier that the man had disappeared into the water.

It took them another three days to identify the corpse as Alex MacKinnon from his military and dental records. He had served in the British Army before starting his own private security firm. Most recently, he had been in the employ of newly elected member of the Scottish parliament and leader of the Scottish First Freedom Party, Fergus Bennett. MacKinnon was single and had no immediate family.

Fergus Bennett announced that he was heartbroken and grief-stricken. Alex had been a dear, long-term friend and colleague, an invaluable member of his team. Alex had left his employ suddenly, only weeks before the recent election, without any warning. Fergus Bennett believed he had been suffering from long-term trauma and stress from his time in the army. The bruising election campaign and the actions of those thugs who sought to demonise and vilify his political movement had taken their toll on all of his workers.

He said that although his friend had always appeared strong and healthy, Fergus knew Alex had been suffering underneath. They had spoken in the past about his struggles after leaving the military. Now his demons had caught up with him and overwhelmed him. Fergus regretted having been unable to do more to stop his friend from taking his own life, if that was in fact what had happened. He demanded better mental health care be provided to veterans and serving military personnel.

Somehow, Fergus Bennett managed to steer the story towards his own political gain. He was now a champion of the British military, despite having never served a day in his life and never previously outlining any policy aimed at the armed forces.

Buried underneath Fergus Bennett's eulogy were circumspect, vague details about Mackinnon's "dismissal with disgrace" from the army, although no specific incident that would have led to this was mentioned. There was a criminal record that consisted of affray and assault, though nothing that had ever landed MacKinnon any prison time. There were rumours about mercenary operations of a dubious nature in the Middle East and Ukraine. No one seemed to know for certain which side Alex MacKinnon had been fighting with when he had ventured overseas.

Millar recognised MacKinnon as the man she had seen on the security camera on the night Riz had disappeared. She messaged Cal and pointed out the coincidence of him turning up dead a few weeks after they had found out he'd had a hand in Riz's death. She wondered if Fergus Bennett was cleaning house now that he had made it further up the political ladder. Cal suggested that would make sense.

Millar replied to say she hoped Cal would take some solace from the fact that another of those responsible for Rose Black's death had met an untimely death, even if Fergus Bennett remained untouchable. Cal did not reply.

Cal told Juliet everything, apart from how Alex MacKinnon had ended up crushed and drowned in the River Clyde.

'And it was this Alex MacKinnon that paid Tariq Rizwan to kill Rose? It was him who chose Rose?' Juliet asked when he had finished.

Cal nodded. 'They picked Rose because she was kind and caring and compassionate. They wanted to destroy someone who was pure and good in order to paint immigrants as evil, a threat that could not be ignored. They wanted to turn more people against immigrants. Riz was set up as part of their plan. They threatened to kill his wife and daughter in Albania unless he did as they asked. MacKinnon paid a man called Konstandin Sula to arrange it. Sula worked for the people traffickers who had trapped Riz. Sula forced Riz to kill Rose.'

'And this Alex MacKinnon was until recently employed by Fergus Bennett?'

'So the newspapers say,' answered Cal.

'Did Fergus Bennett know about MacKinnon? Did he know what he was planning?'

Cal did not answer her. He looked at her and then turned his head and looked out across the sea of gravestones and the yellow-orange backdrop of trees that signalled the coming of autumn to the city.

'I suppose,' he said softly, 'someone should look into that possibility. Perhaps someone who could talk to Konstandin Sula and see what he has to say about it, a lawyer who knows about these things. He's being held on remand ahead of his sentencing. Perhaps he has had time to think about the people who have left him to rot in jail and what he does and does not owe them. A good starting point might be trying to find out who paid for his legal representation – one of the top lawyers in the country.'

Juliet pulled her jacket closed and stood up. She held out her hand. Cal took it and she shook it. 'Thank you,' she said. She turned and walked towards the gate at the end of the path, leaving him sitting on the bench under the tree. Cal watched her leave. She walked past the row of cars parked on the verge. Jenny was in his car, waiting for Cal. She had insisted on coming with him to the cemetery.

He noticed Jenny watching Juliet as she passed by. She was trying to read from Juliet's expression exactly what Cal had told her.

After five minutes, Cal rose and walked back to the car.

'You told her?' Jenny asked him as he got in and started the engine.

'I told her enough,' he answered.

'She looked determined, like she was on a mission.'

Cal smiled to himself as he checked his wing mirror, put the car into gear and pulled away from the verge.

One day Fergus Bennett would pay for what he had done, and it would be a bright, courageous human rights lawyer who made sure that he did.

42

Erjon saw the woman on the balcony and knew it was Leandra. Riz had shown him the photograph of his wife and daughter he carried with him in his pocket. The curls in her hair were just as Riz had described them when he spoke of his beautiful wife and daughter waiting for him at home.

Erjon checked the scrawled piece of paper in his hand to be sure he had the correct address, the pencil markings faded but etched into his memory. He had not been to Durrës before. He had lived in Tirana all of his life, until the fateful day he had embarked on his journey to the west. He wished he had never left Tirana at all.

Travelling across Albania, his country, from the capital to the coast had filled him with joy. He had not appreciated his country until he'd left it behind. He had been told the West would offer him a better life, a better way of living, a better chance to be a success. This was not true. Albania was not perfect, Erjon knew this. He was not the naïve fool he had once been. There was plenty wrong with his homeland, but he now knew that the rich countries of Europe had their own problems and difficulties too.

The sun beat down as he squinted up at the woman on the

balcony. The weather was one of the things he had taken for granted about Albania. He did not miss the constant grey rain and cloud of Scotland. A chill ran through him as he thought of the cold and damp that had infected that place.

Rruga Koder Stan. This was the street, and this was the house Riz had told him about. A squat, square building with three floors, each with a balcony. The balcony walls were painted a lime-green colour. The street was not well maintained. It was narrow and weeds and rubble gathered along the sides of the road. The plots of land varied in shape and size. The houses were irregular – shacks and sheds sat next to two-storey villas. Nothing matched, nothing was uniform. It filled Erjon with joy to see such a place. It was the opposite of the city he had fled in order to get back here, with its rows of identical tenements and houses. The character of his country shone through in the unconformity of its housing and haphazard city planning.

The woman with the blonde-brown curls was hanging out clothes on the drying rack on her balcony. She paused when she saw Erjon looking at her. She stared at him for a minute. Erjon did not look away. As they stood looking at each other, understanding reached her. She nodded her head, folded a child's t-shirt and placed it back in a basket of washing, and then she went inside.

After five minutes, Leandra appeared at the bottom of the stairs. She had a small girl with dark, curly hair with her.

'You must be Zerina,' Erjon said and the girl smiled shyly at him in response. 'Your father said you were a beautiful girl, but he did not tell me just how beautiful you are.'

'You know my father?' the girl said in soft Albanian.

Erjon was unsure how to answer the question. He did not want to break the spirit of this angel. He did not want to expose her to the cruel world that she would have to live in.

Leandra saved him. 'Come on, Zerina. Lead the way to the beach and I will get you an ice cream.'

Zerina skipped ahead of them along the rutted track. Leandra let her get a few yards ahead of them.

'You were with Tariq?'

'I was. You have not told her that her father will not be coming back?'

'No.'

They walked along Rruga Koder Stan, side by side. Erjon took pleasure in the heat from the sun shining on his face. He waited for Leandra to ask him to tell Tariq's story. There was no rush. Erjon knew he would not share some of the details with Leandra.

They reached Rruga Vellazrimi, a wide boulevard with vast open spaces punctuated by rows of villas, a petrol station and rows of small shops along both sides. Zerina was sitting at the bus stop waiting for them.

'You don't mind a bus ride to the beach?' Leandra asked him.

'I would love to visit the beach,' answered Erjon.

Zerina stood on the pebbled beach and threw stones into the Adriatic Sea. Erjon and Leandra kept an eye on her as they walked along the new, modern walkway that stretched along a mile of the waterfront. Behind the palm trees and new streetlights that lined it, high-rise hotels and apartment blocks towered up. An ancient Venetian tower was dwarfed by the modern buildings. In the background was the constant hum of traffic and the sound of car horns. Yet Erjon felt a peace wash over him as he looked out at the water and heard the waves lapping against the shore.

The experience was the opposite of the last time Erjon had been near the sea. Then, he had been full of dread and fear. His future had been uncertain. He had been desperate to escape and return home. He had hidden in the back of a lorry and prayed that he would not be discovered. He had stayed hidden on the boat while it had been tossed around the storm-swept sea.

'The last time I saw Tariq, he thought of you,' Erjon began

tentatively. 'He wrote the name of your street on a piece of paper and told me to find you and tell you what had happened to him.'

'He knew he would not be returning to Albania. He knew something was going to happen to him?'

Erjon thought back to the squalid high-rise flat and the last morning they had all been there. They had been woken up abruptly in the early hours of the morning. Konstandin was in a fury.

'Get up, you lazy pigs,' he had shouted at them. 'We must go now, all of you. It is not safe here now.'

'Where are we to go?' asked Lorik.

'Shut up, you insolent fool. If you had done as you had been instructed, this would not have happened. Now you are all useless to us, worthless. The police are coming for you and if you do not move your fat, useless backsides, you will be arrested and sent to jail.'

In the panic that had followed, Riz had pulled Erjon to one side. 'You must get back to Albania at all costs, Erjon. You cannot stay here. If you do, they will kill you in the end. When you get back, go to this address.' Riz pressed the slip of paper into Erjon's hand. 'Tell my Leandra that I love her, and kiss my Zerina for me. Tell her I was not a bad man and that I loved her very much.'

'What are you saying, Riz? Where are you going? You must come back with me and tell your family this yourself.'

'I cannot go with you. They will come for me soon. They will kill me. I have made them angry. Do not be sad for me. It is what I deserve after what I have done.'

'What we have all done, Riz. What they have forced us to do. None of us wanted this.'

At that moment, Konstandin had seen them. He had pulled Riz away from Erjon and out of the door.

The men had been marched down the stairwell and out into the street. The van was not there. Instead, there were three cars waiting for them. The men were packed into each car. There was not enough room for them all. Some men were forced into the boots of the cars.

In the confusion and the weak morning light, Erjon saw his chance to do what Riz had told him to do. He waited until he was sure no one was watching him and he stole away, running around the corner of the high-rise building then leaping over the wall and crouching down out of sight.

The cars sped away without him. He never found out what happened to the other men.

It took him a month to make his own way back to the south coast of England. Most of the journey he had achieved by stowing away in lorries. He knew the people of this country did not want him to be there. At one service station, he saw the newspaper headline about an illegal immigrant from Albania who had been found dead after a police manhunt. It said Tariq Rizwan had been wanted for committing murder.

Erjon made it to the port and hid in a lorry that went on to the ferry.

It took him another two months to travel down through Europe. It had not been easy, but the closer he got to home, the simpler it had become. He felt people viewed him with less suspicion. He was not afraid to ask for help. An Albanian businessman he met in Mostar had taken him all the way to the border and dropped him off. Erjon had trekked the last few miles through forest and countryside. He did not realise he had crossed the border until he came upon a road sign and saw that it was written in Albanian. He sat down by the side of the road and wept.

Now he was here, in Durrës, fulfilling the promise he had made to Riz thousands of miles away and a lifetime ago.

'He knew something bad was going to happen to him. I did not know what at the time. I found out about it through the news, like you did.'

'I only know what they told me. The men who came to my house.

They told me Tariq had killed a woman. They told me my husband was a killer and a criminal and that he had killed himself because he could not live with what he had done.' Leandra spoke without anger. 'I do not believe them. I know my Tariq would not do these things, and yet it said in the news that he had. That was not the man I loved. That was not the man who left our home to try to make a better life for us.'

Erjon could not bring himself to tell her the truth. He did not know for sure himself. He only knew that Riz had been taken away to do a special job and when he had returned, he had been a different person. 'I know that he loved you and Zerina more than anything in the world and he would do anything to protect you.'

'Including killing someone?' Leandra guessed at the truth. Erjon did not answer her and did not meet her look. 'Tell me what it was like over there.'

'It was not good,' Erjon admitted. 'It was not what they had promised it would be like. There was no job. There was no chance to earn money. Any money we did earn, they took from us. They told us we had to pay our debts to the people who had brought us into the country.'

'You were not happy there?'

'No. It was impossible for us to be happy there. We had all left our loved ones behind and thought we would find a better life, but it was not a better life.'

They walked on further. Leandra asked more questions about what it had been like. Erjon tried to answer her honestly. They reached the end of the walkway as it came to a sudden stop. Beyond it was a rough pebble beach and behind that, a piece of wasteland on which a funfair was setting up.

Zerina came running up to them. 'Can we go to the fair when it opens?' she asked her mother.

'We shall see. Perhaps, if you behave yourself.'

'I would love to go on the rides.' She pointed at a carousel. 'Daddy could go on this one with me when he gets home.'

Leandra put her arm around her daughter. 'That is a nice idea.' Erjon heard the catch in her throat. Zerina looked up at her mother with a puzzled look. 'Why do you cry, Mummy?'

Erjon stepped across and picked the small girl up. She was as light as a feather.

'I am sure your father would love to go on this ride with you. He loves you and your mother very much. He told me this when I was with him in a far-off country.'

'Yes, he went there to earn good money so we could have a better life.' The girl was parroting what her mother had told her many times.

'That is right. He wants only the very best things for you.'

Erjon pulled Zerina close to him in a hug and kissed her lightly on the cheek. 'Your father asked me to give you this kiss on the cheek to remind you how much he loves you.'

Zerina laughed, then pulled back and wiped her cheek where Erjon had kissed her. She ran down to the water again and picked up another stone and threw it into the waves.

'When will you tell her?' Erjon asked.

Leandra wiped away a tear from her own cheek. 'She will guess soon enough, when he does not return.'

'Will you tell her the truth?'

'I will tell her that her father would have done anything to be with her again.'

'They made us all do terrible things over there. We had to do them to survive. I am only here because Riz helped me survive.'

'I wish he had never gone,' said Leandra.

'So do I,' said Erjon. 'Everything he did, he did because he loved you, and because he wanted to protect you and Zerina.'

'He should not have killed for us. It is never right to kill, no matter the reason.'

Leandra did not know Rose Black. She did not know her story. She did not know the hurt Riz had done or the evil that he had discovered within himself. It was better that she did not know. It was better that Zerina did not know.

Leandra walked away from Erjon and went to her daughter. They began retracing their steps along the waterfront, the waves lapping over their feet.

Erjon watched them go. He did not follow them. He had delivered his message as he had told Riz he would.

He looked out over the warm Adriatic Sea and thought about the land that lay beyond it. He vowed never to return there again.

THE END

CAL JACKSON WILL RETURN

ABOUT THE AUTHOR

Iain Kelly lives in Scotland. He works as an editor in the television industry and is married with two children. *Hostile City* is his seventh novel.

For more information visit his website: www.iainkellywriting.com

Follow on social media:

Facebook: iainkellywriting
Instagram + Threads: @iain_kelly_writing
X: @IainK_Writing
LinkedIn: iain-kelly-writing
BlueSky: @iainkellywriting.bsky.social

If you enjoyed reading *Hostile City*, please do leave a review on social media or a website and help others to find the book. It really is appreciated.

ACKNOWLEDGEMENTS

My thanks to the team at Book Guild Publishing and Troubador Publishing for their continued work and support.

To my first reader, Mum.

To Joanne, Chloe and Caden for allowing me the time needed to continue writing.

And to all the readers – those who are finding my work for the first time and are taking a chance on a new author, and especially to those who have been with me since the start and continue to invest their time in my work. Thank you.

ALSO AVAILABLE

FULL SUN
The First Cal Jackson Thriller

Cal Jackson has just been released from prison. Now all he wants is a quiet life.

But when his sister marries into the family of corrupt businessman Francis McArthur, Cal finds himself caught in the middle of an ongoing war between his new family and the police.

When a childhood friend, the mysterious and enchanting Elise Moreau, disappears, Cal's got his work cut out to find her and discover what links her to McArthur.

And that's before the first dead body turns up.

As a heat wave grips Glasgow's mean streets and vibrant night life, Cal is reluctantly forced to act, before he finds himself either back in prison, or buried in the ground.

Praise for *Full Sun*:

– 'A fantastic novel that I couldn't put down.'

– 'One of those rare novels that you wish would never end.'

– 'Well crafted, with some sinister characters and perfectly placed shocks, this is a fine start to a new series.'

– 'The reader becomes quickly immersed in the story and feels utterly compelled to follow the fast-moving events.'

– 'Everything I wanted from a thriller – a gritty story with strong characters and a story that had depth.'

– 'Highly recommended for those who enjoy thought-provoking fiction that speaks to the human experience.'

ALSO AVAILABLE

THE BARRA BOY

1982. Thirteen-year-old Ewan Fraser is sent to the remote island of Barra, off Scotland's west coast, to stay with his aunt and uncle.

Resigned to a monotonous summer of boredom, he is befriended by local girl Laura Robertson, and together they explore the golden beaches and rocky coves of the idyllic island.

But a dark secret that connects Laura to the mysterious outcast Mhairi Matheson and her son, Billy, is hidden beneath the tranquil surface…

A secret that threatens to tear the small community apart.

Forty years later, Ewan returns to confront the truth about the formative summer of his adolescence, and finally learn the truth about Laura and the boy from Barra.

Praise for *The Barra Boy*:

– '[A] superbly written, character-driven story that ranks as one of my favourite reads of the year. The author has a wonderful feel for locations… This is an outstanding novel from an author with a great future.'

– 'Rich in description, superbly controlled pace of reveal… we have lots and lots of praise for this book – highly enjoyable setting, utterly pleasurable to imagine, early introduction of suspense that lasted right through to the conclusion, and satisfying answers to the mysteries that you encounter during the storyline. Great, great work.'

– 'A thoughtful combination of literary fiction and coming-of-age novel, and will undoubtedly remain in my memory for a long while.'

ALSO AVAILABLE

ALL WE CANNOT LEAVE BEHIND

Edinburgh, 1920. Three children are missing, abducted from the poorhouses of the city.

When a body is found near the town of Liberton, Dr Thomas Stevenson, still suffering from the trauma of the First World War, finds himself drawn into the police investigation.

But suspicion falls on the woman with the mysterious past who lives with Thomas. Could she be guilty of the brutal murder?

With time running out and lives at stake, Thomas must prove her innocence, but to do that he has to find the real killer and unlock the truth about her secret past.

A past that casts a long, dark shadow.

Praise for *All We Cannot Leave Behind*:

– 'An incredibly atmospheric piece of writing. [The] description of Edinburgh and every location throughout the novel feels authentic and his characters fit perfectly into each setting. This is a wonderful piece of fiction and a highly recommended read…'

– 'The writing is beautiful and I was left feeling quite emotional as the story unfolded. The characterisation is excellent, I was invested from the start, and I really felt compassion for Dr Thomas and Louise. This is a beautiful work of fiction, which I highly recommend.'

– 'An emotive read that had my heart aching. [Kelly] draws the reader into a powerful, dark, all-encompassing narrative. Kelly writes with a brutal honesty that is all at once gritty and gentle, hard-hitting and empathetic.'

– 'An absolutely gripping read. Great characterisation and a well-researched historical thriller.'

ALSO AVAILABLE

THE STATE TRILOGY

A JUSTIFIED STATE
STATE OF DENIAL
STATE OF WAR

Set in the near future, the assassination of a politician triggers a series of events that threatens to bring down the State government in this explosive dystopian thriller series.

Detective Danny Samson finds himself at the centre of political scandal and cover-ups as he hunts the mysterious killer Gabriella, with the help of special agent Phillips.

Their investigation leads them to the very heart of power, and the disturbing truth about The State.

Unfolding over the following years, *The State Trilogy* will have you gripped from the first page until the end.

Praise for *The State Trilogy*:

– 'The action is pacey and exciting, the characters fleshed out, nuanced and believable, the mystery…is genuinely intriguing and alarming.'

– 'The writing brought to mind Phillip Marlow, *Do Androids Dream of Electric Sheep?*, the world of George Smiley, and Robert Harris's *Fatherland*.'

– 'This is a superbly well written, fast-paced, suspenseful mystery. A page turner as the action…makes you gasp.'